KILLER UNICORN
APOCALYPSE

KILLER UNICORN
APOCALYPSE

E.A. KIEFER

Pancake Massacre Publishing

TO K & P

THANKS FOR ALL THE BOOKS –
THEY MADE ME BELIEVE

I

*"It's not always paranoia... sometimes they're really
out to get you."*

*– The Meridian, matriarch of the Overgruk-
Monoceros coven*

From a distance, squinting across the vast Nyasian outback under the stabbing light of the morning sun, it might
have been possible to mistake the pair of figures standing
on the cliff for unusually large sand ponies, or maybe even
king camels.

From a distance, anyway.

But as one drew closer, they would have seen the beasts'
regal necks... cascading manes... leathery wings... and above
all else, those terrible, resplendent horns. And at that range,
it would have been impossible to mistake a unicorn for any
other creature in existence.

They strode lithely to the edge of the bluff, moving more
like birds of prey than horses. The first was a stallion with

a sheer, black coat that shimmered like a patch of living midnight. His companion was a dark-crimson mare, slightly smaller and with a hateful twinkle in her eyes.

The two of them stood with the sun at their backs, staring at a distant rock formation in the shape of a phoenix. It was an uncanny match for their mistress' vision. She was right. But then again, she was *always* right about these things.

They exchanged a glance. Time to send word to the Meridian.

Marshalling their concentration, the unicorns closed their eyes and opened their minds. A teardrop-shaped pendant draped around the larger unicorn's neck began to glow with a bright, purple hue.

"Great Meridian," he whispered in the intricate and entrancing language of the Monoceros. "We beseech you to answer our call."

There was a pregnant pause, like the instant before a bowstring is released, then the unicorns felt an irresistible energy leap forth from the pendants into their bodies. Even with their mighty pain thresholds they couldn't help but whimper. The energy burrowed inside them like a parasite, penetrating into their blood, diffusing into every fiber and nerve.

And in the space of a heartbeat, the unicorns were no longer alone.

"I am here," a mellifluous voice proclaimed telepathically, coming from all directions at once. "Speak."

"Your premonition was correct, mistress," the stallion responded. "We're at the Phoenix Rock now. We should arrive at our target by sunset, maybe sooner."

"Excellent."

"And what about the humans?" the crimson unicorn inquired. "What shall we do with them when the ring is in our possession?"

There was only the slightest of pauses before the Meridian offered her reply.

"Kill anyone you come across," she said without a trace of empathy. "What you choose to do with them afterwards, I leave entirely up to you. Remember, your deeds this day will determine the fate of your entire race. Do not fail us. Do not fail *me*."

Then – as quickly as it had arrived – the presence in their minds was gone and the unicorns were alone again.

A pair of determined glares met. There was no turning back.

"For the glory, my brother," the crimson unicorn declared. [1]

"For the glory, my sister," her companion agreed.

And spreading their wings, they leaped off the cliff and soared into the air.

2

"There are two ways to get what you want in life: acquire more, or desire less."

– Traditional Nyasian folk saying

It was a spring afternoon in the outback, just a few weeks before the start of the potuber harvest, and Luzi Winterstar was finally going home.

The young woman languished atop her camel as the animal plodded along under the relentless heat of the Nyasian steppe. Holding the reins in her teeth, Luzi removed her weather-beaten keffiyeh and shook it clear of grit. She tried her best to adjust her broad frame in the saddle, but she'd outgrown the damn thing years ago and didn't have the coin to buy another.

Luzi took a moment to tighten the braid in her bone-white hair, an anomaly among her people. Like a greedy phantom, the outback air sucked at the brown, glossy nape of her neck.

If life is soup, then I'm a fucking fork, she pondered bitterly, dabbing at the sweat with the sleeve of her tunic.

As she rode through the desolate outback, Luzi massaged the bags under her eyes. Huge tracts of uninterrupted sand flats stretched out before her, a blank canvas not even the gods knew how to paint. It seemed like only a few years ago that the thought of those open fields had infused her with a hopeful buoyancy. Now, the sole thought on her mind was the long ride ahead – and the monstrous list of chores that awaited the journey's end.

It'd been more than forty-eight lonesome hours since she left home to irrigate the western fields. In her youth, when there were more hands to share the load, the task could be done in a single afternoon. Luzi sighed, knowing those days were long behind her.

I guess it's like mother always said, she reminded herself: *Shit in one hand and wish in the other, and the same one will fill up first every time.*

Luzi's camel grunted loudly, startling the Nyasian from her brooding. She reached up and patted him on the neck.

"When did it all get so ugly, anyway, huh?"

It took a minute before Luzi realized she was waiting for the beast to reply. "So now I'm actually expecting you to answer me?" she said, forcing a chuckle in lieu of a tear. "I must be lonelier than I thought."

And giving the horizon a final, wistful peek, Luzi tapped her stirrups and leaned into the saddle.

***

It was almost dusk when Luzi finally made her way back home.

As she hitched her camel to a post outside the front gate of her adobe cottage, Luzi's attention strayed to a deep notch cut into the wood. It'd been more than three years since she'd left it there in a fit of anger, but the Nyasian could still remember the embarrassing outburst like it was yesterday.

After working in the fields all day, she'd returned home to find her mother outside, chopping wood. The elder Winterstar quaked from overexertion and coughed with each heave of the axe, a sight that made Luzi suck in her breath. Her mother hadn't been laid low by the crimson lung in those days – not yet, anyway. But the bug was already in her blood, and the entire family had known it was only a matter of time before she took a turn for the worse.

"Mother!" Luzi called out, trying to shame her into stopping.

The family matriarch looked up. She wiped sweat from her upper lip and waved her daughter over. Cramped and dusty from the day's ride, Luzi approached, expecting a hello – if not a thank you. But instead, axe still in hand, her mother only offered a gruff nod.

"Sure took your fucking time getting back here, didn't you?" she grumbled.

There was little else Luzi could do but sigh.

"Papa would cry if he knew you were out here chopping wood. You're supposed to be resting. How do you expect to get any better when you're out here sweating in the sun?"

Luzi's mother answered with her axe, splitting a log in two. THWACK!

"Your father's off at the well filling the water barrels and doing the wash," she replied. "He won't be back for at least an hour. What he doesn't know won't hurt him. And it'd better stay that way."

THWACK!

She pivoted around to face her daughter. "How'd the irrigation go?"

"Fine," Luzi said, deliberately trying to keep her answer vague. She tugged on a stand of her hair, a nervous fidget she'd picked up as a young girl.

"So there's no signs of blantises or root slugs, right?" her mother probed, tapping the handle of her axe suspiciously.

Luzi rolled her eyes, familiar with the game.

"Noooooooooo, mother."

"And the wilting in quadrant three. Did that finally stop?"

"Yeeeesssssss, mother."

The elder Winterstar nodded with a grudging satisfaction. She returned to the woodpile and grabbed a new log, then placed it on the chopping block.

"So as long as you made sure to reinforce the hilling before you left, we should be fine... right?"

Luzi paused. She briefly toyed with the idea of lying, but she'd never been any good at it. "It didn't *need* it, mother," she replied at last, bracing for the inevitable fight to come.

The grizzled desert denizen set down her axe. Her brow wrinkled.

"Dammit, Luzi!" she huffed, pointing angrily with her now-empty hand. "I knew you were going to half-ass things out there! I saw it in your eyes when you left. It's the same look you'd get when you were a little girl and I asked you to sweep the house or take a bath. When are you going to grow up? When?"

"By the unholy scrote of Dis!" the younger Winterstar protested, flailing her arms in frustration. "Everything will be fine! You always panic for the dumbest reasons!"

Her mother wasn't mollified.

"If you really believe that, I'm not sure what you need to be lectured about more: farming or responsibility," she insisted. "If any of those roots get exposed, it'd cost us a third of the crop, maybe even half. You should know better by now. This is what puts food on our table, clothes on our backs. We can't afford to cut corners like this. Have some pride!"

Luzi felt her face grow red.

"I was just out there for the entire afternoon – alone – doing chores for three people. And instead of thanking me for the work I *did*, you yell at me for what I *didn't*? No pride? Whose fault is that? You never give me any respect, and I'm sick of it!"

"So now you need an ass-kissing for simply doing your job?" her mother retorted.

"Yes!" Luzi pleaded emphatically, wounded and searching for words sharp enough to cut back. "Maybe I deserve a little bit of gratitude! Is that so much to ask?"

Luzi's pulse quickened.

"You think this is how I want to spend my life? I've got plans, mother. I've got dreams. And I know it's hard for you to believe, but none of them have anything to do with this fucking potuber farm!"

"I just don't get it," she pressed. "What's keeping us tied down to this awful little patch of desert, anyway? You're still well enough to travel. The harvest is almost done. Why don't we sell every last scrap of it at the market and get the hell out of here? I mean, the Landcasters did, and they barely knew how to plow their own damn-"

"Enough!" her mother yelled, trembling with betrayal. "I don't want to hear another word about the Landcasters! I'm not going to have the same conversation yet again with you, Luzi. You want to abandon your father and me? You want to piss on our dreams? Go ahead and do it! But like it or not, this is our home! This is where we belong! This is-"

A fit of hacking and coughing cut her mother off mid-sentence. The effort doubled her up in pain. She bent over, holding her stomach, then spat a large mouthful of red glop on the ground, where it laid like a dollop of wet clay.

"Mama!" Luzi exclaimed, forgetting she was supposed to be mad. "Are you alright?"

The gruff, old Nyasian waved her daughter off and forced herself to her feet. "I'm fine," she muttered as her breath returned. "Just fine."

There was a moment of silence between parent and child. When the elder Winterstar spoke again, it was with the conciliatory voice of someone who knew she was having an argument she couldn't possibly win.

"Luzi, you've grown up to be a strong, stubborn woman... just like me. I'm very thankful for that. But there are still many things you don't understand about how the world works. Inspiration is noticing the world around you – not fixating on what lies beyond. And the sooner you make your peace with that, the sooner you'll understand what I've been telling you all along."

The elder Winterstar gave her daughter a weary glare.

"I was born in this desert. I'll take my final breath here. And that's all I have to say about it."

Her mother's curt dismissal of the conversation rekindled the anger in Luzi's heart. Without warning, the junior Winterstar picked up her mother's axe and slammed it as hard as she could into the hitching post, leaving it wedged deep in the wood.

"Well, I guess that's the difference between us," she snapped. "I'm busy trying to find ways to live, and you're busy trying to find ways to die."

And without another word, Luzi stormed into the house.

She apologized the next day over breakfast, of course, but the damage had already been done. Not long afterwards, Luzi's mother took a sudden turn for the worse, as is common with the crimson lung.

She died three weeks after their argument.

When the family matriarch passed away, it was like a light went off in Luzi's father's eyes. He'd always been the most optimistic member of the household – almost to the point of sappiness. It was one of the things that Luzi loved about him, and he knew it.

"Trees don't eat their own fruit, and rivers don't drink their own water," he'd often tell his daughter, raising her spirits after her mother's latest admonishing. "Life is good when you're happy, but much better when others are happy because of you."

But from that day on, her father trudged through his chores like a golem, until one otherwise uneventful morning, he took a careless step while repairing the roof of their farmhouse and plummeted to his death.

And just like that, Luzi had found herself without a family.

***

It was an injustice the Nyasian ruminated on that evening as she cleaned out the stable, anathema growing in her heart with each shovelful of camel shit.

As Luzi worked, she fiddled with a ring hanging on a chain around her neck, an heirloom she'd been entrusted with on her thirteenth birthday. Crafted from an exotic, golden alloy, it was wrought in the shape of Ouroboros, the serpent which devours its own tail. Like many families who acquire such treasures, the Winterstars had completely forgotten where the ring came from by the time it made its way to Luzi's hands. But its ambiguous origin had no effect on its worth; the ring was the only thing in their possession with even a sliver of real value. That the Winterstars had never sold the thing – not even in their most desperate of hours – spoke volumes more about its importance than any letter of provenance ever could.

For almost a decade, the day Luzi inherited the family heirloom had stood as the proudest moment of her life. "Hold it close and keep it sacred," her mother told her all those years ago, the pride unmistakable in her voice. "For today, your childhood ends."

But as she'd grown from an awkward teen into a woman, Luzi gradually became aware that her mother's gift was more than just a symbol of adulthood. As the sole Winterstar heir, it represented an agreement to take the helm of their farm. It was her covenant, her legacy, her birthright.

There was only one problem... she didn't want it.

From the early days of her youth, Luzi had dreamed of exploring the world beyond the Nyasian outback. Ironically, it was her parents who'd planted the first seeds of wanderlust in her heart by feeding her a steady diet of childhood fables. They eventually stopped telling Luzi stories about the outer lands when they realized their daughter was taking their fairy tales seriously, but by then, the damage was already done.

As curiosity evolved into infatuation, Luzi continued to glean every scrap of information she could about the world beyond Nyasia, mostly from visiting relatives' stories and her sparse-but-treasured trove of books. She learned about the ancient elven boroughs of the northern plains... the undefeatable warrior-mages of the Ragnarian empire... the fabled forest civilization of Abyssinia... the million-book athenaeum of Quiyst... and many of the other endless wonders of the five Great Realms. [2]

With each new destination she discovered, Luzi's appetite for adventure grew more ravenous, more insatiable. Still, as much as Luzi wanted to leave Nyasia behind, and as much as she resented her parents for putting her in this position, she knew she loved them too much to leave.

Even now, years after her parents' deaths, Luzi found herself unable to abandon the farm. It was the only thing remaining of them, after all. Although it meant working from dawn to sundown, she was unable to summon the intrepidness – or the apathy – to write the final chapter on their lifelong dream. But Luzi also knew this was exactly how her mother and father had gotten trapped in Nyasia, as had their parents before them, and so on throughout the gnarled roots of their family tree. It was a prison built of love. And every day she spent on the farm added another bar to the cage.

Suddenly, Luzi stopped work, overcome by frustration. She reached under her tunic and took out the ring, which had never quite fit any of her fingers and had to be worn on a chain instead. The Nyasian gazed at the thing forlornly, letting out a sullen sigh.

Is this who I AM, or just who I've BECOME? she silently fumed.

With a heavy heart, Luzi tucked the ring back under her tunic and turned to finish cleaning out the stable. But before she could lift her shovel, all four of the Winterstars' camels began to low and stamp around nervously.

"Whoa, you big bastards... what's the matter?" Luzi chastised, trying to lay her hand against the nearest animal's neck to calm it down. But the beast and its companions refused to be placated. They continued to buck so vehemently it seemed they might burst out of the stable.

An animalistic fear spread throughout Luzi's body. Her legs tensed. Her neck muscles stiffened. *Something is wrong,* she realized. *Something is very wrong.*

At that exact moment, there was an immense crash from outside of the stable. Luzi heard the crunch of shattering stone and adobe, then an awful clatter, as if a mountain had collapsed.

Dis be damned... what now? she wondered, dread filling her heart.

And without wasting another moment, Luzi dropped her shovel and ran outside.

***

When the Nyasian arrived at the only place she'd ever called home, she barely recognized what remained.

An entire support wall laid in shambles, leaving the guts of the house completely exposed. Chunks of debris and adobe brick were scattered across the outback. A cloud of dust floated in the air – a lurid, twilight ghost haunting the wreckage. It was a sick sight, as if Dis himself had descended from the heavens and gone berserk with his mighty war hammer.

With a panicked frenzy speeding her actions, Luzi dashed over to the rubble, expecting the worst. Her heart pounded as she tried to sort out what could have possibly happened. An earthquake? A crumbling foundation? An infestation of brick-eating desert termites?

But nothing – not even her worst nightmares – could have prepared her for what awaited.

As Luzi turned the corner, a pair of terrifying equine creatures stepped out from the shadows where they'd been lurking in ambush. One had fur of deep crimson; the other was midnight-black.

It can't be! she balked, enraptured by their horrible, gleaming horns.

Unicorns!

As soon as the word entered Luzi's head – as if they heard her thoughts – the beasts turned around and glared at her. Time ground to a halt. Then, like a cat smiling at a mouse, the crimson unicorn's lips curled apart in an evil grin.

And without further delay, Luzi began to scream.

A split second after her cry pierced the air, a puff of blood-colored smoke spontaneously appeared where the unicorns were standing. As Luzi watched dumbfounded, the crimson unicorn stepped into the mist and disappeared. Then, as if by some nefarious sorcery, the beast reappeared in a second cloud of smoke a few feet away.

Raising one of her mighty hooves like a spear, the unicorn lifted Luzi off her feet and pinned her by the throat to a nearby chunk of rubble. The pain was excruciating; the shock even worse.

As Luzi's eyes bulged in horror, the beast spoke. Her voice was caustic, like acid splattering on glass.

"You know, most of my kin consider human flesh to be lower than that of worms or rats," the unicorn hissed in Communia, the shared language used by traders and travelers across the Great Realms.

"Myself, I've come to appreciate the subtle bitterness of ape meat," she added with bared incisors, savoring the effect her words were having. "But I suppose that's just the connoisseur in me."

The unicorn increased the pressure on Luzi's throat. The Nyasian choked in horror, unable to scream. She felt herself spinning, her muscles burning, her heart ready to leap out of her mouth.

"Listen closely, maggot," the unicorn commanded. "I'm going to ask you a question, and I'm only going to ask once – WHERE IS THE RING?"

Luzi racked her brain in a calamitous panic trying to understand the unicorn's demand. *The ring?* she wondered. *What could she possibly–"*

And that's when it hit her.

Fumbling with her last bit of strength, Luzi reached into her shirt and pulled out her family heirloom. Unable to speak, she held the thing out with a trembling arm, like she was trying to ward off a vampire with a clove of garlic. To her astonishment, the gambit succeeded.

"In the name of the Meridian... it's true," the creature whispered, captivated by the sight of the ring. "We're going to rule the world again."

In its preoccupation, the unicorn completely forgot about Luzi. She continued to hold the helpless Nyasian by the throat, oblivious to her need to breathe. But just as Luzi was about to lose consciousness, the dark unicorn spoke, his august, bass-soaked voice the diametrical opposite to his peer.

"Buvöda!" he bellowed. "Let the human go!"

Without loosening her grip on Luzi, the crimson unicorn paused, considering her options. After a moment, she released the young woman, who dropped to the ground choking and gasping for air.

"Why have you interrupted my kill, Uchchaihshravas?" she asked with a calm menace, squaring around to face him.

Her companion didn't answer. He walked over to the still-gasping Luzi and stood in front of her. Fear gripping her heart, Luzi gazed into the unicorn's eyes. But instead of hatred, she saw something else.

Confusion.

Uchchaihshravas gave Luzi a long stare, as if trying to penetrate straight through to her soul. Nobody had ever scrutinized Luzi that way in her life, not even her mother. Finally, he turned to his peer with an iron absoluteness.

"Sister," he said. "We cannot kill this human."

His words proved a complete shock to Luzi... and Buvöda as well.

"What the gods are you talking about?" she queried, cocking her head.

"I know you don't share my visions, but she has some sort of aura surrounding her," Uchchaihshravas hastily explained. "It's a connection to the Deep Magic that I've never seen in a human. Something raw. Something powerful. And if we kill her now, we may never find out what it is."

"So?"

He gestured at Luzi, who was still on the ground, wheezing in pain and frozen in fear.

"You don't understand, sister. I believe the human has some sort of link to the ring. We have to bring her back... alive. I want to contact the Meridian."

"She won't like this," Buvöda replied skeptically.

"I accept full responsibility," Uchchaihshravas said.

Buvöda snorted. "Then you're a bigger fool than I thought. Let's get this over with."

"You... girl," Buvöda ordered, scowling at Luzi. "Move an inch from that spot and I'll make sure you die in so much pain, even poets will be afraid to describe it."

Luzi nodded, hoping the gesture would appease them.

The unicorns bowed their heads reverently. A pair of heart-shaped pendants hanging around their necks illuminated with a magical, purple hue. "Great Meridian," Uchchaihshravas murmured softly. "I beseech you to hear our call."

In an instant – as if she'd been waiting for a message – their mistress was in their minds.

"Do you have the ring?" she demanded curtly.

"Yes, mistress," Uchchaihshravas replied telepathically. "We are at the humans' home now. But we've come across something unexpected."

"Speak," the Meridian said.

"It's the human," he explained with an uncharacteristic desperation. "Somehow, she's unaffected by my curse! I can see her, mistress! I – I can *see* her!"

"I know you gave us orders to kill any human we encountered," he pleaded. "But surely this changes things? With your permission, I would like to take her back to the coven for further study. *Alive.*"

There was a long pause before the Meridian replied.

"I'll admit to a certain curiosity. And on another day, you would have my full support. But this is no ordinary task. The ring is all that matters. It's bigger than you, or me, or even the Overgruk clan. It's far too dangerous to allow this human to live. Kill her immediately and bring me the ring without further delay. Your orders stand."

"But mistress!" Uchchaihshravas objected, stunned by the Meridian's decree. "I've waited my whole life for this! I *must* discover what sort of magic is at work here! I need to–"

The Meridian interrupted him mid-sentence.

"Enough! We will discuss this further when you return. That is all I have to say. Perform your duties, Uchchaihshravas. I know you won't let me down."

With that final declaration, the Meridian exited their minds. As their pendants stopped glowing, the unicorns woke from their trance. They turned to look at each other, blinking their eyes.

"I told you so," Buvöda chided. "Now let's dispose of this meat puppet and go home."

Like a fly caught in a spider web, Luzi could only stare with an impotent fear as Buvöda crept towards her. But as soon as the unicorn's hoof touched the ground, her companion spread his hellish wings out intimidatingly, halting his peer in her tracks.

"Stop! This is wrong! We cannot kill this girl!"

Buvöda stamped her front hooves. "Are you mad? You heard our mistress. Get out of the way!"

Uchchaihshravas didn't budge.

"Buvöda, you know me well. We've hunted together many times, shared many kills, brought much glory to the Overgruk coven. And you know I would never do anything to harm any of our brothers and sisters. But the Meridian is wrong about this human. Dangerously wrong. And if you make me, I will not hesitate to do what I must to protect her life."

Buvöda's eyes narrowed at his threat. She tilted her head towards Luzi.

"You'd betray your mistresses' direct orders, cross horns with a coven mate, and doom your entire race... for *that* pitiful thing?"

Her companion looked at Luzi for a moment. He turned back to Buvöda with a steel reserve.

"Yes."

"I don't believe you," Buvöda said matter-of-factly.

Without further discussion, the unicorn turned to Luzi with death in her eyes. The beast reared back on her hind legs, hefting her hooves in the air. Whinnying maliciously, the unicorn prepared to smash down with her deadly war hammers.

Before she could strike, Uchchaihshravas folded his wings to the side and charged headfirst, his horn aimed like a knight's jousting lance at her heart – just as she knew he would. The split second before he hit his mark, Buvöda vanished in a cloud of crimson smoke. Desperately, Uchchaihshravas tried to twist around and defend his flank.

He was too late.

In the blink of an eye, Buvöda reappeared at his side, landing a devastating horn stab through his lung. A spurt of hot, silver blood jetted from the wound, splashing on the ground and pooling like liquid steel. Buvöda twisted her horn savagely and Uchchaihshravas collapsed in the dirt, gasping for air like a fish tossed onto a riverbank.

With her peer immobilized, Buvöda returned her attention to Luzi. For a brief moment, the two met eyes. The unicorn grinned. Then the beast lunged at Luzi with raised hooves, ready to dash her brains in.

The Nyasian instinctively backpedaled in fear. As she did, her foot caught on a rock. With a violent whoosh, she tumbled backwards, unable to soften her descent with her arms or shoulders.

Luzi slammed into the ground. Something exploded in her skull. The world went pitch black, as if a hood were pulled over her face.

Then – for a long time – there was nothing.

3

"Sometimes anger is the only key that can unlock the door to forgiveness."

– The Compendium of Quiyst, book 4, proverb 17

When Luzi opened her eyes, her first thought was that she'd died and awoken at the Gates of Jannah. But it only took a moment to realize there was no way her head would hurt so badly if she was in heaven.

Or hell either, she moaned, wincing and groggily struggling to her feet.

The Nyasian flexed her arms and legs, groaning with relief when they responded. Her head throbbed interminably, as if she'd guzzled an entire carafe of her father's double-fermented potuber wine. But aside from a whanging head-ache and an ugly bruise on her neck, everything seemed to be in its right place.

The famously bright triple-moon of the Nyasian outback illuminated the desert with a savagely vivid light. Luzi stood among a patch of giant saxaul bushes; a vast expanse of sand stretched in both directions. It didn't make sense. She knew every patch of desert within twenty miles like the back of her hand. But nothing was familiar; not a single landmark was in sight.

By the gory horn of Dis... where am I? she wondered as she glanced around. And then – in the space of a single breath – it all came flooding back.

Unicorns.

Calamity.

Death.

Suddenly, before she could scream in terror, Luzi heard a man's voice call out from behind her in Communia. He spoke with a mellifluous, impossible-to-place accent, something from out of antiquity or a dream.

"Don't panic! I mean you no harm!"

Luzi spun around, her jaw dropping as she laid eyes on the young man who stood in front of her. He was outrageously handsome – chiseled jawline, heroic nose – the sort of face that comes right out of a storybook. Dressed in a black thobe and matching cloak, the stranger had a lean, athletic frame, and his dark-brown skin had the immaculate complexion of a prince who'd never shed a drop of sweat in his life. But by far, his most captivating feature were his deep, umber eyes; they drew Luzi's attention like a flame attracting a moth. It felt like peering into every spectrum of emotion at the same time: despair, anger, lust, bliss.

As Luzi gawped at the stranger's face, an irrational sensation of familiarity swept over her. It didn't make any sense. But the feeling was absolute. It was as if he'd been a background character in her dreams for twenty years, and now she was bumping into him in real life.

I know you, Luzi marveled, racking her brain for any clue of the stranger's identity. *For the love of Dis, I know you!*

"Are you hurt?" the stranger asked, startling the Nyasian out of her internal monologue. "You took a pretty serious bash to the head when you fell. You had me worried, Luzi."

The sound of her own name kicked Luzi's brain into gear. She sucked in a lungful of air. And a second later, the words exploded out of her mouth in an incomprehensible, rambling mess.

"Whoareyouwherearewewhat'sgoingonhowdoyouknowmynamewhathappenedtothosethingsthatattackedusandwhatthefuckweretheyinthefirstplacetheylookedlikefuckingunicornsbutthat'simpossibleisn'titunlessholyshitthey'rerealanditwasn'tadreamatallunlessI'mdreamingnow–"

The stranger held up his hands, pleading for mercy from the verbal onslaught.

"Slowly... slowly. The creature that attacked you is dead. We're safe for now. But there's a lot we need to talk about."

The stranger reached into his coat and retrieved a wineskin from his inner pocket. "Here," he offered. "I found this in your saddlebag. Have a drink. It'll help you pull your head together."

Luzi grabbed the wineskin with a shaking hand and took a deep swig. It didn't help at all.

"Th-this is real, isn't it?" she stammered weakly.

"Yes. I'm sorry."

Luzi shook her head. "For the love of Dis – what happened?" she muttered.

"You were attacked by a pair of Monoceros," the stranger replied somberly. "In Nyasia, you know them as unicorns."

Luzi blinked. The concept fizzled in her brain. "Unicorns? But... they're just myths, children's tales told around campfires. There's no such thing."

The stranger shook his head in amazement.

"Children's tales? Is *that* what they think of the Monoceros in Nyasia these days? No, Luzi. Unicorns are real. And you should be very, very afraid of them.

"The Monoceros are an ancient race of beings born of the Deep Magic, some of the most powerful, merciless creatures in existence. They're strong as Ragnarian steel... wise as a Quiystian mystic... swift as a Rider of Zynn. [3] And their healing abilities, which can repair a pulverized bone or a stab wound in seconds, make them nearly impossible to kill.

"As if those powers weren't enough, every unicorn is born with its own unique magic ability: fire breathing, elemental control, future-sight. I've seen unicorns who can walk on water, pass through solid rock and turn into steam. Some even have the ability to hijack your very thoughts.

"In many cultures – including Nyasia, it seems – the unicorns are but a myth. But I assure you, Monoceros continue to dwell in the dark corners of the world. And there are more of them out there than you'd ever dream possible."

Luzi's voice cracked with anguish and confusion.

"But what do they want with *me*?"

The stranger walked over to Luzi. He reached into his pocket, then slowly unfurled his hand to reveal something Luzi thought she'd never see again... her family ring!

"They came here for this."

Luzi stared at the hunk of metal blankly. "I don't understand. That's nothing, just some hunk of stupid jewelry."

The stranger held the ring out with a wary respect, as if the world's most venomous scorpion sat in his palm.

"Jewelry? If only that were true. But this is no simple bauble – not by a longshot."

"As legends tell, there were five great relics of power created in the primordial days of this world, when it still belonged to the gods. The first is the Weeping Blade, which lies unreachable at the world's core. The second is the Great Sunstone, which can be found in the mountain city of Dama'run. The third is Indra's Bow, the location of which remains shrouded in mystery. The fourth is the Lantern of Fools, which only exists in the realm of dreams."

Luzi felt a shiver run down her spine, already knowing the answer to her question. "And the fifth?"

The stranger glanced down at the ring.

"Many millennia ago, a pair of gods known as Thought and Memory – the Immaculans – placed a piece of their essences into a pair of indestructible wedding bands. As a show of trust, the Immaculans exchanged rings, ensuring their fates were forever linked.

"But all things must come to an end, even the reign of gods. When the ancient ones left this world, the Immaculan Rings were separated and lost. Knowledge of their existence became the province of a precious few. And that was how it remained for eons, until several hundred years ago, when your distant ancestor brought the Memory ring to Nyasia. It's been in your family's possession ever since, incognito all these years... until now."

"What does it do?"

"By itself? Nothing. Alone, the rings are powerless, as inert as lead. But when touched together, they act like a giant prism, capable of infinitely amplifying a person's natural magical abilities. With the power of the rings, a bumbling apprentice magician instantly becomes a master mage. And a master mage? They become a god."

A dark thought flashed through Luzi's mind.

"You said there were two of these things. Where's the other one?"

The stranger paused, as if loathing to ponder the answer to Luzi's question.

"The unicorns who attacked you are members of the Overgruk clan, one of the oldest Monoceros covens in existence. They're ruled by a powerful alpha unicorn called the Meridian, who would like nothing more than to wipe out the human race and create a new age of unicorns. It is *she* who commanded your death. And it is *she* who possesses your ring's companion."

The stranger nodded sympathetically at the sickened expression on Luzi's face.

"Now you're beginning to understand," he said. "If the Meridian gets hold of both rings, she'll be able to use her new abilities to create an end of days for the human race... a killer unicorn apocalypse. And not a soul will survive the 'utopia' that follows."

The stranger paused.

"We only have one chance to avert armageddon. We have to get the ring – and you – somewhere safe before the unicorns find us."

"Us?" Luzi squeaked.

"The Meridian knows where you live," the stranger replied grimly. "When word of what happened here reaches her ears, one of the first things she'll do is send a team of unicorns to interrogate you. Believe me... they *will* find you. And when they do, you'll wish that you killed yourself when you had the chance."

Luzi looked up at the stranger with a sudden suspicion, like a newly deceased soul who just realized she's talking to the devil.

"How do you know all this? Who in the name of Dis are you, anyway?"

The stranger sighed, as if he was about to undertake an unpleasant task. "There's something you need to know," he said. "This isn't my true form."

Luzi's eyes widened.

"What the hell does that mean?"

"I'm a shapeshifter," the stranger explained. "I can take almost any size, hue or identity, including human. I chose to greet you in this form because I thought it would be the most inconspicuous... and the least frightening. But the time has come to show you who I *really* am."

The stranger paused.

"When I reveal myself, you must not panic. Remember, I mean you no harm. Do you understand?"

Luzi could only bob her head in reply.

The stranger shrugged. "For both of our sakes, I hope so."

With these words, an incredible change overtook the young man. His face elongated. His body stretched and bent at the waist. Two, leathery wings emerged from the back of his ribcage. His hands and feet fused into hooves. Finally, as the coup de gras, a two-foot-long horn erupted from his forehead. And that's when Luzi was confronted with the horrible truth: she was looking at one of her would-be unicorn assassins!

The Nyasian's body flooded with a paralyzing mixture of hatred, fear and awe. She froze, like a bug meeting a boot.

"Who *are* you?" Luzi whispered.

"My name is Uchchaihshravas of the Overgruk," the creature replied in a princely voice. "But you can call me U." [4]

***

Luzi had but one question... the *only* question a sane person would have in such a situation.

"Are you going to kill me?"

"Not to sound like some sort of cheap villain in a fairy tale, but if I wanted you dead, you'd already be a stain on the desert floor," U quipped.

A cinder of anger sparked in Luzi's heart, burning away her fear.

"Tell me then, unicorn. You've destroyed my home. You have your ring. Why am I still breathing?"

"Because you're the most beautiful thing I've ever seen!" the unicorn blurted out.

For his part, U seemed as surprised by his answer as Luzi, almost as if he hadn't meant to say it aloud. He swallowed hard and continued.

"I know what I said seems confusing, but let me explain.

Since the day I was born, I've been cursed with a mysterious, magical affliction. My kin call it the *dying eyes*."

He gestured at a tiny, indigo flower near the foot of a nearby Jaxon tree.

"That blossom... how does it appear to you? Colorful? Vivacious? Do you know what I see? A shell of brown petals, wilting on a desiccated stem. And it's the same for anything else I've ever laid my eyes upon. A garden in fruit? I see a mass of barren stems crumbling in the sun. A young maiden's face? I see a worm-ridden mask of rotten flesh. I have never seen beauty. I have known naught but death.

"I've combed the far corners of the known realms for something – anything – that would give me the slightest glimpse into the origin of my affliction. After all these years, I've found nothing but despair."

"But then I met *you*," U continued, his voice lighting up with hope.

"Your face... your body... there's not a trace of death on them," U explained, straining to find the right words to describe what he was seeing. "Every patch of your skin is unblemished by rot. Every hair on your head is lustrous and full. And your eyes. To look into a set of eyes that have life in them–"

He paused, overcome with emotion.

"It was the only thing I've ever wished for, Luzi. So tell me... how could I let them kill you?"

Luzi's forehead wrinkled.

"But I don't understand. It doesn't make sense. I'm no magician. I don't have any secret powers. I'm just a farmer! A goddamned farmer!"

"Yes, you are," the unicorn replied cryptically. "And no, you aren't."

"I've been pondering this all night," he continued. "There's only one logical explanation… it's the ring. Being in contact with one of the most powerful artifacts in the world for so many years must have saturated your body with magic. Somehow, this pent-up magic is overpowering my curse. It's the only answer that adds up."

U rubbed his bottom lip thoughtfully.

"But then again, logic and reality don't always go hand in hand. And I do not assume the truth about you is so simple, Luzi Winterstar. There's a hidden strength that flows through your veins, a power outside the realm of rings, and maybe even magic altogether. I saw it in your eyes when we first met. And may the gods help me, I see it there now."

Luzi stared at Uchchaihshravas, her stomach knotting tighter every second. *This is insane,* she told herself. *All of it. It's crazy. And so am I for even listening to this evil bastard!* But there was an embarrassed vulnerability in the unicorn's voice that kept Luzi from discounting his story. He wasn't offering an explanation; he was giving a confession. And try as hard as she might, the Nyasian couldn't deny there might be some kernel of veracity to what he was saying.

"Why the fuck should I trust you about any of this?" a dubious Luzi asked at last. "What can you possibly do to convince me you're telling the truth?"

There was a brief pause, then U transformed again, this time from beast to man. Luzi watched the change with awe, no less amazed than the first time she saw it. When the transformation was complete, the unicorn reached into his pocket.

For a moment, Luzi feared he was going to pull out a weapon. But instead, he withdrew her family ring and dangled it from its chain.

"You're not my prisoner, Luzi. If you don't believe me, you can walk away at any time you want. Take the ring or leave it behind. I give you my word as a Monoceros that I will not pursue you, either way. But I tell you this... I know my mistress. She won't stop until she has both rings in her grasp and humanity is extinct. And your last moments will be cursed with the awful truth that you could have prevented the apocalypse – if only you'd found it in your heart to trust an enemy."

"It's your call," he concluded. "Do what you think is right."

Luzi peered down at the ring. She'd daydreamed about ditching the goddamn thing for so long. Now, she finally had the opportunity to get rid of it. Only this time, it wasn't just her own fate that hung in the balance... it was the entire world's.

A long moment passed. Luzi shut her eyes.

Father, mother, forgive me.

Reluctantly, the Nyasian took the ring from U and hung it around her neck.

"Fine. You win. But I want you to understand something. I don't give a shit about your curse. I don't give a shit about *you*. I'm doing this for all of the innocent people who will suffer if I take the coward's way out. I'm doing this for all the daughters and sons and fathers and mothers who will lose each other. And the second our business is done – the very moment this ring is in safe hands – I never want to see your goddamn face again."

U bowed his head. "You have my word."

"So tell me, monster," Luzi said, folding her arms across her chest. "What the fuck do we do now?"

***

"Well... that's where it gets a little complicated," U conceded.

"What's so difficult about it?" Luzi huffed. "Let's take this thing to the nearest blacksmith and toss it into their forge. Problem solved."

U shook his head.

"If it were only so easy. The Immaculan Rings weren't created by the tools of mortals. They can't be destroyed by any known forge or magic. You could bury that thing in the middle of a kiln for a month and it wouldn't cause as much as a smudge. Our only option is to get the ring somewhere with an army so large, even my mistress won't dare come after it."

"But that's easier said than done," he added.

"We *could* take the ring to the elves, but they're in the middle of a brutal civil war and we might be executed as spies at first sight. We *could* take it to Abyssinia or Quiyst, but it'd take a month to reach either nation, maybe more. We *could* take the ring to the federal headquarters of the Ragnarok nation, but there's a good chance they'd simply keep it for themselves and torture us to death trying to learn where its counterpart is."

U rubbed his chin pensively.

"The more I think about it, the clearer the answer becomes.

There's only one place it makes sense to take this thing... Dama'run."

"Dama'run?" Luzi queried. "The mountain city of the north?"

"You've heard of it?"

"Only what I've read in books," Luzi replied, shrugging. "It's a huge fortress built within a hollowed-out mountain on the shore of the Oligarth Sea. Governed by representatives from each of the five Great Realms, the city is a neutral ground for all races to coexist and trade, a melting pot of cultures. Anyone is welcome to visit – as long as they have coin or cargo, that is."

U nodded.

"All true. But you're forgetting the most important part: it's invulnerable to attack from the land, sea or air. Inside, an army of five thousand soldiers stand ready to shed blood at a moment's notice, with some of the most powerful mages in the world among their ranks. Not even my mistress would dare to put them to the test, even with the full power of the Overgruk at her disposal."

He paused and glanced out at the steppe.

"Here's the problem, though. Dama'run may be closer than Abyssinia or Quiyst, but it's still thousands of miles away. First, we need to cross the Nyasian outback and pass the Kil-lij Divide. From there it's a long, exposed passage across the Elven Plains to the Dama'run city outskirts, and eventually, to the Vavsoliar Gate."

U moved his mouth silently, doing calculations in his head. "Even if we travel in twenty-hour days, it'll take almost two weeks to get there... maybe longer."

Luzi gulped.

"Two weeks?"

"We could probably knock off a few days if we took the main trade roads," the unicorn ventured. "But our greatest asset right now is anonymity. In fact, it's the only thing keeping us alive. So we're going to have to avoid the highways and stick to the outback. And that's going to eat up some time."

"I don't understand," Luzi said, glancing at the unicorn's massive wings. "Why don't we just fly there?"

U shook his head.

"We can't risk it. The skies are Monoceros territory; it's how they'll be searching for *us*. If we tried to fly to Dama'run, it would be like a gazelle trying to escape a crocodile by jumping into a river."

Luzi crooked an eyebrow. "So how the hell are we supposed to travel thousands of miles in two weeks?"

The unicorn grinned.

"That's the easy part. You can ride, right?"

***

If you live on a potuber farm in the Nyasian outback, you're no stranger to the saddle.

Luzi learned how to ride a full-grown camel when she was four. Since then, she'd climbed aboard horses, donkeys, sand ponies and even a giant jackalope... once... during her cousin's wedding... while smashed out of her mind on potuber wine.

But *nothing* could have prepared her for what it was like to blast across the Nyasian steppe on the bare back of a unicorn.

U and Luzi broke camp at the first trace of daylight, the

wind at their backs and the endless desert horizon ahead. The unicorn had been offended at the mere mention of a saddle, as if he'd been asked to put on a dog collar. So all Luzi could do was to grip his mane tight and squeeze him between her thighs. To her surprise – even without a saddle – the ride was preternaturally smooth, almost as if U's hooves never actually touched the ground. Still, despite the easy gait, moving at such a speed proved to be one of the most physically draining experiences of Luzi's life.

I feel like an ant fired into the air by a crossbow, she lamented as they sped through the outback.

Though he ran at a full gallop the entire time, U didn't show the slightest sign of exhaustion. By the end of the day, they'd traveled ten times beyond what even the most intrepid of steeds could have dreamed possible. And at some point, Luzi became aware it was the farthest she'd ever been from home in her life.

Hell, it's probably farther than any Winterstar has been for a hundred years, she mused as they zoomed along.

Finally, when the last shred of sunlight was gone, the unicorn came to a reluctant stop near a small oasis. "This will have to do until the morning," U said, eying the meager tree canopy. "We'll rest here for the night and leave at sunrise."

Luzi dismounted the unicorn and immediately went to relieve herself behind some bushes. Her exhausted legs buckled as she squatted. She'd come close to pissing herself several times during the ride; U seemed completely oblivious to the human need to urinate.

Luzi gazed across the outback with weary eyes. In the distance, a crow took off from its perch on a rocky crag. It swooped away into the night, silhouetted against the moon until it became just another blur in the darkness. The Nyasian watched the bird with a gnawing jealousy. She had a brief impulse to take off running into the desert after it and put the whole mess behind her. But in her heart, Luzi knew she'd be as good as dead. Without water and hundreds of miles away from the nearest farm, the desert would finish her off long before the unicorns got a chance.

Sighing, Luzi pulled up her pants and returned to the campsite.

When she emerged from the bushes, U had reverted to his human form. He stood waiting with an expectant look on his face, the same her mother would summon whenever she wanted to have a serious discussion.

Deliberately choosing a rock as far away from the unicorn as she can get, Luzi sat down and said nothing, praying he would take the hint. But the Nyasian's hopes were shattered when U meekly approached and sat down beside her.

"Luzi," he asked cautiously. "Can we talk?"

She didn't bat an eye.

"No."

The unicorn shrugged off her reply.

"I haven't gotten a chance to tell you in the craziness of everything, but I wanted to say I truly regret what happened. You didn't deserve what happened back there. Hell, you don't deserve what's happening *now*. And all I can do is beg for your forgiveness."

U's surprisingly naïve request lit a fuse in Luzi's heart.

"Forgiveness?" she exploded, a raw, alien rage hijacking

her heart. "I've lost everything because of you! Do you understand? EVERYTHING!"

"That goddamned farm wasn't much, but it was all I had… and now it's gone!" Luzi roared, the tears welling in her eyes. "You and your bastard kin just destroyed thirty generations-worth of dreams! Everything my parents worked for – everything they sacrificed and bled for! And now you want forgiveness? *Forgiveness*? Well, you're not going to get it!"

Unable to stop herself, Luzi sprung from her seat and lunged towards U. Piloted purely by anger, she flailed at the unicorn with a closed fist, wincing when she connected with his cheek. His flesh was so tough it was like slugging a bag of rocks. *He probably didn't feel a thing*, Luzi realized as her knuckles turned red.

U's next comment didn't make things any better.

"You didn't hurt your hand, did you?" he asked tenderly, not even bothering to rise from his seat.

"Go to hell!" Luzi choked, determined to not let him see her cry.

Without waiting for a reply, she stormed off and flopped down on the ground at the far end of the campsite. The temperature had plunged with the sunset, as it always did in the unforgiving Nyasian outback. Luzi glanced up at the sky, where a trio of bright, yellow moons backlit a canvas of stars. It was the same night sky she'd always known. But now it seemed impossibly cold and foreign, a mocking memory of what used to be.

Cradling her throbbing hand, Luzi curled up into the fetal position. Trying to take her mind off the horror of the present, she retreated into the comfort of the past, reminiscing about all the last moments she never knew would be final.

She sniffed the sweet, worn leather of her father's work gloves. She listened to her mother's dulcimer voice ringing out across the steppe, singing the beautiful lullabies of her childhood. She felt the cool mud on her feet as the three of them splashed around in a summer monsoon... a unit... a tribe of their own.

Gone.

All gone.

Before she could blink it away, a big, fat tear ran down Luzi's face. She felt it on her cheek, warm and embarrassing, somehow even worse than if she'd soiled herself. More tears soon followed, forming a crusty, clownish mask on her face. Luzi didn't bother to stop them. She laid there – red-eyed and broken – unable to put herself back together, even if she'd wanted to.

I tried! Luzi silently lamented, her teeth chattering from cold and shame. *I'm sorry, mama... I tried!*

And before long, like a dog that's been beaten until it can't feel anymore, she drifted into an exhausted sleep.

4

"Angels come, when you cry. Devils come, if you don't try."

– Dada Da Dada, beloved Abyssinian children's bard

It was spring in the Nyasian outback – those brief days before the summer rains – when all of the elements were at equilibrium and everything was right with the world.

Luzi lazily plowed the potuber field, not so much toiling as puttering. The afternoon sun gently shone down with a soft, golden glow, and the rich smell of soil wafted up with each pass of the blade. Luzi sipped on each lungful of air slowly, like she was tasting a fine wine. Standing before the naked splendor of the outback, she couldn't help but be awed. In a few weeks, the weather would take a turn for the worse again, and the crushing routine of farm life would drag her back down into the doldrums. But in that moment – for just a short while – there was no finer place in the world.

As she reveled in her temporary nirvana, Luzi heard the muffled sound of shuffling feet on freshly plowed dirt.

Company?

Luzi turned around. At one end of the field stood her father, his bear-shaped silhouette unmistakable against the sun. At the opposite end was her mother, her wiry frame throwing an oblong shadow across the steppe. Delighted to see them, Luzi waved and called out.

"Mama! Papa!"

Strangely, neither responded. Instead, both plodded towards her at a glacial pace, as if they were asleep on their feet.

Luzi called out again. There was no reply.

Didn't they hear me?

The Nyasian stood with her arms at her side, waiting for her parents to get closer. As they approached, she saw that they were moving unnaturally stiff, lumbering ahead with unbending knees and elbows.

And then – gasping – Luzi saw the reason why.

Her parents were little more than walking corpses, decomposing husks held together by a handful of sinews and tendons. Their dead eyes stared ahead lifelessly, unfocused and uncaring. The grotesque zombies shambled onward like crude puppets guided by a malevolent, spectral hand, leaving a trail of maggots and grave slime in their wake.

Frozen with fear, Luzi watched the things trudge closer. And that's when something even more horrifying caught Luzi's eye... her parents were each wearing one of the Immaculan Rings!

Luzi spun around, hollering at her mother and father in turn.

"Don't do it!" she pleaded, waving her arms in a frantic attempt to get their attention. "You'll destroy the world!"

But the elder Winterstars ignored her and continued to

close the distance. As they reached arm's length, they raised their ghastly digits towards each other. Then, for the first time, they slowly turned towards their daughter. And in a dead whisper, Luzi's parents uttered a single word: "SEREN-DIPITY."

Luzi recognized the phrase immediately. It was a mantra her father used when something bad happened, his perpetual attempt to find the good in things... even when it seemed there was none. A camel died? Serendipity, because it was suffering. No rain for three weeks? Serendipity, because there isn't any mud to track in the house.

But the cryptic message didn't make sense coming from those ghouls. *Why here?* Luzi puzzled. *Why now?*

"Wait!" Luzi implored, begging the specters to halt. "I don't understand!"

Her pleas had no effect. Luzi's parents turned back to each other.

They touched rings.

The world exploded.

A violent wave of energy burst forth from the mated rings, engulfing everything in its path. Nothing survived its rage, not a plant or beast within a thousand miles. And though she wailed and wailed, all Luzi could hear above the awful roar was a single word, moaned over and over.

"SERENDIPITY."

***

Suddenly, Luzi awoke with a gasp.

She was lying on the ground, gazing at a starry sky. The

nippy chill of the nighttime Nyasian outback wafted over her sweat-soaked body, coaxing her back to reality. *Just a dream,* she realized with a relieved shudder. *Just a dream.*

"Are you all right?" a familiar voice asked.

When Luzi whipped around, she saw U staring at her with an eerie, unblinking gaze. He was sitting on the same rock – in the same exact position – as when she fell asleep.

"Have you been watching me this whole time, you fucking creep?" Luzi mumbled, rubbing her eyes.

U shrugged.

"If it makes you feel any better, I wasn't spying on you – just keeping guard. Unicorns have no biological need for sleep. We only do it when we're seeking a spiritual vision, or as you humans call them: 'dreams.' Speaking of which, I was just about to wake you up. You were thrashing around like a gremlin in a gunnysack. Is anything wrong?"

Luzi sat up and took a deep breath to gather her wits.

"I'm fine," she muttered, blotting the sweat from her forehead with her sleeve. "It was a nightmare, that's all."

"What was it about?" U queried, arching an eyebrow with concern.

"None of your goddamn business!" Luzi snapped.

"Don't be embarrassed," U insisted. "Dreams can be powerful things. And we ignore them at our own peril. Trust me, I know."

"Oh, you do?" Luzi scoffed. "Tell me, then... what does a *nightmare* have nightmares about?"

To her surprise, Luzi's comment cut the unicorn deep. For a long moment, U said nothing. When he spoke again, there was a palpable pain he didn't bother to hide... something raw... something honest.

"Did you know that unicorns can't have children?"

Luzi blinked. "No," she admitted, her curiosity overpowering her anger.

U wrung his hands together.

"What I'm about to tell you hasn't ever been recorded by any human scribe, or passed down by any elven oracle's tongue. But I assure you, every word is true."

"Many ages ago – long before the rise of the humans or elves – we Monoceros ruled as the dominant species of this world. In those golden years, tens of thousands of my kin roamed the forests... lounged on beaches... feasted on fresh game in the plains. We were the top of the food chain, the pinnacle of evolution."

"And then came the *Nbzz Xchi*: the Birth Drought," he said, melancholy seeping into his voice like water into a sinking boat.

"About five thousand years ago, back when I was still a young stallion, the unicorn race lost the ability to bear children. To this day, nobody understands why, not even we Monoceros. We have left no stone unturned in our quest for a cure. Magic. Science. Prayer. All have been equally useless.

"After our ailment became known, it wasn't long before we lost our place as the masters of the world. Once feared or worshipped by every culture in the known realms, we became outlaws in our own fiefdoms, hunted at every turn by those we once preyed upon. To survive, we fled to the hidden places: the impassable mountains, the deep underground, the islands at the farthest corners of the world. But we all know it's only a matter of time before the last of us succumbs to battle, disaster or a cruel, slow starvation."

U's eyes gained a desperate sheen in the silver light of the moon.

"You ask me what a nightmare has nightmares about? Here's my answer: extinction. Without the ability to have off-spring, the unicorn species is only forestalling the inevitable. The Monoceros are a doomed race, cursed with lifespans that will drag out our demise for millennia to come. Even if the Meridian *does* get the ring – even if she *does* manage to wipe out the human race – our future is still ruined. Nothing can stop what's to come. And one day, for better or worse, the world will no longer have unicorns in it."

U stopped talking, as if he didn't have the strength to continue. A long silence passed before the unicorn spoke again. When he did, it was with a humility that trembled under the weight of its own gravity.

"Luzi... what I said earlier about forgiveness? I'm not sure if stupidity or pride made me say that. Maybe both. But I know I don't deserve it. That's never been clearer to me than it is right now. I can't bring back your old life, any more than I can save the Monoceros race. The only thing I *can* do is show you I'm sorry. So that's what I'm going to do."

U's eyes narrowed with determination.

"The entire time you've been asleep, I've been trying to figure out an apology worthy of your attention. Such a thing proved more difficult than I'd expected. After all, I have no coin or jewels, no connections to house or trade in Dama'run, not a single worldly possession I can surrender."

The unicorn looked at Luzi earnestly.

"But then it hit me. I *do* have a boon I can grant you. It's something more valuable than gold and more enduring than a diamond. And once you have it, you'll never be at anyone's mercy again... including mine."

Luzi snorted. "Oh yeah? What's that?"

"I'm going to teach you how to use magic," U replied, the corners of his mouth perking up in a faint smile.

****

"Magic?" Luzi remarked, laughing sarcastically. "Ridiculous!"

"I don't understand. What's so funny?"

Luzi wrinkled her nose.

"In case you can't figure it out from the calluses on my hands and the patches on my clothes, I'm a farmer! I don't know a goddamn thing about wizardry!"

"Nor does any mage until their first day of study," U countered. "But even the mightiest flood has its origin in a single drop of rain, does it not?"

The unicorn's eyes flashed bright with a spark of nostalgia.

"Before the Nbzz Xchi, one of my favorite duties was working with the Overgruk younglings, helping them to hone their powers and master the Deep Energy. And if I learned anything during that time, it's that *anyone* can be taught *anything* – as long as they have the willpower to learn."

"Forget what you are, or think you are," U urged. "There's a power lying within your grasp that you've only read about in books until now. The big question is... do you want it?"

The immense casualness of U's question – "Do you want

it?" – echoed in Luzi's heart. Every instinct in her brain screamed to refuse his offer on basic principle. *This is the creature that threatened your life just a day ago!* she reminded herself bitterly. *It's some sort of trick, are you really this stupid?*

But although Luzi's conscience raged against the idea, another part of her psyche offered a vehement second opinion.

How many times have you cursed the gods for putting a shovel in your hands instead of a sword? All these years of pretending you have some great destiny beyond the farm... was it only a bunch of lies? Or do you actually believe it?

Suddenly, as if a sign from above, a twinkle from a cluster of stars caught her eye. Luzi peered up at the night sky to the source.

The Scales of Fortune.

The favored constellation of Nyasian traders, it's fabled that any deal struck under its full light is fated to end fruitfully. Luzi had never lent much credence to the myths herself. But that night, standing under an unfamiliar sky without a friend in the world, there was something strangely comforting about its presence. And the words came tumbling out of her mouth before she even knew she'd uttered them.

"Fine, unicorn... let's give this ridiculous apprenticeship a try. What do I do first?"

U smiled at her eagerness.

"Patience. Our first lesson will be a difficult one, and you'll need some rest. We can start out fresh after the day's journey tomorrow. Get some sleep if you can."

He winked, mimicking a human gesture of empathy he'd learned long ago.

"Because tomorrow, your new life begins."

5

"Empty womb / Malaise of knowledge / The slumber cauldron / We stir the whispering songs / Second coming, or victory in death!"

– Ly the Poet, matriarch of the Hünndiin-Monoceros coven [5]

The cave was primordial and dark, as ancient and imposing as the Overgruk themselves. That was why the Meridian chose it for their home, after all.

Except for a few scattered glowworm colonies, there was no light in those miles of twisted underground: no sunspots, no torches, not a single lantern or candle. But the interminable gloom wasn't a drawback for the unicorns; Monoceros do not need light to see. Indeed, over the thousands of years they'd been living in exile, many members of the coven had begun to *prefer* the darkness. And throughout that entire, awful cavern, there was only one space where any true illumination existed... the Meridian's chamber.

Her sanctum lay deep in the heart of the cave, where none except the upper echelon of the Overgruk coven were permitted to tread. There, a hundred magic-imbued basins blazed with a spectral flame, reflecting their golden light off the walls of the chamber and bathing everything inside with an unnatural, regal brilliance. There was no gate, only an open mouth of the cavern through which anyone could freely stroll. But no sane creature in the known realms would have dared to enter her lair uninvited.

Not while *she* dwelled inside.

Two heads taller than any of the other Overgruk, the alpha unicorn was immaculately proportioned, as if cut from marble. Her platinum hair and cascading mane shimmered like an angel. Her pitch-black eyes absorbed light like a sponge. Those who have seen her in repose have described her as "beatific." Those who have seen her in combat have called her "terrifying."

None – friend or foe – have ever called her "ordinary."

The Meridian casually strolled through her subterranean chamber. Dozens of podiums carved of polished bone were placed throughout the lair, each with awe-inspiring treasures resting on top of them: a bottled Jinn... one of the seven Ouramos wands... a pair of Phrygian gauntlets... the fabled helm of Rostam... a preserved medusa head... the jaws of a true dragon. [6]

The Meridian paused and stared at the coven's treasures, all eyes and memory. She'd collected many of the mementos herself, back in the days when she used to do her own killing. But no new trophies had been added to the collection for a thousand years, maybe more. It was sad.

No... not sad, the Meridian mused, correcting herself. *Shameful.*

Suddenly, her nose twitched at the musk of an approaching

unicorn. The scent was old, familiar. Soon another Monoceros crept forth into the chamber, moving slowly as her eyes adjusted to the light of the Meridian's den. Copper-colored and with a long, wiry body, the unicorn seemed to have a spiteful smirk perpetually cut into her face. One of her eyes was gouged out; a gaping, empty vacuum was all that remained.

Karkadiann.

The unicorn approached the Meridian and lowered her head respectfully.

"You called for me, mistress?"

"Our worst fears have come true, old friend," the Meridian replied, her voice as supple as a summer breeze yet bold as a clap of thunder. "We've been betrayed. Uchchaihshravas has taken the ring and slain Buvöda. They are on the run, with the future of our race in their possession."

"They?" Karkadiann queried.

The Meridian's lips curled.

"The Nyasian still draws breath," she said, every syllable feeling like acid on her tongue. "Uchchaihshravas has ignored my direct order and spared her life."

"Where are they, mistress?" Karkadiann snarled, grinding her teeth. "I will tear open their bellies and smear their entrails in the mud. I will stomp their skulls into shrapnel and gnaw on their brains. I will–"

"I have no doubt you would do all this and more, my friend," the Meridian interrupted. "But I know not where the vermin have scampered. The traitor has smashed his sigil, and he's too far away to locate with my powers. When you combine this with his shapeshifting abilities, they'll be next to impossible to find. So I've been forced to enlist... aid."

"Aid?"

The Meridian gave her subordinate a steely glare, knowing what her reaction would be.

"I have issued a bounty request to the Boogeyman."

"Mistress!" Karkadiann gasped. "Forgive my insolence. But are we truly so desperate that we would entrust our future to *that* abomination?"

"The gap between hope and reality that we face is too large to cross on a bridge built of assumptions," the Meridian explained. "The Boogeyman has never failed to deliver a mark in his career as a bounty hunter. His power as a Dragnir to travel through dreams is one that even we Overgruk don't count among our arsenal. If there is anyone who can hunt down Uchchaihshravas and his human confederate – and quickly – it is he."

"Still, I suppose that strange fruit has grown in desperate places before," the Meridian conceded. "We must be prepared if the Boogeyman should fail. I want you to assemble a full murder of our swiftest warriors. Be ready to depart the cave at a moment's notice. But under no circumstance will you leave without my permission... is that understood?"

"Yes, mistress."

"Don't take it personally, old friend," the Meridian consoled, seeing the disappointed expression on Karkadiann's face. "I know you're still sore about Uchchaihshravas' victory in the ring all those years ago. And I know you've been dreaming of a rematch for centuries. But this is no time to let our egos get in the way of destiny. Not when we stand to lose so much."

The alpha unicorn paused.

"Do you remember how it was in the early days, before we lost the ability to give birth and were driven underground? The world was different then. *We* were different. We roamed in fields of green, feeling the cool of the grass on our forelocks. We soared into sunrises high on the summer breezes."

The Meridian looked up, meeting her servant's eyes.

"We laughed, Karkadiann. Do you remember? We *laughed*."

"I remember," Karkadiann said quietly, her anger dissipating at the memory.

The Meridian didn't release her subordinate from her gaze.

"What transpired between you and Uchchaihshravas is in the past. Our brothers and sisters deserve justice more than you deserve pride. Remember this if jealousy clouds your vision, my loyal lieutenant. Now go. Assemble your peers. And I promise that when I have both Immaculan Rings in my possession, the glory which awaits us will burn so brightly it will set the world on fire."

"Your command is my conviction," Karkadiann said. "I will see it done."

With a short bow, Karkadiann disappeared the same way she came. The Meridian watched as she slipped away like a shadow on the edge of a sunset.

And with a smile lifting her lips, she turned back to her trophies.

6

"Are you sure you still want to do this?"

U and Luzi stood among a grove of Jaxon trees, a vivacious moonlight reflecting in their eyes. Their second day of riding had been just as grueling as the first. And U's question echoed in Luzi's head with a pragmatic poignancy... she was completely fucking exhausted.

"Like I told you last night, learning how to use magic isn't easy," U continued, trying his best not to sound condescending. "You've been going nonstop for two days, now. Maybe you should get some sleep. We can always start our lessons tomorrow."

For a brief moment, Luzi couldn't help but consider the unicorn's proposal. Fatigue was painted like ceruse on the Nyasian's face. Her legs felt like rubber; her stomach growled like a demon dog. And there was nothing she'd have rather have done than close her eyes and let it all slip away. But when Luzi thought about the creatures pursuing them – and what they planned to do if they caught up – it filled her belly with a fire that slumber had no possibility of extinguishing.

"I'll sleep when I'm dead," she told U, shaking off her weariness. "Let's get to it."

"Fair enough," U replied with a nod. "I suppose I should start at the very beginning. What do you know about the Ubamota?"

"Uh-oh," Luzi quipped, trying not to groan. "Why does it feel like a long batch of exposition is coming my way?"

U couldn't help but smile. "Don't worry, I'll make this as painless as possible."

"Ubamota are the tiniest living things in existence. If you split a drop of water in half a billion times, you still wouldn't come close to the size of one. They lie at the center of every-thing, even our own bodies, existing in every possible climate and environment throughout the known realms. They don't have sentience – not any more than a mushroom or a worm, anyway. However, these otherwise modest creatures are the source of all magic in the world.

"Instead of breathing out air, like you or me, Ubamota exude an energy more powerful than lightning... greater than the binding forces... stronger than the fury of the heavens themselves. This energy is called the 'Deep Magic.' It's in-visible and odorless, completely undetectable unless you're looking for it. But anyone who can harness it can break the laws of nature as if they were made of glass.

"Some creatures have an instinctive ability to manipulate the Deep Magic. Gorgons turn their victims to stone. Kitsune can shapeshift. Naga control the weather. For them, it's as natural as eating or breathing. They don't *think* about it; they just *do* it."

"Humans are a different story," U continued. "You're all born with the gift of being able to tap into the Deep Magic. But you need to learn how to use it or the ability fades away in a few years. This is one of the reasons why almost all human mages start training when they're toddlers."

U shrugged.

"It isn't impossible for an adult human to learn how to use magic – only difficult. But you don't have the months of intensive study that would usually be required of an apprentice your age. So we're going to have to try something unorthodox to jumpstart your abilities... and you're not going to enjoy it."

The unicorn pointed at a sash hanging around Luzi's waist. "I need to borrow that, if you'd be so kind. And your canteen, too."

Luzi hesitantly handed over the items.

"Now what?"

"Now I'm going to kill you," U replied matter-of-factly.

"Let me explain," the unicorn interjected, cutting off the Nyasian's protest before it could begin. "You see, when humans die – or they *believe* they're dying – they let down all the mental walls they've erected in their minds over their lifetime. They exchange the possible for the impossible. And at the moment of their deaths, they become capable of absorbing the Deep Magic once again."

"The same should be true for you," U theorized. "There's a good chance that if we trick your body into thinking it's dying, you'll be able to rekindle your ability to channel

Ubamota energy. It'll be like restarting a campfire from a bed of hot coals."

"Such a thing is easier said than done, however," the unicorn admitted. "I can think of a thousand ways to take you to the brink of death. A dozen would leave you unmaimed. A handful would also leave your mind intact. But only one can be done with the materials we have on hand: the Trial of Mizuchi."

"The Trial of Mizuchi?" Luzi asked in a dubious tone. "What the fuck is *that*?"

"One of the oldest tortures in recorded history," U replied. "It involves no magic whatsoever, just two simple components."

He held up the cloth and the canteen.

"First, you lay the subject down. Then, you take a wet cloth and drape it over their face. Finally, you take a pitcher of water and run it over their nostrils and mouth, tricking their body into thinking it's drowning."

Luzi blanched. "It sounds awful."

U nodded somberly.

"I'm not going to lie. This isn't going to be easy. The trial is a torture designed to break the minds of hardened warriors. You'll feel scared... helpless... alone. But I'll be here the entire time. And I give you my word: you will be fine."

He paused dramatically and grinned. "Unless you die of a heart attack, of course."

"U!"

The humor disappeared from the unicorn's face.

"Luzi... you don't have to do this," he assured. "You have

nothing to prove to anyone – least of all me. We can forget the whole thing if you want. Just say the word."

But of course – it was far too late for that, Luzi knew.

Sighing, Luzi laid down on the ground. She glanced up at U expectedly.

"Well... what are you waiting for?"

With expert speed and precision – as if he'd performed the task many times – U wet the remaining scrap of cloth and draped it over her face like a death shroud. Then he placed his hand on Luzi's forehead, using his immense strength to effortlessly pin her down. *By the rotten orbs of Dis, what've you gotten yourself into?* the Nyasian whispered to herself, a paralyzing claustrophobia buzzing in her brain.

"We're almost ready," U said in a calm, deliberate voice, positioning the canteen above her head. "I just have one last question. Do you trust me?"

Luzi inhaled sharply. She tried to nod but couldn't move. Instead, she blinked twice.

U smiled reassuringly. "Then prepare to be reborn, Luzi Winterstar."

And without further delay, he began to dump water onto her face.

There was a sharp shock as the first deluge entered Luzi's nostrils and flooded her sinuses with a stinging rush. She felt her body seizing, her muscles clenching. It was the world's worst hiccup, the devil's acid reflux. As she choked, Luzi desperately struggled to free herself. She felt herself gagging and trying to spit up water, but there was nowhere for it to go. Fear surged through her arteries like venom. She tried to scream for U to let her go, but couldn't draw enough air to make a sound.

Something's wrong! she panicked. *Stop! Stop!*

But as Luzi's body began to go into shock, something strange started to happen. A warm energy radiated through her belly, like the first sip of hot tea on a cold, winter day. It swelled through every synapse and nerve – pure sunlight injected into her bloodstream. Soon, an irresistible light appeared all around her, as if descended from Jannah. Like a moth drawn towards a flame, Luzi felt herself floating towards it... melting into it. The panic faded. Her struggle for air ceased.

And then – just as she found peace – the world whooshed back with a horrifying clangor.

Luzi found herself lying unbound in the dirt. For a minute, she did nothing but gulp air, like a thirsty dog quaffing from a bowl. Finally, she looked up at U with moist eyes and a feeble smile.

"I think we're gonna need more water," the Nyasian joked weakly, wiping spit off her face with her sleeve.

U grinned sympathetically. He extended a hand to Luzi and lifted the young woman to her feet.

"You did incredible," he complimented. "I've seen hardened murderers emerge from the trial blubbering like babies. You should be proud of yourself. No matter what happens next."

"There's *more?*"

The unicorn's tone darkened; his smile faded.

"I know your head is still spinning. But I need to walk you through one more lesson while the experience is fresh in your mind, or you've endured all this misery for nothing."

"Think back to the last moment before I revived you," U probed. "What did you feel?"

"Panic!" Luzi immediately replied, choking at the mere thought.

"No, no, that's the *reptile* part of your brain," U responded, shaking his head. "Dig deeper. What did the *human* part feel?"

Luzi closed her eyes, searching her memory.

"There was a warm, white light," she finally said, unsure of how to describe it. "I've never felt anything like it. It was as if I was in the presence of some greater force, something omnipotent and–"

Luzi stopped in mid-sentence and cocked her head at U, suddenly making the connection.

"By the unholy taint of Dis... *that* was the Ubamota, wasn't it?"

U nodded.

"Why do you think so many of your species see a bright light at the moment of their deaths? It's the Ubamota energy racing through their systems, flooding their bodies with pure mystic energy. To perform magic, you need to be able to charge yourself up with this energy at will. Luckily for you, the hard part is done. Your body has been reawakened to the Deep Magic. We just have to teach you how to bring it to that same place again."

The unicorn waved at Luzi encouragingly. "Let's give it a try. Close your eyes."

This is crazy, Luzi thought. But trying her best to suspend her lingering disbelief, she shut her eyes, took a deep breath and relaxed.

"Concentrate," U whispered, his voice hushed with a

hypnotic softness. "Let down all the walls you've erected in your mind over the years. Become a dry sponge, an empty vessel. The energy is all around you. It's in the air. It's in the trees... the sand... the rocks. All you have to do is let it in."

The Nyasian took another deep breath. The unicorn's voice began to fade in the back of her mind.

Let it in... let it in... let it in.

After a moment, a pleasant sensation began to blossom inside of her stomach. It was a soft but enveloping feeling, like being immersed in a warm bath. Luzi could sense it flowing through parts of herself she wasn't normally aware of... her hair... her toenails... her eyelids.

The Deep Magic.

"I feel it," Luzi whispered.

"Good," U replied. "But we're not done yet. There's one last step: you need to purge the Ubamota energy from your body."

"How?"

"Simple... relax and allow it to diffuse into the air around you. Imagine it just like breathing. Only instead of exhaling through your mouth and nose, you're exhaling through your entire body."

Following U's instructions, Luzi slowly released the energy inside her. There was a mild tingle as the excess warmth left her body, like taking the first step outside on a cold, winter night. And a few seconds later, it was as if she'd never absorbed the Deep Magic at all.

Luzi opened her eyes. She blinked a few times at U, as if waking from a trance.

"That was fucking amazing," she muttered at last, unable to hide her awe. "What's next?"

The unicorn grinned.

"Let's stop tonight's lesson here. Practice for a little while longer, then get some sleep – you've earned it. You can pick it up again during the ride tomorrow."

Luzi bristled at the order, as if he was her father commanding her to bed. "Stop sandbagging me," she insisted. "I'm not some little popinjay. We don't have to-"

The unicorn cut her off.

"Believe me, I don't doubt your fortitude in the slightest, Luzi. I *know* you're a badass. But this is an essential lesson. If you can't keep continually charged with Ubamota energy, your magic will be disastrously unreliable. Most apprentices spend months doing nothing but Deep Breathing before making the leap to actual spellcasting. Have patience, I beg you. We've got a long road ahead of us before we reach Dama'run. And you've got a lot more to learn before you stand a chance of surviving combat with a unicorn."

For a moment, Luzi considered continuing the argument. But in her heart, the Nyasian knew U was right.

"Fine," she grudgingly conceded. "But just remember one thing. None of this will matter if the Overgruk find us first."

U glanced out on the horizon, envisioning his brothers and sisters flying across the sky with fire and venom in their veins.

"I guess we've finally got something we can agree on," he said solemnly.

7

Rising at the first hint of sunrise, Luzi and U slogged through another punishing day of travel before they stopped to rest amid the cover of some Jaxon trees.

"Did you practice charging up with the Deep Magic during the ride?" U asked as they prepared for their evening training session.

Luzi nodded.

"It's coming much easier. It took me almost a half-minute to fully charge when I went to sleep last night. Now, I can do it in a few seconds."

"Keep practicing," the unicorn replied, stretching his arms to limber up. "Deep Breathing needs to be instinctual, something you do without thought or premeditation."

"Still, we have a lot to cover and not much time to do it," he added. "So this will have to do for now. Because tonight,

I present the most important bit of magic you'll ever learn... how to make substantives."

"How to make *what*?" Luzi questioned, no longer ashamed by her own ignorance.

U extended his hand in reply. There was a brief flicker – like a spark appearing from a flintstone – and a miniature bird magically appeared in his palm. It looked exactly like a real animal down to the finest detail, except it was made from a strange, golden light unlike any she'd ever seen from sun or candle. As Luzi watched in awe, the bird transformed into a wolf... a griffin... a snake... each of them as intricate of detail as the last. Finally, with a theatrical flourish, U clenched his hand into a fist. When he opened it again, his creation had vanished, leaving no trace behind, not even a wisp of smoke.

"Okay, you got me," a mesmerized Luzi muttered. "How in the name of Dis did you do that?"

"The Deep Magic can be used many ways," U explained. "One of them is to form solid objects, like you saw me do now. In the magic schools, these are called *substantives*. And they're not limited to little trinkets, either. With enough practice, a skilled mage can conjure keys that fit any door, bridges that can cross a river, or weapons that can cleave the thickest armor... the only limit is their own imagination."

U surreptitiously peeked at her, like he was about to impart a secret.

"The key to creating substantives is grasping one simple concept: *perception is reality*. In its pure form, the Deep Magic is both energy and matter. It's only the perception of the magician that makes it manifest as one or the other. If you perceive of the Deep Magic as energy – like you did yesterday

– it will be so. But the opposite is true as well. If you perceive of it as a solid object, it will take that form instead."

"I don't get it," Luzi said, already lost.

"Let's put it another way," U continued, rubbing his chin. "Imagine that you shut a spider and a fly in a box together, then close the lid so you can't see inside. Tell me, is the fly alive or dead?"

Luzi deliberated for a second before answering. "Both," she finally said. "There's no way to know until you open the box."

U nodded encouragingly.

"Exactly! Until that exact moment, the fly must be both alive and dead – existing in two states of being at once. The only thing that makes it one or the other is when you intervene. Your perception of the event is literally what creates it."

"You mean... I can just *wish* something into existence?" Luzi asked with wide eyes.

U clicked his tongue.

"Wishing? What you're suggesting is impossible. There is no wishing involved here. These concepts are as tangible as the air you breathe or the ground underneath your feet. The Deep Magic is as real as the flame that cooks your meals or the water that you drink. And if you don't realize this, you'll fail before you begin. Do you understand?"

"I guess so," Luzi reasoned tentatively.

"Well, there's only one way to know for sure," U challenged. "Let's give it a try."

"First, charge yourself up with Ubamota energy," he instructed, gesturing for her to take a breath.

Luzi took a breath and let the Deep Magic flood into her body. "OK," she said after a few moments. "What now?"

"When you're ready, slowly release all that stored up energy like you've been practicing," U replied. "But this time, instead of letting it dissipate into the air, focus it into a shape. Let's start with something easy... a ball, perhaps."

Luzi held out her palm like U had done. Exhaling audibly like a flautist, she started to release the Deep Magic. At first – to her chagrin – not a damn thing happened. But after a few seconds, there was a strange glint in the air, like a heat wave across a hot patch of sand, or the shimmer of sunlight on water. Tiny sparks of light flickered above her hand, then started to congeal... become denser... take shape. And suddenly, there was a sphere of golden energy resting in the center of her palm.

Luzi gaped at her creation with wonder. Unable to contain herself, she glanced at U, a childlike look of delight spreading on her face.

Despite his best attempt to remain stoic, the unicorn couldn't help but return her goofy grin.

"Not bad," he conceded. "Not bad at all."

Distracted by his praise, Luzi began to lose her concentration. The orb in her palm started to flicker and fade.

"Stay focused!" U insisted. "If you daydream while spellcasting, your substantive will collapse back into energy. Remember, it's only your willpower that's holding it in this form. And if your mind or body should break, so will the substantive."

Luzi nodded. She gritted her teeth and bore down; the golden ball re-solidified.

"Very good," U encouraged. "Now that you've got the

theory down, let's see how far you can take this. Follow my lead and do your best to keep up."

One by one, the unicorn called out items for Luzi to create, gradually increasing in complexity. At his cues, Luzi created a brick... a wheel... a hammer... a pair of shears. Impressed, U watched his pupil as she performed each instruction, growing more adept at wielding the Deep Magic with each pass. *It's like she's been doing this for years*, he mused.

Finally, U raised his hands. "That's enough. Let's move on to the final part of tonight's lesson."

Luzi let her substantive disappear. "And what's that?"

The unicorn gave her a sly grin.

"We need to figure out what your armum is."

Waving his hand, U conjured a long, thin-bladed sword, similar to the type those of the Abyssinian nation favored. But this was no ordinary weapon. It gleamed with a golden hue, making it seem otherworldly – something a god would wield.

With the effortless movements of a seasoned warrior, U raised his magic sword and slashed at a nearby boulder. It cut through the rock like a knife through cake, leaving a firestorm of sparks trailing behind in its wake.

U held out the spectral blade to a slack-jawed Luzi.

"A weapon made of Ubamota energy is sharper than the most expertly crafted cutlass. It's harder than the most menacing war spike, more accurate than the finest-calibrated crossbow. And it's damn near the only thing that's tough enough to kill a unicorn.

"Every battle mage has an Ubamota weapon they can summon without hesitation, something they've trained to use with lethal precision. Some of us favor swords. Others prefer maces, or halberds or spears. I even knew a mage whose idea of a deadly weapon was a pitchfork. In the magic world, we call these *armums*."

The unicorn dematerialized his sword and looked Luzi in the eyes.

"The question we need to figure out now is simple," he said pointedly. "What's *yours*?"

"I- I don't know," Luzi stammered, stalling for time.

But U didn't relent.

"Try to picture it... try *hard*!" he urged. "What if you had to protect yourself from another unicorn? What would you choose? A morning star? A three-sectioned staff? A butcher's knife? Think, Luzi! Think! Because one day – maybe soon – both of our lives might depend on it."

Just then, an image popped into Luci's head: *Aunt Throy's war shield*. A large, thick circle of bronze with a dagger-thin edge, the battle shield had hung on the wall of her relative's home since before Luci was born. According to her aunt, it was a relic from one of their distant ancestors, a mighty warrior who died while defending his homestead from outback raiders. Luci remembered marveling at the shield when she was a visiting child, being filled with wonder every time her aunt told its story. And though she was never allowed to try it on, the shield became a symbol of courage that would never lose its sheen.

"You have something in mind?" U asked, seeing the sudden look of familiarity on the Nyasian's face.

"Yes," Luzi said, surprised at her own conviction. "I do."

"Show me."

Acting quickly – as one does to jot down the details of a dream – Luzi summoned the Deep Magic and started creating. It came easily, as if it were already half-completed in her head. And in less than a minute, a golden war shield was strapped to her forearm.

Luzi examined the weapon with pride, surprised by her own handiwork. She hefted the shield high. It was unnaturally light, as if it were made of balsawood, but Luzi could tell there was a strength to it beyond any steel or iron.

"A war shield?" U commented, raising a curious eyebrow at her creation. "An unusual choice. But I've got to admit that it suits you."

The unicorn pointed at a large tree stump nearby. "Go ahead. Try it out."

Shifting her feet, Luzi raised the shield into striking position. She paused, balancing the weapon in her hand. Then, rearing back as if she was about to hurl a discus, Luzi swung forward with a right hook. Splinters and sawdust flew into the air as her shield sliced cleanly through the tree stump – a surefire killing stroke.

By the burly nuggets of Dis... did I just do THAT? Luzi marveled, gawking at her spectral weapon.

U clapped his hands approvingly.

"Congratulations, Luzi. You've discovered one of the most important bits of magic you'll ever use. Practice summoning your armum for another hour and get some sleep."

The unicorn nodded at her shield. "And tomorrow, I'll start showing you how to actually use that thing."

***

The next few days were made up of two activities: traveling at day and training at night.

The daytimes were the hardest. Trapped riding, there was nothing to do but reminisce. And inevitably, Luzi's contemplations strayed to her former life. At times, the weight in her heart felt so immense, it seemed impossible that U was able to carry her.

But at night – engrossed in her magic – Luzi could forget about the ghosts that plagued the waking hours. It was an outlet for her anger and helplessness, a way to fight back against an enemy she couldn't see. And so, she poured her heart into every drill... every motion... every lesson.

There was no alternative except madness.

As fortune would have it, the Nyasian couldn't have hoped for a finer teacher. U's knowledge of the art of war was unparalleled, a lethal combination of scholarly insight and thousands of years of battle experience. Over the next two days, U ran through the basic shield fighting techniques with Luzi: the press, the hook, the block. He taught her how to stand, how to defend, how to retreat... how to breathe.

To help herself learn, Luzi juxtaposed each new move with one of the repetitious motions she'd done thousands of times during the course of her daily work on the farm. A punch block became "opening the gate." A shield snatch became "scything the weeds." An overhead strike became "hammering the nail."

To Luzi's surprise, once she made the connection, the rest of it came naturally. She was amazed at the coincidence. It was as if – by complete accident – her days on the farm had trained her for what was to come.

And with every new move Luzi learned, a part of her wondered what else she'd underestimated about her old life.

***

After yet another grueling day of travel, the duo stopped for the evening, a full canopy of stars illuminating the skies overhead.

"So what's on the menu tonight?" Luzi asked, trying not to sound too eager. "More substantive exercises? Some new combat drills, maybe?"

"Not tonight," U replied, his cautious tone sending a chill down her spine. "You've come a long way in these past few days. But there's one final lesson you need to master... it's time to teach you how to kill a unicorn."

"Slaying a unicorn isn't an easy feat for a human," U continued. "Monoceros can heal from almost any injury: burning, stabbing, crushing, freezing. We're resistant to nearly every known disease. We can survive for days without breathing, months without drinking, years without eating. In fact, there are only two certain ways to kill a unicorn short of total disintegration... cut off the head, or remove the horn."

"Sounds pretty straightforward," Luzi commented, trying to sound confident.

U chuckled.

"I promise you, it's as far away from 'straightforward' as getting horseshoes on a hippogriff. But don't take *my* word for it. Try it out for yourself."

Suddenly, a flash of golden light flared, and a Deep Magic replica of Buvöda was standing an arm's length away. Just like any of U's other substantives, it looked exactly like the real thing, right down to the late unicorn assassin's cruel grin and unrepentant stare.

As Luzi stared at the monstrosity with dread, her palms began to sweat. Her legs buckled; she felt the confidence of the last few days instantly evaporate.

"Go ahead," U prodded encouragingly, unaware of the pounding in her heart. "Take your best swing."

The Nyasian took a shaky breath, then manifested her shield with an immense effort. As sweat beaded on her forehead, she reared back to strike. Just then – right at the moment of truth – Luzi felt her shield hand start to quiver. At first, it was only a quick shudder. But the twitching didn't stop. It kept building until her whole hand was trembling, like she was in the terminal stages of crimson lung.

Her armum fizzled out with a pathetic *WHUMMM*.

"What's wrong?" U asked, finally understanding something was amiss.

The Nyasian didn't reply at first, biting her lip in a tense attempt to stay silent. But when the unicorn repeated his question, she looked up with glassy eyes, blinking to keep the tears from forming.

"Dis be damned!" she gushed at last. "Are you going to make me spell this out, U? I'm scared, all right? I'm fucking *scared!*"

Luzi balled her fists in frustration and kicked at a clod of dirt.

"For years, I made fun of my parents for how small their

lives were. Now, here I am, with the fate of the world in my hands, and I've never felt tinier in my life. The truth is, I wish I could just throw this damn ring on the ground and walk away from it all. I don't want to be a hero. I just want to be *me*. Guess that makes me a real coward, huh?"

U paused as he considered her words. Then, after a moment, he reached out and took Luzi's hand, squeezing it reassuringly.

"The Monoceros have a saying: *Even a coward can't abandon their own story*. And you know what? It must be true. Because if it weren't, I would have given up on myself millennia ago."

The unicorn gave his companion a smile, warming the chilly evening air of the outback. The two shared a moment of silence, naked in their vulnerability under the bright Nyasian moonlight. Finally, U let go of her hand, as if just realizing he'd been holding it all along. He turned back to the substantive, giving Luzi an encouraging nudge.

"Why don't you give it another try? And this time, remember... this is *your* story, Luzi Winterstar. It will end how *you* want it to."

Luzi wiped her palms on her robe and swallowed, trying to moisten her suddenly bone-dry mouth. She glanced at the phantasmic Buvöda, then back at U.

"Okay," she agreed, nodding.

Luzi slowly approached U's substantive, manifesting her armum and hoisting it into position. The Nyasian paused for another moment, focusing her energy. Then, just as she'd been practicing, Luzi pivoted on her foot and pitched her body forward, aiming for her target's neck.

Her cut was clean and powerful. Her follow-through was full and deliberate. And the result was inevitable.

Death to a unicorn.

"Excellent!" U crowed as she dematerialized her shield, the pride unmistakable in his voice. "What did I tell you? Heart of a warrior! Heart of a warrior!"

Luzi felt a cathartic swell rush through her head. She looked into U's fathomless brown eyes, almost forgetting they belonged to that of a unicorn, not a man. She wanted desperately to hate him in that moment. It would have made everything so much simpler. But as hard as she tried, Luzi could no longer summon the same animosity that once flowed so freely through her veins.

You're one of the worst things that's ever happened to me, she admitted bitterly. *But Dis help me... you're also one of the best.*

8

"It's better to light a candle than curse the darkness."

– Mandala Bakshi, survivor of the Quiystian 'Red Purge'

On the seventh day after the attack at her home, Luzi and U arrived at the border of Nyasia and the Elven Plains... the legendary Killij Divide.

Luzi caught sight of the massive mountain range shortly after sunrise. On first glance, it seemed only a short ride away. But as the pair drew closer to the foothills, U was forced to take anfractuous routes around sprawling fields of huge boulders and impassable gullies, slowing their progress to a crawl. As they crept through the unforgiving terrain, Luzi gazed warily at the rocky mountaintops in the distance. The towering peaks loomed on the horizon, a row of jagged teeth ready to chew the two of them up and spit them out like sunflower seeds.

"How the hell are we going to get over these things, anyway?" Luzi asked as they rode, feeling ludicrously small, like a speck of sand in the center of a dune.

"We're not going *over* them," U replied cryptically. "We're going *through* them."

"Will you please stop speaking in riddles, you enigmatic fuckhead?" an exasperated Luzi pleaded.

U grinned.

"We're headed for the Tuvan Passage, a tunnel that cuts through the mountains and emerges in the Elven Plains. The elves carved it out of the rock many centuries ago, way back when they still traded with your countryfolk."

"A tunnel?" Luzi remarked, blinking with surprise. "I've lived in Nyasia all my life and never heard a whisper about a passageway through the Killij Divide."

"I know it's already a distant part of your people's history, but I assure you, it's true," U confirmed.

"The elves carved it out of the rock many centuries ago, back when they used to barter in the Nyasian markets for motta, the herb your people call rockroot. To humans, the stuff is little more than a cooking spice. But to the elven physiology, it's a medicine rivaled only by the most powerful magic.

"Motta is nearly impossible to grow anywhere other than Nyasia and has a shelf life of just weeks, which is why the elves built the tunnel in the first place. In fact, there's a good chance that's how one of the Immaculan Rings made its way to Nyasia... as trade bait."

"I suppose it's a moot point," U added with a shrug. "The elves stopped interacting with your countryfolk after the Nyasian motta blight about four hundred years ago. The tunnel was abandoned shortly afterward. In those long centuries since, neglect and time have undoubtedly turned it into a crumbling tomb. It's little more than a haven for ghosts at this point, I'm sure."

U craned his head to look at Luzi.

"It wasn't always like this, you know. There was once a thriving trade route here, a living landscape of commerce with a character and disposition as real as any person. But everything went south when the motta disappeared." [7]

The unicorn snorted.

"It's amazing how quickly allies can become strangers when there's no profit to be had."

***

Luzi and U rode for another hour, until finally – just as the sun peaked in the sky – they reached a colossal passageway in the mountain.

Luzi gazed up at the thing in amazement. As tall as a tree and three times as wide, the dome-shaped tunnel extended for what seemed like miles; there was no way to tell where it ended. It was easily the largest feat of architecture she'd ever seen – a monument to overachievement that left her head spinning.

Dis be damned... it must have cost a thousand souls to dig this monstrosity! she marveled.

It wasn't hard to imagine the tunnel as a bustling corridor of commerce, filled with merchants and carts and cargo. But even from outside, Luzi could see U was right: the once-mighty passageway was disintegrating beyond repair. Without someone to mend the roadway, centuries of exposure to the elements had turned it into a minefield of potholes that would have made wagon travel nearly impossible. Large chunks of stone that had broken from the crumbling roof lay haphazardly throughout the tunnel, with others threatening to follow them from above at any moment.

It's entirely possible this goddamn thing will collapse on our heads before we reach the other side, the Nyasian realized uneasily.

"It's... big," Luzi offered, not knowing what else to say.

U gazed into the darkness.

"Yes, it was once one of the Ten Wonders of the Great Realms," the unicorn said with the wistful recollection of someone who had seen it in its glory. "Long, long ago, anyway." [8]

Luzi stood at the entranceway with her arms tucked in at her sides. The tunnel loomed before her, as apt a metaphor for her own spiritual murkiness as any poet could dream up. The irony didn't escape her. She'd dreamed about discovering what was on the other side of the world since she was a child. And now that she was on the brink of leaving Nyasia, it should have been her moment of triumph.

But as Luzi stared into the darkness, the truth of the matter hit home. Despite finally getting a chance to carve out her own legacy, all she *really* wanted was for things to return to the way they were before any of it happened. The numb comfort of surrendering to mediocrity is a powerful aphrodisiac – and Luzi was not immune to its lure.

I'd trade the whole of my future for one more day of the past, she lamented.

"Well..." U said, startling Luzi from her thoughts. "I guess we can't stare ourselves to the other side. Shall we?"

Luzi took a final, foreboding look at the tunnel.

"Let's ride," she affirmed with a curt nod.

And slowly, cautiously, they crept forward into the unknown.

***

As they entered the passageway's shadowy confines, Luzi spotted hundreds of strange lamps mounted to the walls, which stretched down the length of the tunnel. The crystal containers were filled with a goopy, amber substance that was unlike anything she'd ever seen... not quite solid... but not quite liquid.

As Luzi and U approached the first lamp, the goop began to emit a brilliant light, powering right through the thick layers of dust coating the crystal. The glow was bright enough to illuminate the path for a dozen feet in every direction. As they passed, the lantern switched off and the next one down the line commenced shining... and so on... and so on.

"What sort of magic is this?" Luzi asked, eyeing the lamps warily as they proceeded down the tunnel.

"That yellow sludge you see is called everlight," U told her. "It's a substance that's derived from Ubamota energy and reacts to the presence of living creatures. Some say it can hold a charge for up to 100,000 years, maybe more."

Luzi and U continued at a plodding pace through the tunnel, neither of them speaking a word. The place was a mausoleum. Dust and cobwebs coated the passageway like a thick covering of snow; U's hooves kicked up tiny clouds of it with every footstep. Here and there, Luzi saw an insect or mouse scuttle off into the darkness at the edges of the everlight. But otherwise, there wasn't a single sign of life save for their own shadows.

U wasn't exaggerating, Luzi thought as they continued through the tunnel. *Nobody's been down this way for years... except ghosts, maybe.*

Suddenly, Luzi caught a glimpse of a rectangular shape in the darkness ahead. Certain that her mind was playing tricks on her, Luzi squinted against the blackness, trying to clear her vision. *Is that what I think it is?* she wondered, rubbing her eyes. But there it was, plain as day: a Nyasian covered wagon.

Her heart thumping, Luzi leaned down and told U what she saw. But the unicorn didn't share her concern.

"Yes, I see it too," U quietly replied. "Don't worry. I don't smell, hear or see anything alive up there at all. Let's keep moving... for now."

As they slowly approached the wagon, Luzi could see that he was right. It was covered in a thick layer of dust and cobwebs, just like everything else in the tunnel. As they got closer, Luzi saw the cart had a broken axle, almost certainly the reason its owners abandoned it. Several pieces of luggage were still tied to the wagon's roof, discarded along with the useless vehicle. Many of the items must have been painful to leave behind: spare parts, several sets of clothes, three barrels of now-rotten grain, a keg of tuber wine, a full set of farming tools.

These people were in a hurry, Luzi realized, a queasy feeling stirring in her gut. *Almost as if they were-"*

Suddenly, the Nyasian spied something among the wreckage that made her heart skip a beat: a child's rag doll. It was a simple thing, nothing unusual on its own. But the mere sight of it made Luzi's jaw drop.

It can't be! she gasped. *What are the odds?*

She focused on the doll's dopey expression... the crooked stitching near the ears... the checkered dress with the distinctive burn mark on the side. There was no doubt about it, Luzi knew.

It was Ilsa's.

"U... please... can we stop for a moment?"

"This isn't a good place to linger," the unicorn said, peeking around cautiously. "What the gods for?"

Luzi paused, hesitant to say the words.

"Because I know who this cart belongs to," she declared grimly.

U halted in his tracks. Luzi could feel him stiffen. He looked around the tunnel for a long moment, checking for any possible danger.

"Quickly," he said at last, kneeling down for her to dismount. "And don't let your guard down for a second."

Luzi hopped off U's back and rushed directly over to the doll. She picked it up and scrutinized it under the lukewarm luminosity of the everlight. Waves of nostalgia and memory crashed over her, stealing her breath.

Changing into his human form, U walked over to Luzi, keeping a careful eye on the darkness around them.

"Something familiar?"

"This cart belongs to a family called the Landcasters," Luzi explained, cradling the fragile doll in her hands. "They were our closest neighbors on the eastern side of our farm... if you call a two-day ride close."

"About a decade ago, their fields had a terrible blantis infestation," Luzi continued. "It was devastating, totally wiped them out." [9]

"My parents offered to help them recover but they refused. Too proud, I guess. A month later, we discovered the whole family had packed up and moved away, just left their farm behind like it was a bad memory. Nobody ever saw or heard from them again."

Luzi felt her throat get thick.

"All our neighbors used to make fun of them, speak about them like they were failures or something. But not me. To me, they were lucky, freed from the shackles of the farm and set on the road to adventure and fortune. I used to name drop them all the time to my mother. I'd ask her, over and over: 'Why can't we be more like the Landcasters?' It drove the old lady crazy. I guess that's exactly why I did it."

Luzi gazed forlornly at the doll as the memories swelled in her heart.

"Anyway, they had a little girl named Ilsa. And this doll was her favorite possession. I never saw her without it. All this other stuff they could have burned, but this doll... she *never* would have abandoned it."

"Can I see that for a moment?" U asked curiously, leaning closer.

Luzi glanced at the unicorn, surprised he should care. Then she nodded and passed it to him.

U took the toy and held it in his hands, scrutinizing it carefully, as if it was a puzzle. Then he grabbed the doll by both arms. And before Luzi can utter a word of protest, he ripped it open like a sack of flour.

"What the shit?" the flabbergasted Nyasian sputtered. "What'd you do that for?"

In reply, the unicorn took the torn halves of the doll and held them out. "It seems your neighbors had a few secrets of their own," he quipped.

Inside the toy – tucked amid the stuffing and rags – were a dozen large diamonds.

U handed the doll to a wide-eyed Luzi. She hefted the secret payload of jewels in her hands. Even in the dim light of the tunnel they sparkled with a stunning clarity. It was a small fortune for a Nyasian farming family like the Landcasters. *It must have taken them generations to collect these*, she realized.

Just then, an unsettling thought crossed Luzi's mind. She turned to U with an ashen expression. "Wait... why would they leave these behind?"

U shrugged.

"Maybe they were attacked by bandits. Maybe they fell prey to one of the many wild beasts that roam these lands. There's no way to know for sure."

The unicorn paused. "But with the value of those stones, I'll tell you one thing. Whatever the reason, it must have been *severe*."

The word "severe" hung in the air. And eventually, Luzi realized it was just U's way of gently saying that they were dead.

You bastards, Luzi mourned forlornly, glancing at the broken-down wagon with a growing despair. She'd always imagined that the Landcasters had escaped Nyiasia to some great glory or happiness. It'd been one of the fantasies that saw her through all of those long days in the potuber fields.

Now, the thought that her former neighbors might be dead – and probably never even made it out of the outback at all – made Luzi cringe with foolishness.

What a silly asshole you are, Luzi Winterstar, she lamented, ashamed at her naivety.

"Luzi, I know this is emotional for you, but we have to go," U insisted, interrupting her internal monologue. "It isn't a good idea to linger here... for many reasons."

The Nyasian stared at the doll in her hands one last time. Then she took out the jewels, put them in her pocket, and placed the tattered keepsake back where she first found it.

"You're right," Luzi said curtly, facing U with a faux-courageous strength. "Let's get the fuck out of here."

U would've had to be blind not to see the tempest of emotion lurking behind Luzi's eyes. But he ignored it – half out of pity and half out of necessity. Morphing back into his unicorn form, he allowed Luzi to remount him, then started down the tunnel again.

As they went, Luzi stole one last peek at the cart. Her eyes lingered on the ragdoll, a pitiful little grave marker for a dream deferred.

May mercy find you, Luzi prayed sadly. *WHEREVER you are.*

***

Luzi's first clue they were nearing the tunnel's exit wasn't the light... it was the air.

An hour after they passed the Landcasters' wagon, Luzi noticed the fine hairs on her arm tingling with moisture. As they continued onward, the humidity got thicker, richer – a slowly building nutrient soup. It was invigorating, a complete change from the thirsty, arid air of Nyasia.

"It's the breeze from the plains," U explained. "We're getting close. It shouldn't be long now."

Soon, Luzi began to spot fuzzy, green moss growing on the walls of the tunnel. It had a viridescent tinge Luzi had never seen in Nyasia, where almost everything was blue or brown. She reached out with her hand and touched the moss as they passed, feeling its dampness on her fingers.

"It's so *green*," Luzi commented.

"If you're impressed by that, wait until we get outside," U replied coyly.

The unicorn's words proved to be an understatement. As they exited the tunnel into an open field, Luzi was dazzled by the sudden onslaught of color. The sky was a deep, intoxicating shade of blue. A shaggy grass covered the rolling hills like a verdant mattress. Dozens of species of flowers dotted the landscape in clusters, each with their own spectacular hue of red, yellow or purple.

But it wasn't just the colors that dropped Luzi's jaw; it was the absolute tenderness of it all.

A soft wind blew over the meadows, caressing her skin. A fertile scent wafted from the earth, richer than any field she'd ever plowed. The sun in the sky was gentle, nurturing — a world apart from the blazing outback of her homeland. In the distance, a plump, furry, six-legged animal plodded along with its cubs, barely taking notice of Luzi and U as it passed by. Dozens of rodents and rabbits leisurely trotted through the brush with the same indifferent attitude. Several large-breasted fowl lazily flapped their wings a stone's throw away, moving so slowly it seemed they could be plucked right out of the air.

Life doesn't struggle here, Luzi noted with awe. *It thrives.*

"Welcome to the Elven Plains," U said with a grand sweep of his arm. "Or as the elves call it, *Zhe a Nek...* the Homeland."

The unicorn glanced at the sun's position in the sky. "We have another hour of light before it gets dark, so let's take advantage of it. We can break for camp at nightfall."

Luzi hesitated. It was so serene – so utterly perfect – that part of her didn't want to leave. *I just need one moment of peace,* she silently pined. But the Nyasian knew there was no time to linger. The ring weighed heavy around her neck, and the killers who pursued them had no plans to stop and admire the scenery.

You're not a tourist... you're a refugee, Luzi reminded herself sternly.

***

When the setting sun finally began to sputter out, U stopped for the night near a large, mossy boulder formation. A creek ran in a semicircle around the rocks, forming a mini-grotto that also made a surprisingly cozy shelter.

"Yeah, yeah, I know... stay alert," Luzi told the unicorn with an eye roll as she went to fill her canteen.

When she reached the water's edge, Luzi noticed several small bushes, each plump with fist-shaped, fuzzy fruits. As she got closer, the Nyasian caught the faint-but-unmistakable smell of cooked steak. She licked her chapped lips. Her stomach – seven days empty – growled like a rabid crocotta.

"You're in luck," U called out from over her shoulder, as if he could read her mind. "This patch of meatplants seems to have ripened early this year. It's a good thing, too. You must be starving."

Luzi felt a flutter of hope in her vacant belly. "These things are *edible*?"

In reply, U picked one of the fruits off the plant and tossed it her way. Steadying her stomach, Luzi took a tentative bite. But it was only a moment before the Nyasian's face lit up like a child eating candy. She'd never had anything like it; the skin tasted like an apple, but the flesh was like a cut of medium-rare steak. Luzi devoured the rest of the meatplant in a few eager chomps and reached for another... and another... and another.

After her hunger satiated enough for her to slow down, Luzi saw that U wasn't partaking in the feast. "Aren't you having any?" she asked, wiping a smear of juice from her chin.

"Thanks for the offer, but no," he replied. "Unicorns need flesh to survive. While they may smell like the real thing, meatplants aren't actually *meat*. They're no more nutritious to me than bark off a tree."

Luzi shrugged and grinned.

"Suit yourself. But like my father always said, you don't always have to eat because you're hungry. Sometimes, you just do it because it's fun."

And for the first time since Luzi left home, she laughed.

***

After the Nyasian was done helping herself to a half-dozen

more of the delicious fruits, she rested silently as the last of the sun slipped over the horizon. As she digested her smorgasbord, Luzi gazed at the gallery of stars dotting the sky over the plains. They were impossibly crisp, as if some astral being painted them into existence with a cosmic brush.

Suddenly, one of the lights started to move straight towards them. Pulsating, iridescent colors emanated from the thing as it drew closer. Certain it was a trick of her road-weary eyes, Luzi blinked and squinted for another look. But sure enough, there it was... getting larger in the sky with every passing second.

A shooting star? she wondered.

Then another of the things emerged alongside the first. And a dozen more after that. Within a minute, there were hundreds of the unidentified flying objects – maybe thousands – all headed straight towards them.

Luzi turned to U, her forehead wrinkled with concern. But the unicorn waved his hand dismissively.

"Don't worry. It's only a swarm of hummingdragons on their annual migration. They're totally harmless. Think of them as flying jellyfish."

"Flying *what*?" Luzi asked.

"It's not important," U said, remembering that the Nyasian had probably never seen an ocean in her life.

"The hummingdragons migrate every spring across the Elven Plains to their spawning grounds at the foothills of the Killij Mountains. Right now, there are hundreds of other swarms floating over the plains, all just as large as this one. They'll pass us by in a bit if we leave them alone."

It wasn't long before the swarm was floating directly above

them, lighting up the night sky like an armada of fireflies. Slightly larger than hummingbirds, the creatures were aptly named; they looked almost exactly like miniature dragons. Instead of wings, however, each had several rows of tiny, fluttering fans on the sides of their torsos. Bioluminescent glands in their stomachs glowed and pulsated as they approached.

Luzi couldn't help but be captivated. It was a majestic sight, something straight out of one of her storybooks. And slowly, her fear began to give way to awe.

U watched as the Nyasian gazed up at the sky.

"Do you know the myth about how the hummingdragons came to be?" he asked quietly, trying not to disturb her. "According to an old elvish legend, they were created by Zimm-Ra, the lord of the sky, as a wedding present to his bride, Daya-Ixl, goddess of love. They say that if you catch one and make a wish, it's destined to come true... as long as your heart is completely pure."

"That's crazy," Luzi scoffed. "Nobody's heart is completely pure."

"Storytellers need to be allowed to lie, I suppose," U said, shrugging. "Anyway, like I said, it's only a myth." [10]

Just then – caught in an errant thermal current – one of the hummingdragons strayed from the swarm, wafting towards Luzi until it fluttered an arm's length away. The Nyasian watched the thing with silent awe as it floated through the air, softly balancing itself on a serene zephyr. There was an endearing beauty to the humble little creature. It had no worries... no fears... no sorrow.

It simply existed.

Something heavy abruptly shifted in Luzi's heart. Since

leaving home, the world had taken on a sinister veneer that had become impossible to dispel. Everyone was out to get her. Everyone was a killer. And nobody was on her side. But as she stared at the tiny, blinking creatures in the sky, the Nyasian felt the fog lifting, letting her see straight again for the first time in a week.

No matter how much evil there is in the world, there's always going to be beauty to counterbalance it. And no matter what fate has in store for me – whether I live or die – somewhere out there, innocence will persist. Even if it's just a flicker of light in the dark.

A breeze shifted and the hummingdragon was carried back towards the swarm. Luzi watched it go, her eyes as large as saucers.

"You know what? Maybe I was wrong about purity," she said softly as the creature floated away on its gentle exodus across the plains. "I mean, have you ever seen anything so beautiful?"

U watched Luzi stare at the night sky. The young woman's snowy hair was resplendent in the starlight, her face lit up with a beatific joy. The unicorn felt something unfamiliar stir within him. And for once, *he* was the one at a loss for words.

"No," U said at last. "I haven't."

And the two gazed silently at the twinkling of the hummingdragons until the swarm passed them by.

9

Romula Zazzau stood amid the Nyasian outback with her crew of warriors, frowning under the cruel, unrelenting desert sun. The mage's obsidian-black hair – habitually cropped close for battle – offered no protection from the elements. Her wizard robes felt stifling; perspiration slicked her wrinkled skin. She didn't remember it being so unbearably hot in the borderlands. But then again, it'd been a long time since she had *any* reason to come to the Nyasian outback.

Even if you were 30 years younger this would still be hell, she lamented as a huge dollop of sweat rolled down her face.

Several days had passed since the attack, that much was clear from the smell. And Romula knew that if she could detect the decaying flesh strewn about the battlefield, surely the others could as well.

They were too late. Much too late.

The Dama'run bureaucracy strikes again, she thought, cursing the council for wasting so much time approving their mission. *You can always count on those bastards to do the right thing... after they've tried everything else first.*

Sighing, Romula turned her attention back to her crew, who were bantering back and forth as they searched the rubble for signs of their quarry.

"Let me know if you see any survivors," a regal-jawed young man remarked to the others, blinking away sand from the corners of his eyes.

"Sure thing, Anian," a reptilian creature replied, chuckling as he hopped nimbly among the debris. "I'll make sure to scrape 'em off the ground."

A pair of forest pixies hovered in the air, wrinkling their noses at their comrade's joke. "Don't be cruel, Cobby," one of the Fae chastised, flicking her gossamer wings disapprovingly as she balanced on a stray breeze. Her companion agreed, nodding silently in accord.

The reptile snickered.

"Lighten up, you two. I don't have a cruel bone in my body, and I'll fight anyone who says otherwise. Isn't that right, Awf'l?"

A hulking, eight-foot troll beside him smiled, her crooked teeth jutting out from her overbite. "Ghuurkkhk?" the troll grunted inquisitively, lifting a massive chunk of adobe and peering underneath.

"See? At least *someone* knows how to take a joke."

"Gots to be funny tuh' qual'fy as a joke, I reck'n," quipped a barrel-chested, jovial-eyed mountain man, his backwoods accent as thick as his beard.

"Did they teach you that in hillbilly school?"

"Nup… that wuz extra cr'dit."

"Everyone cut the chatter," Anian interrupted, glancing at Romula's dour expression. "You all know the stakes here. Let's focus on our jobs."

Ignoring the playful middle fingers and chorus of "boos" aimed his way, the young man sidled up to Romula, ready to give his report. But the mage kept her gaze fixed on the rubble.

"You've got to keep them sharper than this," she advised sternly. "You're going to be in charge of this crew one day when my luck finally runs out, Anian. Maybe it's time you start acting like it."

The Quiystian rolled his eyes.

"This again? You know that isn't why I joined the Scions, Rom. If I wanted to lead *anything*, I'd have stayed at home in the palace all those years ago. Anyway, I wouldn't worry about it. You're waaaaayyy too stubborn to die. And you're probably the only one that doesn't know it."

"Fair enough," the mage conceded, cracking the tiniest of smiles. "So tell me. Did anyone find any sign of the ring?"

"Not a damn trace. But we finished digging that corpse out of the rubble, like you asked. You were right, it's a Monoceros – what's left of it, anyway."

The grizzled old mage raised an eyebrow. "A unicorn? There hasn't been a sighting of one of those soulless devils around these parts for centuries, maybe more. This isn't good."

"You don't think they have the other ring, do you? Anian asked cautiously, as if he didn't want to know the answer.

"Well... *somebody* does," Romula replied pensively. "And I'd say whoever sent this unicorn is as good a bet as any."

The mage shook her head, trying to clear it of the growing doubts that clouded her judgement. "We've got other things to worry about at the moment, though. What about the girl? Did Cobby find any trace of where she went?"

Anian nodded. Even after several days, the scent was strong enough for the keen-nosed reptile to pick up with ease.

"There's a trail headed northeast in the direction of the Elven Plains," he said, pointing at a few faint depressions in the sand. "From the looks of it, one rider and a steed. And they were off in a goddamn hurry, too. I wonder if-"

"We're wasting time," Romula interjected, cutting Anian off. "There's nothing left for us here. If we find the girl, we find the ring. It's as simple as that."

"Gather the others," she concluded, snapping her fingers. "It's time to ride."

Anian knew not to question his mentor when she gave an order. But despite his better judgement, he couldn't avoid posing a final question.

"Rom, I've got to ask. We were told that the Nyasian wouldn't be a threat. The council said she'd be alone, defenseless. So tell me... what the hell killed that unicorn?"

The elderly mage paused, trying to walk a tightrope between fear and bravado for the sake of her crew.

"I don't know," she admitted at last. "But I have a feeling we'll find out soon enough – we're *always* discovering bold, new frontiers of misery. Now let's get moving. We've got a job to do."

10

"People can change, sure. But snakes? That's a different fucking story."

— *Jon Covfefe, high court advisor to the throne of Ragnaron*

By the time the sun peeked above the horizon the next morning, Luzi and U were already well into another day of travel.

As they crossed the plains, Luzi replayed her moment of peace with the hummingdragons in her head. The experience had reminded her of the possibility of good in the world – and with it, the chance of a future. Still, the epiphany raised more questions than it answered. For the short term, the plan was simple enough: reach Dama'run alive. But presuming they actually made it to the mountain city, then what?

You have no skills that can possibly be of use, Luzi reasoned. *You have no place to live... no connections... no leads. In fact, there isn't a single person there who gives a shit if you live or die. How can you ever call such a place home?*

The more these doubts snowballed in her head, the more

Luzi wondered what a home was, anyway. A roof over your head? A bed to sleep in? Or something more?

As they rode, Luzi reminisced about her family's farm in Nyasia and its simple blessings. A fresh potuber casserole and a draught of perfectly aged wine. Hills with sunsets so gargantuan they sting the eyes. Freshly tilled soil beneath bare feet on a warm spring day.

But as much as she pined for these things, Luzi knew in her heart they didn't define a "home" any more than a rug on the floor or a lamp on a shelf. There was an element she couldn't put her finger on. Something intangible. Something simple.

And that's when Luzi realized what was missing: her family.

She remembered lying in their hammock with her mother as a child and snoozing in the sun. She remembered the arm wrestling matches her father would let her win as a child. She remembered the countless sunsets and meteor showers and starry nights, all three of them laughing and sharing the bounty of the heavens together.

Maybe a home is just the people who you surround yourself with, Luzi finally understood, teetering on the brink of an important enlightenment. *Maybe–*

Suddenly, U skidded to a bone-jarring stop, scattering Luzi's thoughts like marbles and yanking her stomach inside out. Puzzled, she looked around for the cause. But they were in the middle of a field; there was nothing in any direction but grass and wildlife.

By the pulsating gonads of Dis, what now? she wondered, fighting to regain her equilibrium.

The Nyasian glanced down at U. He stood motionless,

staring straight ahead and holding his head high. His ears were perpendicular, his muscles taut.

"What?" Luzi whispered tensely, surprised at his abrupt anxiety.

In reply, U nodded at the field ahead of them to the northeast.

"Up there. About a hundred yards out. To the right of that bush."

Luzi turned to where the unicorn gestured, pressing her hand against her forehead to block out the sun. At first, she saw nothing. But then – just at the periphery of her vision – she spotted a miniscule lump sticking up against the horizon, a small thing splayed out on the ground that she missed on first glance. And with a start, Luzi finally realized what she was looking at.

"Stone the crows!" she exclaimed incredulously. "Is that a *kid* laying out there?"

U nodded. "From the smell of it, an elf child," he said, sniffing at the air.

Luzi squinted, watching the figure for movement. She leaned down towards U.

"Hey, I think that kid's hurt."

But the unicorn didn't reply. Instead, he kept peering intently at the horizon around them, acting as if Luzi didn't speak a word.

"Hey!" she insisted, her voice rising with urgency. "I think that kid's hurt!"

"Ssshhhhhh!" U whispered, finally acknowledging her. "You're right. But for the sake of both our lives, keep your voice down!"

His words of caution didn't placate Luzi.

"Well? What are we waiting for? Let's go help!"

U hesitated, glancing around like he expected assassins to emerge from the bushes at any second.

"Hold on. Something's wrong. Think about it. What's this child doing out here alone in the middle of nowhere? Why right in our path? This smells every bit like a trap... and not even a clever one."

The unicorn flared his nostrils.

"No. I don't like it one bit. I never should have stopped in the first place. That was *my* mistake... I take full responsibility."

"Wait a second," Luzi interjected incredulously. "Are you saying what I think you are?"

U shook his head, disappointed with his own lack of prudence.

"We need to get out of here – right now. We've already put ourselves in danger by lingering this long. Let's get out of here and double around. It'll cost us some time, but there's nothing we can do about it."

"We can't leave a helpless child to die!" Luzi protested. "What kind of heartless bastard are you?"

"We can argue about this later," U pleaded, desperately trying to keep from yelling in frustration. "Right now, we need to mov–"

Suddenly, before U could do anything to stop her, Luzi tumbled off his back and dashed over to the child. For a moment, all the unicorn could do was gape helplessly at her unexpected bravado. Then, like a mouse about to creep into a snake den, he gave the surrounding plains a final, cautious scan. *Abandon hope, all ye who fucking enter here!* he cursed to himself in Monoceros.

And without further delay, he galloped after Luzi as fast as he could.

When U caught up to her, the Nyasian was kneeling on the ground next to the child's unconscious-but-still-breathing body, her brow furrowed with worry. He was an elf, just as U had thought. The boy was young – no more than seven or eight-years-old – and almost indistinguishable from a human, apart from his pointed ears and pinto-toned, black and white skin.

"He won't wake up!" Luzi lamented, wringing her hands together.

Warily, the unicorn turned his attention to the child. His face was turning a sickly grey; his lips were cracked and split with thirst. He laid still as a corpse with little evidence to the contrary.

And that's when U saw the blood.

"Gods be merciful," he said solemnly. "This child was stabbed."

Luzi's eyes widened. "Stabbed? How do you know that?"

"Let's just say that I've seen my share of battle wounds – and then some," the unicorn replied. "But go ahead, lift up his shirt and see for yourself."

Gingerly, Luzi pulled aside the torn edges of the child's deerskin vest. "Oh no," she muttered, her heart sinking. It was an ugly sight. The weeping wound was two fingers wide, deep enough to see the pink of the muscle. It was the sort of injury that carried a certain death sentence without the aid of a healer... and a good one, at that.

"See where the flesh is bruised?" U asked Luzi, gesturing to a purple swelling around the cut. "That's impact damage from a spear tip. I'd bet my life on it."

"A fucking *spear*?" Luzi exclaimed in an anguished voice. "Who the hell would stab a child?"

U worriedly glanced around the surrounding plains. "I don't have the faintest idea," he admitted. "And that's exactly the problem."

Luzi reached down and gently touched the child's clammy face. There was no reaction, not even a flinch. It was like brushing her hand against a corpse. She looked up at U, the full extent of the injury finally sinking in.

"He's really hurt bad, isn't he? What are we going to do?"

U peeked at the boy. He slowly turned back to Luzi with a grim expression.

"I know you don't want to hear this, but there's virtually no chance this child will survive," he told her with a surgeon's sympathy. "And it will be a slow and unpleasant death, to boot. This child has two, maybe three days of excruciating pain ahead of him before he finds his final peace."

U paused, fumbling for the right words. "That is... unless..."

"Unless what?"

"Unless we ease his passing."

It took a moment before Luzi caught up to U's euphemism. "Wait a second... Are you suggesting we fucking *kill* him?"

"It may not look like it, but fate was smiling on this young-ling when it rendered him unconscious," U replied. "I've seen battle-hardened warriors bawl like babies and plead for death with these sorts of wounds. If this child ever wakes up, his last moments will be abject agony and utter fear. Why would you want him to endure that awful suffering on the miniscule possibility we might get him to a healer before he dies?"

"So there's a chance he might live?"

U shrugged.

"There's *always* a chance of *anything*. Nothing is impossible, only improbable. But the odds this child will survive are astronomically small, the stuff of miracles. And to get even that slim chance, he'll have to endure pain I wouldn't wish on my worst enemy."

"Can't we take him with us? There's got to be a village nearby we can leave him at."

The unicorn shook his head. "It's not that simple." He pointed to a small cluster of tattoos on the side of the child's neck. "Do you see those? I'd recognize the patterns anywhere. This child is a Yali."

"Yali?" Luzi repeated. "What does that mean?"

"There are hundreds of elvish boroughs, each with its own customs and laws," U explained hurriedly. "For the most part, these boroughs operate independent of each other under the authority of their own ministers and shamans. But every now and then – strictly for defense and trade – the elvish boroughs come together and make decisions as a cooperative. This gathering is known as the Rundermust.

"The elves have kept peace and protected themselves as a nation this way for millennia. But a few decades ago, a coalition of elvish boroughs who call themselves the Yali, or 'The Truth' in elvish, announced they were merging to form a separate, sovereign nation. The other boroughs refused to allow this, fearing the Yali's combined might. Negotiations failed. And a brutal civil war followed that still rages today."

"That's where the problem comes in," U concluded. "We can't take this child to any village loyal to the Rundermust. He'll be killed on the spot... and likely us along with him."

"So we'll take him to Dama'run," Luzi countered. "There's got to be a healer in the city who can–"

"No," U said, furrowing his brow. "He'll never make it. The wound is too severe. We might kill him just trying to move him."

Luzi bit her lip. "There's got to be *something* we can do!"

U glanced at the child somberly.

"I can think of just one other solution... Erund Mar. It's a small Yali trade village near the border of the Rundermust. The inhabitants have a reputation for being relatively tolerant of outsiders, unlike many of their kin. And it's almost certainly this child's only chance at survival."

Luzi nodded enthusiastically. "Then that's where we'll go."

But U cut her eagerness down like a farmer scything wheat.

"Not so fast," he warned. "Just because I said it's his only chance doesn't mean it's a good idea. Erund Mar is at least a day's ride from here, maybe two days with this kid in tow. And trust me, with the Overgruk that pursue us, that's a luxury we can't afford."

"Luzi, I feel bad for this child, I really do," U said, noticing the expression on her face. "But remember what will happen if the unicorns get their hands on the thing that hangs around your neck. We aren't just risking our own lives, we'd be risking the lives of millions of other children across the known realms. Think of how many things can go wrong if we take this detour. Picture how many ways this story can end in tragedy. We need to get back on the road without this... burden. And we need to do it *now*."

Logically, Luzi was forced to admit U was right. It was simple math, after all. There was no getting around it; the only move that made any sense was to ditch the kid and take off running. But as much as she tried, Luzi couldn't find the heart to follow through with her brain's demands.

A lot has happened these past days, Luzi told herself. And you'll again never be the person you were a week ago. But willingly leave a child to die? That's murder, no matter how many of layers of logic you wrap it in. If you let this kid perish, you'll be leaving a piece of yourself behind you'll never see again. Can you live with that?

Luzi looked down at the elf. As if on cue, the child's pinky trembled. It was the sole sign of life from him they'd seen so far. And with that one, tiny twitch, Luzi knew what she had to do.

"I'm sorry," she said, turning to U. "But I'm not going to leave this kid behind."

The unicorn's frustration finally got the best of him.

"Gods be damned, Luzi! Why are you making *me* be the villain here? Have you forgotten the apocalypse we're trying to prevent? Have you forgotten the risks? We can't take this child along with us! We just can't!"

When Luzi replied, it was with a thousand times more confidence than she ever thought herself capable of.

"You're right. *We're* not going to take him anywhere."

"Wait a minute," U said suspiciously. "Luzi..."

Luzi looked the unicorn dead in the eyes. She reached into her tunic and pulled out the ring.

"Here. Take it and go. Get this goddamn thing somewhere

it can't do any more harm. I'll take this kid to Erund Mar myself. I'll carry him if I have to. Just point me in the right direction."

"This is crazy!" U started to object. But in reply, Luzi just dangled the ring in U's face.

"This isn't a debate," she insisted. "I mean it. Take the fucking thing. I never wanted it in the first place. And I don't want it now."

Luzi paused. "I couldn't save our farm. I couldn't save my parents. I probably can't even save myself. But I *can* save this kid. And that's exactly what I'm going to do."

"Luzi..."

She didn't budge. "Go ahead, U. I'm serious. I won't leave him to die."

Luzi glared at the unicorn defiantly. "Or maybe compassion is a trait only *humans* are capable of understanding."

Just as she intended, the words sliced into U like a bullwhip. The two of them stood there for a long moment, each unwilling to budge. Finally, the unicorn's chest heaved with a tremendous sigh.

"Very well," he relented. "We'll try it your way. Let's get this child bandaged up. We've got a long ride ahead of us."

Luzi raised an eyebrow, surprised at U's change of heart. "Thank you," she finally mustered, unsure of what else to tell him. But instead of looking grateful, the unicorn shook his head.

"No," he warned gravely. "There's nothing to be thankful for here at all."

***

They rode nonstop the rest of the day, a million unknown dangers dogging every step. It was a race against time, every second stretched into a thousand years.

The unicorn tried his best to keep a steady gait and avoid any hairpin turns. But Luzi saw that the effort robbed the spring from his step; he traveled at only a fraction of his previous speed.

Meanwhile, Luzi clutched the boy to her chest as they galloped across the plains, trying desperately to keep him from jostling around and aggravating his wound. The Nyasian was terrified he would die right in front of her; she'd never felt so helpless.

Can things possibly get any worse? Luzi lamented, looking at the sky and cursing the heavens.

Then, as if the gods decided to answer, it started to rain.

Like all those who dwell in the desert, Luzi's love for the rain bordered on spirituality. It was in her blood, like a tulip bulb craves the spring dew. But that night, speeding through a strange land with a dying child in her arms, the downpour took on a sinister persona she'd never known. As the dark began to creep in and her teeth started to chatter with the mounting cold, the rain became Luzi's enemy for the first time in her life. It slashed. It stung. It soaked.

And when they finally came across an abandoned trapper's cabin around twilight, the sight was almost too good to be true.

Nestled against a tree at the top of a small hill, the dilapidated cabin was half-rotten, like a log going soft with age. There were no surprises when they opened the door; the inside of the shack was as crummy as the outside. The smell of mildew clung tenaciously to the air, and a thick layer of damp dust coated every surface. It was little more than a bed, four walls and a roof... and a leaky, moss-ridden one at that.

But to Luzi, it seemed like a palace.

After laying the child down on a plank bed in the corner, Luzi shook the grime off an old, tattered blanket and gently draped it over him. Then she took out her canteen and tried to give him a drink. But he didn't move a muscle, not even when she poured a sip of water on his sun-cracked lips.

Luzi stood at the elf's side helplessly, watching him slowly breathe in and out. Silently, U shifted into his human form and joined her.

"He's dying, isn't he?" the Nyasian asked, straining with despair.

"Yes," the unicorn confirmed, hanging his head.

"Is there anything we can do?"

"I'm sorry," U replied, his voice flat with shame. "But I know of no healing techniques that would help this child beyond what we've already done. It seems my only talent lies in taking lives – not saving them."

There was a sadness in his voice that caught Luzi's attention. As she looked at the unicorn, she saw he was telling the truth. *He really does care that he can't save this child*, Luzi realized.

And in that moment, something in her heart shifted.

"U," she said quietly, reaching out and touching him on the arm. "I need to tell you something. What I said earlier... about unicorns not being capable of feeling compassion... I was wrong."

The unicorn's eyes widened with surprise at her sudden empathy. He opened his mouth to speak, but Luzi didn't yield.

"Please, hear me out. I wouldn't be standing here today if not for your help. It's taken me a long time to admit that. But it's true. You've risked everything for me, and all I've given you in return is hate. Every step of the way, I've refused to recognize the good you've done because of the evil that you haven't. Even when it comes to this child. But I do know one thing: you *are* capable of empathy. We *all* are. And I'm sorry I said otherwise."

"Thank you," U said quietly. "If only you could convince the Meridian of that."

"Maybe we could."

U shook his head sadly.

"No," he said, frowning. "The Meridian's hate for humanity is a fuel that will never burn itself out. She can't change her destiny, now – she doesn't know how. And she'd swim through an ocean of broken glass if she knew it would mean the end of the human race."

Luzi paused, mulling over his words.

"U?" she asked. "Why do the Monoceros hate humans so much? What did we ever do to you, anyway?"

Her inquiry stopped the unicorn cold.

"It's not what you *did*," he admitted at last. "It's what you *represent*... change."

"Scholars say the Great Realms have seen three separate eras over its long history. First came the Age Cosmic, when gods such as the Immaculans roamed the world. Second came the Age Fantastic, when the world belonged to the creatures of the Deep Magic, including the Monoceros. Finally came the third era – the one we live in now – also known as the Age Ephemeral.

"To humans and the others who have only known the Age Ephemeral, time is a one-way road... it can only move forward. But for those who survived the Age Fantastic, the past is all we have. And many of us still dream of returning there one day."

U lowered his voice reverently, as if he was reading from a holy scripture.

"There are many Monoceros who believe there will be a day when our species rises again, a glorious, bloody revolution when we regain our ability to have children and take back what was once ours. And on that day, all humans will be slain and the world shall begin a fourth age: the reign of the unicorn. They call it *Io-X'likon'sh* – the Second Coming."

Luzi raised an eyebrow. "I'd call it something else... genocide."

U frowned.

"I know unicorns seem like evil creatures to you. And yes, we have committed atrocities in the name of survival. But can the human race claim any different? Would *you* have the grace to quietly shuffle into extinction if you were in *our* place?"

The weight of U's truth settled in Luzi's heart. As much as she hated to admit it, the unicorn had a point.

They sat for a moment in silence.

"I just don't get it," Luzi said. "Haven't the Monoceros ever tried to sit down and talk this whole thing out? Haven't we humans ever tried to do the same? There's got to be some sort of truce that can be reached... some sort of peace?"

U sighed, as if he'd pondered the same question and come to a discouraging conclusion.

"I suppose there was once an inkling of a chance, long ago. But the things we have done to each other since – the things we believe each other *capable* of doing – have made it all but impossible. And it would take a true miracle to change our collision course now."

"Still, the Deep Magic is a powerful thing," U added, rubbing his chin thoughtfully. "Some say it has its own subtle way of safeguarding reality, balancing good and evil to ensure that the world survives itself. I've never given those stories much credence before. But these past few days have made me reconsider many things I thought were impossible."

The unicorn paused.

"After all, the universe led me to *you*, didn't it?"

There was an odd tenderness in his voice that captured Luzi's ear. She looked at U. A faint, rosy tint was spreading across the skin of his cheeks, almost like the reflection of a sunset on a lake. It was a familiar gesture, but one she couldn't place right away. And then it hit her. *Sweet mother's milk... he's blushing!*

The realization caught Luzi completely off-guard, like getting nipped by a live coal while sweeping out a hearth fire. She and Uchchaihshravas sat for a while, ruminating on his words like they were hundred-year-old Abyssinian merlot.

"Umm.... U?" the Nyasian probed after a moment. "I've been meaning to ask you something. And I need an honest answer. Do you think you can do that for me?"

The unicorn nodded sincerely. "Of course."

"If you hadn't seen me as 'alive' a week ago – if your death vision didn't exist – would you have killed me?"

U averted his eyes, as if he could delay the conversation by not acknowledging it. "I want with all of my heart to tell you no," he said at last. "But that wouldn't be honest, would it?"

"I guess not," Luzi admitted, trying to disguise the disappointment in her voice.

U touched the Nyasian lightly on her shoulder.

"I don't want you to be scared of me, Luzi."

"I'm not," she replied, tensing up with defensiveness. "You know, I could kill you now if I wanted to – just remember that. You don't have any power over me, U. Not anymore."

The unicorn just shook his head sadly. "Oh, Luzi. Is that what you've thought all this time? That I have some sort of power over you?"

"Try to understand," U continued. "Like many humans, the Monoceros believe in an afterlife... in a *soul*. But we also believe that nobody is born with one – it has to be earned. And ever since I met you, I've been forced to confront a savage truth. In spite of all my thousands of years, and all the terrible deeds I've committed in the name of duty and honor, I haven't done a single thing that would qualify."

The unicorn looked up with wide eyes, a heroic timbre rekindling in his voice.

"But maybe if I can save you – *just you* – I can leave this world with an act of compassion instead of hate. Maybe this is the real reason you overpower my cursed vision. Maybe you're a blessing from the gods, a final opportunity at salvation after a lifetime of death and blood."

Uchchaihshravas wrung his hands together anxiously.

"You say you're under my power. But don't you see? If you'd have chosen to stay behind on your farm, I would have remained at your side. If you'd have fled to Quiyst or Ragnaron or Abyssinia seeking asylum, I would have followed you there. You're the one holding the reins on this journey. You have been all along. And if you told me to throw myself into a volcano, I'd do it without a single flinch."

This last revelation – that U would be willing to die for her – resounded in Luzi's head like a church bell. Suddenly, nothing made sense. In a heartbeat, everything seemed to catch up to her... all angles... all dead ends... all possibilities.

"Maybe you're right," Luzi admitted, a confession on the tip of her tongue. "So much has happened in such a short time, and we haven't had a chance to talk about any of it. I don't know about you, but-"

Suddenly, like a fox catching wind of a hound, U started sniffing at the air, cutting Luzi off mid-sentence.

"Wait... something's wrong."

"What's happening?" Luzi asked, an abrupt panic building in her stomach.

But U just gestured for silence. Without another word, the unicorn strode to the door, pushed it open and walked outside into the rain. The hairs on her neck perking up, Luzi followed him, watching as he stood near the front of the cabin looking outward on the horizon.

"It seems our journey to Erund Mar is over," U said, a deadly seriousness creeping into his voice.

"What do you mean?" Luzi demanded to know. "Why?"

U gazed towards the stormy horizon.

"Because of *them*."

11

"It is what it is... but it doesn't have to be."

– Astinus Shy, leader of the Shy Barley Riots

Adrenaline spiking her veins, Luzi craned her neck to look where U was pointing.

For several moments, she couldn't see anything amid the rain and storm clouds. *For the love of Dis, that unicorn's eyesight is good,* Luzi jealously observed, squinting in concentration. [11]

Eventually, she was able to make out a faint group of tiny blobs coming toward them in the sky. From afar, they resembled a flock of hawks or eagles. But as soon as they got closer, Luzi could see they weren't birds at all – they were some sort of huge, dragon-like beasts. Even more surprising, they carried riders on their backs.

"Who are they?" Luzi asked nervously.

"It looks like a platoon of Rundermust elven soldiers, probably members of the Gongqui borough," U replied. "Those creatures they ride are called wyverns."

Luzi blanched. Alarmed, she glanced at the cabin, where the elf child was still asleep.

"They're here for *him*, aren't they?"

U took another long stare at the rapidly approaching cloud of doom. "There's no reason to bother wondering," he declared. "They'll be on us soon, and I'm sure they won't be shy about letting us know why."

"So what are we standing around for?" Luzi interjected, getting ready to move. "Let's get the fuck out of here!"

But U just shook his head.

"It won't do any good. Unicorns are fast, but so are wyverns. And there's no way I can outrun an elven war party with two riders on my back, even if I take to the air. We're going to have to fight or talk our way out of this."

"I vote for *talk*," Luzi deadpanned, raising her hand.

"Let's hope they feel the same way," U warned. "The Gongqui aren't known for using magic, but they're some of the fiercest soldiers in the Rundermust. And they're notorious for their mistrust of foreigners. So be ready for a fight."

Luzi nodded and started to manifest her armum, preparing for battle. But U motioned for her to hold.

"I don't want them to know we're mages yet," he explained. "I'd rather they believe we're a couple of helpless travelers who simply ran into this kid by accident."

The unicorn paused pointedly.

"For now, at least."

In a few minutes, the elves came swooping down atop their beasts and landed in a semi-circle around the cabin. Clad in deerskin vests and pants, their sleek bodies were covered in heavy swaths of mystic tattoos. Each was armed with a spear made of a gleaming, silver metal, which they carried with a well-practiced ease.

The elves' mounts were even more horrible up close then they were at a distance. The gigantic, winged serpents were almost all torso, with stubby legs that would have been almost comical if not for the beasts' razor-sharp teeth. The wyverns hungrily ogled Luzi and U, kept at bay only by the command of their masters.

The elves dismounted their beasts and surrounded the cabin, pointing their weapons at Luzi and U menacingly. Worried, Luzi looked at U for a sign to attack. But instead, he calmly extended a hand to the elves in greeting.

"Nish Dvenj!" the unicorn exclaimed confidently, addressing them in their own tongue.

Hearing their language coming from a human stopped the elves in their tracks. They stared at U with surprise, but didn't lower their weapons. Undeterred, he repeated his earlier greeting, this time more emphatically.

"Nish Dvenj!"

After a long pause, one of the elves stepped forward. Taller than the others by a full head, she carried a massive war hammer that looked like it could pulverize Luzi's skull into powder with a single swing.

"Dvenj aa? Tnik Biik?" she dubiously inquired of U, as someone would greet a never-before-seen cousin at the reading of a deceased uncle's will.

"Biik!" he reaffirmed ardently.

Unsatisfied with U's overtures, the elf turned to Luzi – "Etska, cho tnik Biik?" – chuckling disapprovingly when she saw that Luzi didn't speak her language.

"You're going to force me to speak Communia on my native soil?" she criticized, switching languages so Luzi could understand her. "This is not an auspicious beginning to our relationship, *outsiders.*"

"I am Bo-Zuni, captain of the Gongqui guard for these lands," the elf continued. "You are trespassing in a live military zone. I have some questions. You need to answer them swiftly and truthfully. And you will only get one chance on the latter point. Do you both understand?"

U nodded. "We do."

The elf's eyes narrowed. "First things first. Where is the child?"

U exhaled through his nose; Luzi bit her lip.

"He's in the cabin," U admitted.

Bo-Zuni glanced from Luzi to U, nodding approvingly. She waved her hand to one of the elves, who trotted off in the direction of the hut.

"I appreciate your honesty. We're off to a good start. Now tell me... who are you, and why are you trespassing on Gongqui soil?"

U's reply came easy and casual.

"We're travelers from Nyasia, trying to pass through the Elven Plains on our way north to Dama'run. While crossing your lands, we found a severely injured Yali child in the wilderness. If we left him, he would have died. So we did the only thing we could. We took him with us."

"And exactly where were you planning on taking this youngling?" Bo-Zuni inquired suspiciously.

"To Erund Mar."

The elves tensed up at the mention of the Yali outpost. A fresh round of muttering broke out among them.

"Erund Mar?" Bo-Zuni asked U with a raised eyebrow. "You're joking, right?"

U remained as cool as a fjord.

"If this is a joke, I don't get the punchline."

Bo-Zuni stared at U for a moment, tilting her head slightly as she tried to figure out if he was playing stupid. "Don't you know?" the elf eventually responded, raising an eyebrow. "Erund Mar no longer exists."

This time, it was U's turn to be surprised.

"What do you mean, it no longer exists?"

"Just what I said," Bo-Zuni replied with a chilling calm. "It's been obliterated."

"For the past several years, Erund Mar has been used as a crucial staging and supply point by the Yali militia. The Elvish Rundermust has always been tolerant of the village, even after the war started. We knew they weren't warriors... they were merchants. But those villagers helped to deliver weapons and supplies that have been instrumental in the deaths of thousands of my countryfolk. And in my mind, that makes them as guilty as the soldier who wields the spear.

"The Rundermust sent the people of Erund Mar three separate demands over the past year. 'Stop giving aid to the Yali militia, or face slaughter to the last man, woman and child.' The village was issued a final warning at last month's full moon. They refused to heed the plea. And despite our best efforts, it became clear that an example needed to be made."

Bo-Zuni's next words came with the cold, calculating logic of a soldier.

"Five sunrises ago, my platoon was among an elvish brigade that burned the entire village to the ground during a sweep and clear effort. We killed the elderly. We killed the infirm. We killed the babes in their cribs and their parents in their beds. Not one living soul remains alive who once called that village home."

The elf pointed to the cabin. "Except *that* child."

"Two days after the battle, while combing the area for military intelligence, my platoon and I came across a set of bloody tracks from a Yali child leading to a river outside the village. When we saw a canoe missing from its moor, it was easy to surmise what happened... and what needed to be done next."

Bo-Zuni shook her head with a grudging respect.

"It was a smart move using the river, I'll give the little shit that much. We nearly lost his trail several times before he landed on shore. We managed to follow his tracks to an open field, where he apparently collapsed in the dirt. But instead of finding a dead body, imagine our surprise when we found something else in its place – hoofprints."

Luzi peeked at U. He remained calm, looking straight ahead at Bo-Zuni with his trademark solemnity.

"So here we are. What now?"

Bo-Zuni looked at the other elves, then back to U and Luzi. "I have good news and bad news. Which would you like first?"

"Good," Luzi blurted out.

Bo-Zuni peered pointedly at Luzi. "I am now one hundred percent certain you are not Yali spies."

The elf turned to U.

"We *were* going to torture you. But after our little chat, I don't think that's going to be necessary. After all, why would a spy tell me that he was headed to a village which no longer exists? Even the daftest of saboteurs would surely come up with a better lie."

Luzi didn't know whether to feel relieved or terrified. Apparently, U didn't either.

"So what's the *bad* news?" U queried, a razor's edge to his voice.

Moving quickly – as if she'd been waiting for the moment to come – Bo-Zuni raised one of her hands in a fist. The other elves brandished their weapons, following the signal of their leader.

"We're still going to kill all three of you," she declared.

***

Luzi felt her stomach go cold. She began to protest, but U reached out and pressed her arm lightly.

"Why are you doing this?" U asked Bo-Zuni. "We're no threat to you. And neither is that child."

"A promise was made to the people of Erund Mar: *Stop helping the Yali or none of you will survive*," the elf replied. "If we let this child live, our promise will be broken. The Yali will think we don't have the ability – or the guts – to follow through on our ultimatums. And that's the very day we lose this war."

Despite her best efforts, Luzi couldn't help but object.

"You're willing to kill an innocent child just to keep a promise?"

The elf clicked her tongue, as if she was admonishing an infant.

"Ah, you humans," she chastised. "Always trying to judge the ethics of a war you haven't shed a drop of blood for. Well, I have news for you. This child isn't the first innocent life this conflict has claimed. And it won't be the last."

"The spectre of what we've done is bad enough. But to give it flesh? Such a symbol can become more powerful than an army. What happens here today is larger than one child, or one village, or one battle. This is about letting the Yali know that we will do whatever it takes to win this war. Even if that includes slaughtering every last one of them."

A long silence followed.

"And *us*?" U questioned warily.

The elf gave Luzi and U a withering stare.

"This may surprise you, but there are those among my kin who do not agree with our methods. They have been pushing to end the war at all costs, and have found receptive ears with some powerful allies in Ragnaron and Quiyst. Letting a couple of humans loose to spread the word of what happened here today would cause... complications."

"For what it's worth, I do believe your story," Bo-Zuni admitted. "It's unfortunate that you are being punished for trying to do a good deed, and for that I'm sorry. I cannot stop what is about to come. But I *can* make it painless – if you'll both allow it."

The elf paused, waiting for a reply from Luzi and U. None came.

"Let me put it another way," she said. "You're unarmed, outnumbered and outpowered. Even if you manage to kill one or two of us, there's no possible victory here. Surely you understand that?"

Silence.

"Damn the gods, I'm done asking nicely!" the elf declared with a growing frustration. "This is your last chance, outsiders. Are you going to submit quietly? Or do we have to do this the ugly way?"

Nothing.

Bo-Zuni shook her head disapprovingly. "Well... fuck both of you, then. Sometimes I don't know why I even try."

The elf waved to her companions. "Kill them all!" she exhorted.

Spurred on by their leader, the Gongqui slowly advanced towards U and Luzi. The Nyasian looked to her companion, watching him for a cue to manifest their weapons and attack. But to her surprise, U continued to stand there completely frozen, like a rabbit before a pack of coyotes. *What's he doing?* Luzi wondered, watching him with a growing frustration.

For a moment, the Nyasian wondered if she should make the first move herself. But before she did, something about the elves caught her eye. And that's when she finally understood U's plan. The advancing warriors were brashly overconfident, clearly having discounted U and Luzi as a threat. Most had their weapons half-raised, expecting Bo-Zuni or one of the others to deliver the actual killing strikes. And none of them had the slightest idea about the hellstorm that they were about to unleash.

Sneaky bastard, Luzi conceded, glancing over at her "helpless" companion.

As the elves closed to within lunging distance. Bo-Zuni

took a big step ahead of the rest of the pack. The muscle-bound elf approached U, her meaty hands curled around her huge war hammer. She hefted it high above her head, cocking back her shoulders to strike.

And that's when the unicorn finally made his move.

As Bo-Zuni lifted her hammer – in the split second when it was impossible for her to attack – U manifested his armum sword. He struck like a viper, a blur of motion too quick to be seen. And before Luzi could blink, the elf's head was lopped off at her shoulders.

"Now!" U yelled to Luzi as Bo-Zuni's lifeless body dropped to the ground.

Without further hesitation, the unicorn dove into the crowd of elves with a merciless fury that took them completely flatfooted. U effortlessly cleaved through the elven warriors like he was harvesting wheat. There was a savage, unearthly grace to each movement; he was a perfect killing machine. And before a single elf could even raise their weapon, he'd already destroyed four of them.

For a moment, Luzi was left frozen in abject shock. But an awful thought soon jarred her back into the fray. *The boy!* she remembered.

With a rising panic, Luzi manifested her armum and ran to the cabin, the fire growing hotter in her lungs with each step. But when she arrived at the door – to her dismay – she wasn't alone.

An elf warrior stood over the child, his spear raised like a fisherman about to stab a trout in a river. He was a scrawny young man, not far removed from childhood himself. But the warrior who stood before Luzi that day was no juvenile. Not anymore. There was a cold conviction in his eyes – no fear – just a single-minded, animalistic desire for blood.

"No!" came Luzi's frenzied yell, as if she could stop what was about to happen by sheer willpower.

If the elf could understand Luzi's anguished cry, he didn't show it. With a sickening thrust, he jammed the spear into the center of the child's heart.

Flesh parted way to metal.

A life ended.

Luzi released a loud yawp. But it wasn't anguish that echoed in the air this time... it was anger. With a blind fury, she rushed the elf, her shield raised high. Her opponent pulled his spear from the child's chest and spun to face Luzi's charge.

Contrary to everything she'd practiced over the past week, Luzi's first swing was a wild haymaker. It was a hate-filled strike that the elf easily dodged, exposing her right side – a target that her adversary attacked with a violent stab. It was only by sheer luck that Luzi was able to twist away and avoid the edge of his spear, taking a nick on her arm that drew a tiny sliver of red.

Luzi recovered her balance. *Remember what U taught you!* she screamed at herself.

The elf took another jab with his spear, trying to gig Luzi like a fish. The Nyasian angled her shield to slightly cross the incoming blow. The force of the collision buckled her forearm muscles. But just as U had instructed, Luzi aimed her shield to slightly cross the blade. Flexing her knees, she pushed forward, deflecting the elf's weapon.

As the elf regained his balance for another whack, Luzi saw an opening in his defenses. Before he could react, Luzi charged ahead like a ram and barreled into him with her shield, bashing as hard as she could. Her move caught the dumbfounded elf completely off-guard, knocking him onto his back. He landed with a loud thud, his spear clattering on the ground beside him.

Acting with an instinct she didn't know she had, Luzi leaped onto the elf and straddled his chest, pinning his arms with her knees. For an infinitesimal click in time, Luzi and her foe met eyes. Then – without further hesitation – Luzi brought her shield down on his head as hard as she could.

And with that single blow, Luzi became a killer.

When the deed was finished and the elf's body stopped twitching, Luzi got up and rushed over to the child. In her heart, she knew exactly what she'd find. But the mere sight of his lifeless corpse was enough to put her into shock.

Luzi barely noticed U finish off the remaining elves. She didn't see the wyverns begin to hungrily feed on the remains of their former masters. She didn't hear the snarls, the screams, the scrape of teeth on bone. She could only stand there dumbfounded, a numb ache spreading through her body and branching into her brain. And when U finally killed the last Gongqui warrior and returned to the cabin, Luzi was still in the same exact spot, staring at the child's body.

The unicorn watched her for a moment before speaking.

"Luzi... we have to leave," U said quietly. "It's not safe here."

The Nyasian said nothing.

U repeated his request and was met with more silence. It wasn't until the unicorn was getting ready to repeat his plea a third time that Luzi answered him.

"They're dead," she said, looking at him with tortured eyes. "They're all dead."

"They left us no choice," U replied with a calm certainty. "This was self-defense. You understand that, right?"

Luzi just shook her head miserably.

"Don't you get it? We tried so hard to save that kid. We risked our lives. We placed millions of people in jeopardy. I killed someone. Dis be damned, U... I *killed* someone! And for what?"

She balled her fists with frustration and shame.

"If we can't save one child's life, what odds do we have of saving the world? You're one unicorn against an entire coven. And me? I'm just... just..."

The Nyasian trailed off into silence, afraid to complete her sentence.

For a long time, U said nothing. "Do you know the difference between a warrior and a murderer?" he finally asked.

Luzi blinked blankly and shook her head.

"A warrior weeps for the dead," U said, offering her a sad smile.

With a gentle nudge of his hand, the unicorn lifted Luzi's chin. "We *will* make it to Dama'run. We *will* get the ring to safety. And the sun *will* shine again. You have my word."

Luzi blinked back moisture in her eyes. "Okay," she said, slowly regaining her composure. "What now?"

U gingerly placed his hand on her arm. "Can you ride?"

Too choked up to respond, Luzi could only nod. Without further hesitation, the unicorn tenderly led her outside into the rain, which continued to slice down on the battlefield. Uchchaihshravas changed into his Monoceros form, then kneeled down and looked up at Luzi, bidding her to mount up.

The Nyasian took a final swipe at her wet eyes with the sleeve of her shirt. With a heavy heart, she climbed aboard the unicorn's back, clutching a handful of his mane for balance.

"Just hold tight," he told Luzi. "I'll do the rest."

And with a flex of his mighty leg muscles, the unicorn was off like a harpy out of hell, galloping across the plain so fast that the downpour barely touched them.

12

"Ah, fury... How blunt are thy fangs when compared to those of shame!"

– Last words of infamous mass-murderer Mason Mannering

They were restless. They were hungry. They were eager for blood.

And that's a very dangerous combination when unicorns are involved.

It had been days since Karkadiann and her team of alphas assembled on orders of the Meridian. For some of them, the desire for action was almost unbearable. Several had taken to relentlessly pacing the cavern, like master musicians with broken hands unable to play their instruments. But their mistress had been clear in her decree: "Don't take a step outside this cave without my word."

And so they waited.

Every good leader knows how far she can push her troops before they lose heart, however. So as a sign of respect, the

Meridian broke her own rule and allowed a hunt – the first in nearly two decades.

In time, a group of beta unicorns entered the chamber, their ears tucked low in a show of respect. Each hefted a much-cherished prize in their jaws: meat. The smell of flesh temporarily distracted the hunting party's attention. Mammal meat had been rare ever since the Meridian placed strict regulations on stalking outside the cave. Even the daftest of the Overgruk understood the reason for her edict – discovery of the coven would almost certainly cost their lives.

But that didn't mean they liked it.

The Meridian's idea to create subterranean insect farms had provided enough protein to stay alive all these years... and that was *something*. Still, not even the most stalwart among them could ignore the primal hunger that consumed their every waking hour, and which could no longer be satiated with beetles and larvae.

One by one, the betas laid their kills at the feet of Karkadiann's hunting party. Deer. Boars. Perytons. As they relinquished their erstwhile meals, each couldn't help but grimace. The meat hunger gnawed in them, the same as their higher-ranking brothers and sisters. Still, the betas surrendered their contributions without pause, selflessly, as any good squire would do for their knight. Not that they had a choice. In Monoceros society, there is little mercy for the weak – and even less for those foolish enough to pity them. [12]

No words of thanks were expected or given. The betas left the chamber the same way they entered: with their noses lowered in deference.

And without further hesitation, Karkadiann and her crew tore into their suppers.

Those who have seen unicorns eat and lived to tell the tale have often expressed surprise at the crude gusto with which the otherwise regal Monoceros dine. For several minutes, all that could be heard was the slobbering of lips and the crunching of bones. But as the frenzy died down and sense returned to the unicorns' heads, so too did their tongues. And it wasn't long before the party turned their discussion to the fallen one.

Uchchaihshravas.

"Where do you suppose he and the human are now?" a blue-furred unicorn asked the others, her muzzle stained purple with blood.

"By now?" another unicorn replied with a muted interest, like a bookie inquiring about odds at a gladiator match. "Anywhere, brother. For all his perfidiousness, the traitor's no fool. With his shapeshifting skills and the Nyasian's anonymity – not to mention a week's head start – there's virtually no chance of tracking them down."

"I hate to admit it, but you're right," a third unicorn agreed. "Perhaps the Boogeyman really *is* the better choice for this mission,"

"Sacrilege," an olive-toned unicorn hissed. "The glory belongs to us, sister, and us alone."

The blue-furred unicorn laughed. "If anything, the honor of ending the traitor's life belongs to Karkadiann. After all, who has more claim to challenge Uchchaihshravas than the one who gouged out her–"

The unicorn trailed off as she recognized her social faux

paus. The others held their breath and glanced at Karkadiann, expecting the worst. But despite their captain's reputation for violence, the impertinent anecdote went without retribution.

"The Meridian has a thousand reasons for everything she does," Karkadiann said simply. "It's our job to provide answers, not questions. I've been promised that we will be given our chance for glory if the Boogeyman fails in his task. Until then, we wait for her command. Obediently."

Karkadiann gave the others an icy glare. "Is that understood?"

The unicorns nodded solemnly in unison.

"Good," she replied. "Now eat your goddamned food."

The hunting party quickly dug back into their half-finished carcasses in a show of obedience. A silence fell over the group as they slurped and chomped, losing themselves in the delight of flesh feeding.

The only one who bothered to look up from their meal was Karkadiann. Almost imperceptibly – so the others won't notice – she angled her head to gaze east, towards the Overgruk combat chamber. The unicorn thought of that long-ago night when she entered the ring with Uchchaihshravas. She remembered the clash of hooves... the gnashing of teeth... the piercing of a horn.

She remembered his mercy. She remembered his pity.

And as Karkadiann chewed a mouthful of meat, her empty eye socket clenched tightly with hate.

13

"Drinking poison from a golden cup is still fatal."

– Enza of Thrais, founding headmaster of the Dama'run Academy of Philosophy

The sickness didn't hit Luzi until hours after their battle with the elves.

It came on slow at first, just a headache and soreness – almost like catching a cold. Luzi didn't say a word to U, not wanting to slow their pace. But it wasn't long before worse symptoms began to surface: sweats, coughing, shaking, nausea. And when her vision started to go blurry, Luzi could no longer deny that something was seriously wrong.

"By the hateful grace of Dis, stop!" she begged as they swiveled around a particularly steep curve.

The moment the unicorn came to a halt, Luzi tumbled off his back and emptied her stomach into the mud and grass. *What the hell is the matter with me?* she wondered miserably as the rain poured down on her head.

While Luzi coughed and wiped her mouth clear of vomit, U moved to the Nyasian's side to examine her.

"What's wrong? Are you sick? Those damn meatplants. I knew they weren't ripe. Maybe we should find somewhere out of the rain until we can... hold on... *what happened to your arm?*"

The abrupt concern in U's voice surprised Luzi. She glanced down at the spot where the elf nicked her with his spear.

"This?" she mumbled, peeling back her sleeve to reveal the tiny cut. "It's just a scratch I got during the fight. It's not a big deal, really. Hell, it's not even bleeding anymore."

But instead of being reassured, U only seemed more worried.

"This changes everything. We need to figure out what to do, where to go. Damn the gods, how could I have been so ignorant? This is all my fault for not catching this sooner."

"What?"

"It's important that you don't get alarmed by what I tell you next, do you understand?" U said, speaking with a deliberate calm that only made Luzi's anxiety worse.

"Dammit, spit it out! What's wrong?"

"I think you've been poisoned."

"Poisoned?" Luzi squeaked.

U nodded solemnly.

"The Gongqui are known for dipping their spears in resin from the teppa plant, which produces one of the deadliest toxins in the world. There are almost no known remedies, magical or not. Even a tiny cut can be enough to kill.

"The poison has just one natural cure – an herb called

foxfern – but it needs to be taken within a day or two. Lucky for us, foxfern is also a common treatment for bedbugs around these parts. Any respectable inn would have a fresh supply on hand at all times."

U glanced to the north, shielding his eyes from the pouring rain with the ridge of his hand.

"There's a small trade village a few hours from here called Westwend. In town, there's a boarding tavern I've visited before in my travels through the plains. I'm positive they'll have what we need – they have to."

Luzi squinted at the unicorn. All of the sudden there were three of him. She wasn't sure which one to speak to, so she faced the one in the middle.

"Won't it be dangerous? The Overgruk are still looking for us."

"We don't have any other choice."

"But the ring!" Luzi insisted, mustering all of her strength for the effort.

U gave her a sideways glance. "Luzi... do you really think I've done all this for a *ring*?

His comment ended the Nyasian's weak protest. She didn't know how to reply, so she just nodded.

"Save your strength for the ride," U suggested, kneeling down. "You're going to need it."

Unable to argue further – even if she'd wanted to – Luzi steadied her stomach and climbed back onto U, grabbing a handful of his mane to steady herself. "Just please, for the love of Dis... watch those fucking curves," she muttered.

"I'll do my best," U promised sympathetically, digging his hooves into the earth.

And without another word, they were gone.

***

For Luzi, the rest of the evening passed in a nauseous blur. They traveled for hours, with nothing to mark the time but drenched clothes and steadily dampening spirits. Finally, just as the Nyasian felt herself nodding off with exhaustion and sickness, they reached the first sign of civilization they'd seen in a week: a dirt road.

The pair continued down the path – not encountering another soul the entire time – until the lights of a small village became visible in the distance.

"Courage," U urged, feeling Luzi wobble on his back. "We're almost there."

True to his word, it wasn't long before they arrived at a tavern on the edge of town. Despite the dark and silence in the rest of the village, the tavern was gleaming like a lighthouse. A cheerful fracas of clapping mugs and drunken shouts rang in the air, masking their arrival. Luzi's hazy vision was able to make out a large sign on the front of the establishment: The Phangorian Inn. [13]

U stopped and glanced back at Luzi. "I need to change into human form before someone sees us. We're going to have to walk the rest of the way. Can you make it?"

"Do I have a choice?" she weakly deadpanned.

The Nyasian steeled herself and dismounted. Her legs trembled as they hit the ground, but they held... barely.

Glancing around to make sure nobody was watching, U transformed into his human persona. He offered Luzi his arm to lean on, but she waved him off. Side by side, they walked up to the tavern, slowly making their way to the vestibule. But before U could grab hold of the door handle, it swung open abruptly, nearly smashing him in the face.

With a series of crashing thumps, a burly man with a scraggy beard and spinning eyes came staggering out of the inn into the night. The goon stunk like his blood was made of booze. He was slurring something fervently, but Luzi couldn't tell what language it was – if any.

Luzi felt the last reserve of adrenaline surge in her heart. She readied herself for a fight. But before she manifested her shield, U reached out and put a hand on her shoulder.

"Wait."

The unicorn's instinct proved wise. Instead of attacking, the stranger pushed past them and stumbled to a nearby hedge. He slumped down on his knees, and for a moment, Luzi thought he was about to start praying... until he started heaving into the bushes.

Luzi and U looked at each other. The unicorn rolled his eyes. And with that inauspicious start – like they were walking straight into the setup of a bad joke – they entered the tavern.

If U was shooting for inconspicuous, he sure hit his mark – what a fucking dump! Luzi judged, gazing at the inside of the bar with dismay.

The entire place was filthy, a mulligan stew of brutal smells and sights. The inn's thick, stone walls were coated with a grey film from decades of pipe and kitchen smoke, and a lingering mushroom scent in the air wrinkled Luzi's nose. A thin layer of straw on the floor helped to sop up the mud and various other spilled liquids, but it hadn't been changed all day from the looks of the caked mess that remained. There wasn't a piece of furniture without a battle scar; not a single mug or plate was absent chips or grease.

The tavern's filthiness was rivaled by its noise, almost as if they were competing to see which could make it more unpleasant. As soon as they crossed the threshold, Luzi's ears were assaulted by the chaotic cacophony of a half-dozen languages spoken all at once, carrying on unceasingly, like the roar of ocean waves against a beach.

A group of drunken elves were gathered at the bar, partaking in a boisterous game with a crimson liquid and a hollowed-out gourd. A cluster of giggling old ladies sat in the corner, puffing up sweet-smelling clouds of pipe smoke. And a dozen other local villagers occupied tables throughout the inn, each too absorbed in their own conversations to pay any attention to a couple of strangers straggling in from the rain.

The voices blurred into a single medley:

"A fuggin' loiter-sack! That's what the guild has sent me! Where do they get these people? The id'jit can't even work a bellows properly! An' that damn guildmaster – don't even get me started on THAT cud-muncher…"

"They've got the best roast cockatrice in the entire known realms. It's so juicy, it just slides off the bone. And that's just the first course. Lemme tell you about their braised basilisk…"

"Know what he told Paz-Ul just ten minutes ago? 'I'm NOT too drunk for another round!' Know where he's saying that from now? Outside in tha' bushes!"

"That's the trouble with investing in the Ragnarian shipping industry. There's no way that inflation will balance out enough

in the fiscal year to avoid forcing a trade deal with Quiyst, and then blah and money and and blah and you'll really see the effect of Abyssinia's isolationist policies on the blah when it comes to finance blah money money blah blah money money money blah blah blah..."

"He called me a cutthroat, a skinflint, a liar and a bad card player. So I said, 'Hey! Who you callin' a bad card player?"

"*Gourd up! Gourd up! Gourd up! Gourd up! Gourd up! Gourd up!*"

Trying their best to blend into the crowd, U and Luzi made their way to the kitchen. There, a friendly, heavyset elf with bags under his eyes was directing the inn's staff with the seasoned acumen of a ship's captain. The elf looked nothing like the Gongqui they'd fought earlier; he didn't have a single tattoo and stood at least a head shorter.

The innkeeper waved at Luzi and U with a dirty dishrag and greeted them warmly in Communia.

"Welcome to the Phangorian! My name's Paz-Ul. Full quarts of ale are on special today for two britt apiece – that's a tweenie bit of gold if you're from the outlands, or half of a kachma if you're on the Dama'run standard. And before you ask, we don't give credit. Now what can I do for-" [14]

The innkeeper trailed off as he saw Luzi shuffling along like a zombie. The smile evaporated from his face when he saw her waxy, sweaty skin.

"Is she contagious?" he asked U nervously. "Listen, I don't want any trouble – I've got customers to protect here."

"Gods above, keep your voice down!" U insisted quietly, glancing around to see if anyone overheard them. "This girl has been poisoned with teppa. We need a bundle of foxfern, a pitcher of water and a private room, and we need them *right now*."

The innkeeper's expression softened. He looked at Luzi with a newfound compassion.

"Teppa? But how… never mind… it's none of my business."

Paz-Ul turned back to U, regaining some of his former composure. "You're fortunate. We have what you need. As long as you have the coin to pay for it, that is."

The elf returned U's icy glare.

"Don't give me that look. I sympathize with your situation, I really do. But this isn't a fuck'n charity, you know."

Just then, Luzi remembered the Landcasters' secret stash of diamonds. She fished one out of her pocket and laid it on the bar.

"Will *this* pay for what we ask?"

"By the Deep!" Paz-Ul commented loudly, gawking at the precious stone with wide eyes. "Where'd you get that?"

U quickly pressed the jewel into the innkeeper's palm and motioned for him to keep quiet. "It doesn't matter," he hissed. "There aren't any more where that came from, so don't bother asking. Now end this charade, damn you! Are the scales balanced between us?"

Paz-Ul discretely examined the diamond in his hand and nodded, impressed with what he saw.

"Balanced and more. Much obliged."

The elf quickly stashed the stone in an iron chest behind the bar. Then he raised his rag and waved it at a corner table. "Leema!"

In a moment, a satyress emerged from the crowd carrying an empty drink tray. Despite her illness, Luzi couldn't help but cast a curious look her way. She'd seen books with pictures of satyrs, the half-human, half-goat hybrids who hail from the outlands at the edge of Abyssinia. But Luzi never dreamed she'd meet one in real life.

"Take our new guests to room six and bring them a bundle of foxfern," Paz-Ul told the satyress waitress. "Be swift – we've got a busy night ahead of us."

The innkeeper turned back to his guests.

"Leema will guide you to your quarters. If you need anything else, seek me out and I'll fly to the task."

He looked at U with a sudden seriousness. "And if things should take an unfortunate turn, kindly let me know, will you?"

U nodded curtly, eager to end the conversation.

Leema took a lantern off a nearby hook on the wall and smiled at Luzi and U.

"Right this way, please."

They followed the satyress up a staircase to the right of the kitchen, her hooves clopping on the stairs as they ascended. Leema chatted absentmindedly as they went, blissfully unaware of the severity of Luzi's illness.

"You got here in the nick of time, this is the last room in the house. There've been so many more boarders lately because of the war. Most of the other inns around these parts have started closing their doors to anyone not of elfin blood... it's kind of sad, really. Mr. Ul has been talking about building an extension to the Phangorian for a while now. But the Rundermust has been taxing the inn to hell and back lately. Sometimes I think the only reason they allow us to serve humans at all is because they need the money so badly." [15]

The satyress led them down a hallway towards the guest rooms.

"We don't have a couple's room free right now. I hope you don't mind squeezing together?"

"A single bed is fine, I'll sleep on the floor," U immediately replied. "And to be clear, we're not a couple. We're just traveling companions, that's all."

The Nyasian felt her cheeks flush. U's insistence that they "weren't a couple" stung for some strange and uncomfortable reason. *What's wrong with you, Luzi?* she wondered, surprised at the unfamiliar emotions broiling in her psyche.

The satyress glanced back at U and Luzi with a sheepish smile.

"Oh, my days! Please don't tell Mr. Ul that I was so stupid. It's none of my business in the first place. I won't make another peep about it. Ah – listen to me blather on. Honestly, if we were in a book right now, you'd bury half of anything I say in the footnotes." [16]

"Anyway, here we are," Leema said as they arrived at the end of the hallway, anxious to change the subject. She held her lantern aloft and pushed the door open with her free hand. Luzi peered inside. The windowless room was small but cozy, warmed by the kitchen below.

Leema set the lantern down on a table.

"Does it meet your approval? I can always check and see if one of the other boarders would be willing to switch. There's a Ragnarian trader in room three who was just complaining about a draft in his-"

"It's fine," U brusquely declared, trying to get rid of the chatty satyress. "The foxfern?"

"I'll fetch it right away," Leema said, finally taking the hint. "I'll get a pitcher of water and a washing bowl while I'm at it. Is there anything else you need?"

U shook his head. "Just privacy. Be quick, I beg you."

The satyress nodded and disappeared quickly back the way she'd come. The unicorn shut the door behind her. And finally, Luzi and U were alone again.

Stretched to the absolute limit of her endurance, Luzi flopped down on the bed with a heavy gasp. She felt her body begin to shut down, every muscle fiber hopelessly taxed beyond its maximum capability.

Luzi closed her eyes. The Nyasian was dimly aware that U was asking her a question, but she could no longer focus on the words. It was all fading away beyond her grasp – now and forever more.

And in the space of a blink, everything went black.

***

That night, walking the boundary between life and death, Luzi dreamed of an old Ragnarian fable called "The Century of Centuries." It was a tale that her parents used to tell her as a child... one she knew word-for-word... her mother's favorite.

It went like this:

It was a tranquil summer evening in the seaside village of Lemuria – just like any other – when a crew of mariners returned early from their expedition, racked with exhaustion and without a single fish.

"Death!" they cried, horror curdling their voices. "Death is coming!"

Their ululations ground the village to a halt. A town meeting was called on the spot; all but the sickest and youngest were summoned to attend.

"While setting our lines this morning we came across a fleet of warships headed down the northern coast," the panicked anglers told the other villagers. "There were at least two dozen vessels, maybe more, each flying a black sail emblazoned with a wolf skull. And they're headed straight for Lemuria!"

The village chief – a large, elderly woman named Hrotha – stepped forward with a grim look on her face. She locked eyes with Ivo, the most trustworthy of the sailors and a father of six.

"A wolf skull on a black sail… are you absolutely certain of this? Would you stake your life on it? More importantly, would you stake the lives of your children on it?"

The crusty-but-wise seafarer didn't hesitate.

"I would."

Hrotha's expression sank even lower. "Then may the gods save us… it can only be the Abbadon."

A handful of the older Lemurians cried out in fear at the name. But the moniker carried no meaning to most of their younger neighbors.

"I don't get it," one young man in the crowd asked, speaking for the majority. "Who are the Abbadon?"

There was a moment of dread before Hrotha replied.

"Death," she said at last. "They are death."

"Long ago, the lands of a tribe of fearsome warriors in the north went fallow, poisoned by neglect and drought. Re-naming themselves 'Abbadon' – the people who gnaw bones – they abandoned their homeland and took to the oceans in

an armada of mighty warships. Like locusts from the under-
world, the Abbadon have traveled the coasts ever since, going
from village to village and destroying everything they don't
steal. They leave no survivors, have no mercy. And anywhere
they go, despair follows."

"Nobody has ever seen them within a thousand miles of
Lemuria," Hrotha explained glumly. "I'd long ago dismissed
them as a legend – or at least a terror that I'd never see in
my lifetime. But it seems we aren't destined to be that lucky
after all."

A chill passed over the village. Hrotha was one of the wis-
est and worldliest among them. And they knew she wouldn't
say such things unless they were true.

"Let them come!" a woman in the crowd cried out, trying
to act brave. "This is our home! We'll defend it from anyone
stupid enough to try and take it!"

But Hrotha just shook her head.

"The Abbadon have slain whole villages, laid entire armies
low. We don't stand a chance against them in combat. If we
try to fight, every one of us will die. If you've ever believed a
sentence I've uttered, please believe *that*."

There wasn't a single Lemurian demented enough to
question her. The village was populated with farmers, fishers
and craftspeople. Many were well beyond their combat years;
many others had not yet reached them. And the majority had
never held a blade in their lives... unless you count hatchets
and fishing spears.

As the crowd began to panic, Hrotha held up her hands,
pleading for calm.

"All is not lost, I have a plan," she promised. "About

a two-day sail south of Lemuria, hidden among a chain of rock-strewn islands, there's a cove that's been a secret in my family for generations. It has fresh water, wild fruit, small game... everything we need to live until the Abbadon have moved on."

"Hold on a minute, Hrotha," interjected the village constable, Guntar, his eyes growing wide. "Are you suggesting we evacuate the entire village?"

The village chief nodded solemnly. "That's *exactly* what I'm saying, yes."

Hrotha turned to Ivo. "How long do we have before the Abbadon arrive?"

"They were headed for the southern cape, so they'll have to sail around the Horn of Huxley," the fisherman replied. "But they will certainly be upon us within a day – perhaps sooner."

"A day!" Guntar gasped, unable to temper his dread. "That means we'd have to evacuate by sunrise tomorrow! Do you know what that will take? We need to round up food, water, clothes, tents, tools. It's impossible, Hrotha!"

A fresh wave of panic spread through the village.

"He's right!"

"We'll never make it in time!"

"We're doomed!"

As if he'd been biding his time for the right moment to speak, a wainwright named Nestor stepped forward from the crowd. A diminutive man with beady eyes, he nonetheless had a way of talking that captured one's attention, like a carnival barker at a sideshow.

"Maybe we don't try to move the *entire* village then."

The murmurs died down.

"What are you talking about?" Hrotha asked tentatively.

"It's simple," Nestor replied. "There are those among us who will take much more time to evacuate. The sick. The infirm. The elderly. But what if these factors were removed from the equation?"

The villagers looked at each other, none of them willing to vocalize what Nestor was proposing. Finally, Hrotha said what the others would not.

"Nestor... are you suggesting we leave them behind?"

The young man set his jaw. "Although it breaks my heart, it's the only choice. And you know it as well as I do, Hrotha."

With the acknowledgment of this awful alternative – even though many among them had already been thinking the same thing – the crowd began to wail. "Blasphemy!" many called out.

But Nestor stood his ground.

"Blasphemy?" he fired back. "Blasphemy is condemning a thousand innocent lives to save a hundred. This is just math. I'm trying to *save* lives, not *take* them! Damn it, don't any of you understand?"

Nestor pointed to a young boy in the crowd standing beside his parents. "Shall we doom this child – and a dozen more like him – because an old man is afraid to meet his end? Tell me, where is the justice in that?"

Some of those in the crowd with children began to yell out in support.

"He's right!"

"Hear him out!"

Nestor turned to the crowd, cajoling them to follow his lead. "Who has more of a right to live? A young girl or an old woman? A man who can drag his daily meal from the ocean, or a sponge who cannot? Who? Who?"

"He's right!" more villagers yelled, sizing up the old and the sick in the crowd with sinister, predatory glares.

But just as the tide of opinion started to shift, a meat-wall of a man named Olaff – one of the few true warriors in the village – stood up in a fury.

"Coward!" he hollered, his stout face turning red. "I know you, Nestor. Your parents have both passed. You're an only child, without progeny or partner. It's easy to say 'leave them behind' when you don't have anyone to say goodbye to. But what about the rest of us?"

Olaff pointed to an elderly man beside him.

"Would you leave my father to the mercy of the Abbadon? Maybe *he* can defend my mother, who hasn't been able to walk since her accident? Or how about the hundreds more who will pay the price for your survival, our brothers and sisters and aunts and uncles? How about them, you goddamn coward?"

Nestor didn't bat an eye.

"You don't get to volunteer *my* life for a pointless cause," the wainwright snapped.

"Pointless cause?" Olaff bellowed, shaking his fist. "You little shit stain! When I'm done with you there won't be any-thing left for the Abbadon!"

Tempers flared and ears shut on both sides of the debate. Neighbor turned on neighbor, each Lemurian siding with Nestor or Olaff and none giving ground to the others. But just as the argument was about to rip the village in two, a grizzled voice rang out above the din, clear and commanding as any general.

"Stop this madness now... all of you!"

Several villagers whipped around at the sudden admonishing, eager to have words with their accuser. But even Olaff paused when he saw the source of the command... Rayna the hermit.

The grey one's origins were one of the biggest mysteries in the village. The old woman had come to Lemuria almost three decades ago from the outlands, and hadn't spoken more than a hundred words since arriving. But that didn't stop people from gossiping.

She was a former captain in the Ragnarian army, drummed out for committing war crimes. She was a mercenary from the far east, on the run from a gruesome past. She was a cold-blooded murderer, escaped from prison and living incognito among her future victims.

Regardless of the details, the core of the rumors were always the same: Rayna was a woman whose past was soaked in unspeakable violence. And there was no doubt in anyone's mind that she had seen dozens of people to the afterlife – maybe hundreds – before retiring to her lonely little perch on the ocean bluff.

The whispers about Rayna's former life weren't hard to believe, looking at her in the bold twilight sun that day. The old woman stood straight as a pine tree, her eyes gleaming with an unquenchable fire that threatened to set the world ablaze.

When she spoke, the crowd fell mute.

"He's right, you know" Rayna said, gesturing at Nestor. "There isn't time to save everyone... not without sacrificing some. There's no getting around this, and the sooner we all realize it the better."

The veteran paused dramatically. "But there may be a way to keep our casualties to a handful... if we have the guts, that is."

Every ear in the village hung on her next words.

"The Abbadon have the advantage of numbers," Rayna continued, slowly turning in a circle to face the crowd as she spoke. "But we have a resource they don't... the land itself."

"What lies to the east of Lemuria? A rock-strewn coastline that would mean certain doom for a craft as large as an Abbadon war ship. And what lies to the north and west? Mountains so steep and treacherous that even goats and lizards shun them. The only place for the Abbadon to safely port and mount an attack will be in the south. Which means they'll have only one way into the village: Dyonder Pass."

Rayna held her hands parallel, mimicking opposite walls of a crevasse.

"Once they hit that narrow strip of valley, they'll be forced to consolidate their ranks and attack no more than a dozen at a time. There – at that singular rallying point – a force of a hundred warriors will be able to face a thousand on equal terms. And it's *there* we'll make our stand."

Hrotha raised an eyebrow. "Make our stand? What do you mean?"

The old woman's eyes blazed. "To buy time for the others to escape, a small force of us – perhaps a hundred spears' worth – will stay behind at Dyonder Pass and hold off the Abbadon for as long as we can. Meanwhile, the rest of the village can evacuate as planned."

Rayna looked at Nestor pointedly. "Everyone."

The villagers exchanged dubious looks and murmured. Hrotha shared their reluctance.

"I appreciate your advice," she said. "But this is a suicide mission. The Abbadon are too many, too fierce. Whoever makes their stand at that pass is going to die."

"True," Rayna agreed. "But luckily, this is a battle we don't need to win. All we need to do is slow them down long enough for our own ships to navigate through the eastern seaboard and escape to the cove."

Several in the crowd began to murmur.

"And who will lead this doomed army?" Hrotha pressed, unconvinced.

"I would be a true coward if I didn't volunteer, wouldn't I?" Rayna replied without the slightest pause. She turned to the crowd. "But I can't do it alone. Who will stand at my side?"

A long silence spread among the village. The young men and women of Lemuria avoided Rayna's gaze as if she were a medusa, able to turn them into stone with no more than a glance. And that was when a wrinkled hand rose from the crowd.

"I will!"

The village turned to look at the unexpected volunteer.

"Father!" Olaff exclaimed, his mouth agape. "Are you crazy? You can't do this! The middle of a battle is no place for–"

"For *whom*?" his father interjected, giving his son a sour look. "An old man?"

Olaff paused. "Please... I didn't mean–"

But his father wouldn't be stopped.

"I will not go quietly into the night like a frightened babe," he insisted. "Not while I can still make a difference for the ones I care about. I've had a chance to live a full life. And if I can sacrifice my last remaining years so a child might have the same opportunity, I can dream of no nobler way to depart this world."

"You were right about *that*, at least," he told Nestor, who shrank from his words like a vampire before a sunrise.

"If you're going, I'm coming with you!" Olaff insisted. But his father stopped him with a stern look.

"No," he said simply. "Get your mother to safety. You're her only chance. And not just her... the others as well. They will need people like you in the months to come. *You* are my true gift to them, Olaff."

He placed his hand on his son's shoulder.

"Be the light that they deserve. And one day, you will look back on this moment with pride, not sorrow."

"I will, father," Olaff said, wiping away tears with his giant paw of a hand.

The old man turned to Rayna with a steely gaze. "What say you, hermit on the hill? Will you allow me the honor of standing at your side?"

But before the veteran could answer, another hand raised in the crowd. This time, it was Jain, the old widow who collected dung chips in the pastures to sell for cooking fuel.

"If that old fart is gonna fight, so am I!" she declared boldly.

Then another wrinkled hand rose, that of a potter whose family died of the plague the previous winter.

"Me too!"

Another elderly hand shot up. Then another. And soon, every octogenarian in the village who could still hold a spear had their hand in the air, stretched to the heavens in an inspiring show of solidarity.

Rayna turned to a slack-jawed Hrotha.

"It looks like we have our army," she said with a smirk. "Now if you don't mind, we have a battle to prepare for."

The sun was just beginning to rise the next day when the Abbadon arrived.

Rayna and her troops looked out at the approaching army from their position at the pass. Even Rayna had to steel her courage at the sight. At least a thousand demons marched towards them with all the fury of the damned, their black banners waving in the air and their cold steel gleaming in the morning light.

Garbed in chain mail and armed with a deadly broadsword – the only mementos from her former life she'd taken to Lemuria – Rayna gazed back at the warriors at her flank. Exactly ninety-nine stood behind her... a century of centuries. There hadn't been enough armor in the village to cover them all, so many of the ad-hoc warriors had simply cobbled together makeshift suits from items they had in their homes: pots and pans, stove lids, saddle leather. It would have been a funny sight – if it hadn't been so deadly serious. But not one of the Lemurians showed an ounce of fear on their faces. They stood proud... brave... ready to die.

One of the warriors – a skinny, hard-as-nails fishmonger named Ziro – looked Rayna's way. The old man nodded and smiled. Rayna returned the grin.

May the gods bless you all, she thought, beaming with pride.

As per the Abbadon reputation, there was no attempt to negotiate, no ambassador sent forth with terms of surrender.

Instead, the dark army simply moved into formation and marched forward, an unstoppable wave of death incapable of the tiniest hint of mercy. There was little the Lemurians could do but wait. They were dead on their feet the moment they strayed from the safety of the pass. It was their shelter; it was their tomb.

The Abbadon advanced until they arrived within arrow range, then abruptly stopped. As a row of their archers moved forward into position, the invaders began to clang their shields and chant: "Run! Run! Run!" It was a fearsome display, one that had sent many foes into catatonic fear. But the Lemurians stood fast.

There was nothing to threaten them with except survival.

"Raise your shields!" Rayna called out. "Remember why we're here!"

When their archers were ready, the Abbadon's forward commander gave a signal. Several volleys of deadly arrows rained down upon the Lumurians. Some of the missiles found their marks – unprotected eyes, vulnerable necks, exposed groins. But for all but a few unlucky warriors, their armor and shields held fast.

They were still alive.

Somehow, they were still alive.

After the barrage of arrows ceased, there was a smothering silence, like the lull after a hurricane. Then the surviving villagers let loose with a deafening yell of defiance that even the rear of the Abbadon ranks could hear.

In a few moments, a brash old woman with a mane of silver hair pushed her way to the front of the Lemurian line. She stepped forward and laid her axe on the ground.

Reaching into her pocket, she removed a ball of yarn and a pair of needles. And then to the dark army's complete shock, she calmly began to knit... as though she didn't have a care in the world.

The would-be terrorists were sent into a fury by their erstwhile prey's utter lack of panic. Giving the signal to charge, a red-faced Abbadon commander led his forward infantry onto the battlefield with the intent of crushing the resistance in one fell swoop. Bellowing with madness, the Abbadon hurtled towards the Lemurians, all the while expecting the elderly warriors to finally succumb to fear and flee.

They did not.

Just as Rayna predicted, the dark army's numbers were neutralized by the narrow valley pass. Goaded into a disorganized charge, the Abbadon began to bottleneck at the entrance, unable to take advantage of their archers or push their way forward. And the Century of Centuries made them pay dearly for each time they tried.

Having never held swords before, many of the villagers had simply opted to take their farming tools into battle. It proved to be unlike anything the Abbadon ever faced. Garden spades decapitated. Fishing nets ensnared. Machetes disemboweled. And all across the battlefield, the Abbadon howled in pain as the Lemurians hurled fiery urns of cooking oil into their midst.

As she anchored the Lemurian frontline – her sword gleaming in the sunlight – Rayna marveled at the way her muscle memory came flooding back. Despite decades of inactivity, it was as if her instincts never left her. She gained in strength with each swing of steel, each clash of metal on metal.

It was like she was young again.

For hours, the two sides smashed into each other, wave after wave of invader falling upon the unyielding Lemurians. Despite the deluge of violence, they held fast, like deep-rooted trees in the midst of a typhoon. No finer effort had ever been made by an army, professional or militia. No finer soldiers had ever graced a battlefield with their blood.

But the Abbadon were legion. They were too well-equipped, too battle-hardened. And eventually, death got tired of waiting for its invitation to the party.

An axe-wielding Abbadon chopped through the handle of Jain's fishing spear, carving its owner in half with the same stroke. A brute with an iron-banded war club shattered Olaff's father's spine, leaving the old man laying limp on the battle-field. A pack of invaders gleefully hacked up Ziro, spreading his guts on the ground like children playing in the mud.

Rayna, however, didn't go so easily. In the end, it took more than a dozen of the fiercest warriors the Abbadon could summon to wrest away her mighty broadsword and take the stubborn old woman down. But none of that mattered. She'd done what she came to do.

As she lay mortally wounded among the other brave Lemurians, Rayna weakly turned her head to the eastern horizon. There she caught the faint outline of dozens of ships, their sails full and boisterous as they raced towards freedom. Suddenly, all of the tragedies and pain that brought her to Lemuria in the first place seemed so silly, like mosquito bites that stopped itching long ago.

I guess it took death to remind me what being human is truly about, Rayna mused, as darkness washed over her.

The dying warrior took her final breath. Her eyes closed. Her fists unclutched.

And that was the end of the Century of Centuries.

14

"Love is like an expensive dinner... delicious until you get the bill."

– Mad Martha Planchett, president of the Dama'run Brothel Guild

Luzi woke up to the scent of cheap lamp oil, the astringent odor dragging her back to consciousness like a fistful of smelling salts. There was a brief moment of panic – then relief – when she realized she was still at their room in the Phangorian Inn.

I've really got to stop waking up like this, she told herself groggily.

"Thank the gods!" she heard a voice cry out.

Luzi tilted her head to see U standing at the foot of the bed, anxiously shifting from foot to foot. "You're awake!" he gushed. "How do you feel?"

Luzi blinked the sleep out of her eyes and drew a deep lungful of air, expecting the worst. But to her surprise, not a bit of sickness remained.

"Actually... I feel just fine," she said, amazed at the unexpected transformation. She started to stand up, but U gently guided her back down on the bed.

"Easy," he cautioned. "Don't overdo it. Your body has gone through hell. You need to let it recover slowly."

"What happened?" Luzi inquired, rubbing her temples with her palms. "The last thing I remember is lying down and falling asleep."

U shook his head in amazement.

"You're tough as nails, Luzi Winterstar, I'll give you that. And clearly, you're not ready for your swan song yet.

"I managed to get a dose of foxfern in you right after you passed out. At first, I was afraid we might be too late – your breathing had already slowed to a crawl. But after a few hours, the medicine took hold and your body began to fight against the poison. From that point it was just a matter of time. And patience, of course."

The unicorn paused.

"It wasn't easy. Having patience, I mean. You've been unconscious for a long time. To be honest, I was just about to cross the threshold from worry to panic."

Luzi raised an eyebrow. "What do you mean? How long have I been out?"

U spoke calmly, trying not to alarm her. "Two days."

"Two... fucking... days?"

Like a panicked monk discovering they're late for morning rituals, Luzi threw off the covers and rolled out of bed. But her wobbly legs – unused for 48 hours – buckled under her own weight.

"Easy," U coaxed.

"But we have to ride!" she insisted with a shaky voice. "The unicorns! The ring!"

"It's the dead of night and pitch-black outside," U replied. "We'll look suspicious as gargoyles in a chicken coop if we try to sneak out of the inn now. So do both of us a favor and get some rest. At the crack of dawn, we'll hit the road with a vengeance – I promise."

Luzi nodded and sat back down, satisfied with his answer.

"Here," U said, handing her a mug of water. "I'm sure you're thirsty."

Nodding thanks, Luzi took a deep chug, not realizing how parched she was until the liquid touched her lips. As Luzi drank, she noticed U was staring at her intently, as if on the verge of blurting out some terrible secret. Combined with his uncharacteristic fidgeting, it put a nervous feeling in the Nyasian's heart that she couldn't ignore.

Luzi took a final quaff of water and set the mug down.

"All right – don't give me any bullshit," she warned in a no-nonsense voice, like a condemned prisoner inquiring about her execution date. "What's wrong?"

The unicorn didn't respond right away. When he finally spoke, it was with a quiet desperation that could have been mistaken for weariness by the casual ear.

"Luzi... I need to make a confession."

"I didn't mean to do this so soon after you woke, and for that, I'm sorry," U explained. "But there's something I need to tell you. And I promised myself that if you survived, I wouldn't keep my true thoughts hidden for a moment longer."

"By the almighty sack of Dis, don't be so dramatic!" Luzi

exclaimed. "It sounds like you thought I was going to die or something!"

The unicorn's reply chilled Luzi to the core: "I did."

"You have to understand, I was convinced you were taking your last breaths right in front of me," he explained, wringing his hands as he spoke. "I thought that was it... I thought... I thought I'd lost you."

"Do you understand what I'm saying?" he pleaded morosely, letting the words drop from his lips like lead weights. "I thought I'd *lost* you!"

"I know it sounds crazy," U continued. "But I feel like this whole journey has been orchestrated just to bring us together. I feel connected to you in a way I've never felt for anyone before – unicorn, human or anything in between. And it's not the ring, or my cursed vision or anything else. It's something much deeper, something more profound."

The unicorn hesitated, as though he couldn't believe what he was about to say.

"There's an ancient Monoceros word that describes feeling lonesome for someone you don't know: *kaanj'aa*. The closest equivalent in Common tongue would be 'love at first sight,' although that's a pale shadow of the word's true meaning.

"Do you remember the first day we met? I'd never experienced anything like that before in my life. When I looked into your eyes, it was as if I was a lyre and you were the fingers on my strings. It changed me forever, right then and there. And if that's not proof kaanj'aa exists, I don't know what else possibly could. Ever since I met you, I've been trying to sort out what it all means. But no matter what approach I take,

I end up asking myself the same question. And I can't live another moment without knowing the answer."

He looked at Luzi with vulnerable eyes. "Do *you* feel it, too?"

At first the Nyasian couldn't speak; it felt like she'd been poked in the larynx with a sharp stick. A thousand voices in Luzi's head shouted at her to ignore his question... for both their sakes. But eventually, the truth burst forth uncontrollably from the depths of her psyche, like a flooded river overtaking a dam.

"Yes," she confessed. "I do."

Luzi shook her head in shame at hearing the words aloud. "Listen to me. This isn't right. I mean, I'm a *human*. And you're a fucking *unicorn*! It's disgusting!"

She looked up at U apologetically. "Ummm, no offense."

U laughed.

"None taken. Trust me, Luzi, if any of my coven mates could hear me speaking right now, they'd be just as revolted as you are. Such a thing is virtually unheard of among my kind... especially with a human. [17]

"There are many among the Monoceros who believe – even to this day – that we are the pinnacle of evolution. And sometimes, I'm inclined to believe them. After all, we're stronger than you, Luzi. We're smarter than you. We're faster and hardier and more disciplined. And our culture was already ancient when you humans were still crawling down from the trees and learning to walk upright. Sometimes your race forgets that."

"So what do *you* think? Are humans as stupid and weak as your kin believe?"

"I won't lie," U admitted. "If you asked me that question two weeks ago, I would have said yes. I once thought humans a simple, self-destructive race. The best of you lack conviction, while the worst of you are consumed with passion. And at times, it seems like there isn't a single one among you that truly cares for anyone but themselves."

The unicorn gazed at Luzi with tenderness in his eyes. "But I was wrong."

"So what changed your mind?" Luzi quietly asked.

"*You* did. Risking your life to save a child you don't even know? Telling someone who was sent to kill you that he's capable of compassion? Trying to stop a genocide, even if it means dying yourself? Any dumb beast can be strong. Any mindless automaton can be fast. But only a truly evolved being can feel empathy – and *that's* what you showed me humans are capable of."

"Love is a necessity, not a luxury," the unicorn insisted. "It is the cog that drives the windmill of the world. Without it, civilization cannot survive. And in the end, it's the only thing that will redeem anyone... human or unicorn."

They shared a moment of silence so pregnant it needed its own crib. Suddenly, an impulse sparked inside Luzi, bypassing her brain and heading straight for her heart. She felt herself moving towards U... stretching out her arms... closing her eyes.

And without stopping to think about what she was doing, Luzi leaned in and kissed him.

Their lips may have stayed locked for a minute or an hour. There was no way of telling; the moment existed outside of time. They became two tuning forks struck in unison, trembling under the taboo urge they'd finally succumbed to. It was a kiss. And yet, it was more.

It was *life*.

Eventually, without knowing who pulled away first, Luzi felt their lips separate. As their connection severed, she crash-landed back in reality.

"Oh no," Luzi stammered as she regained her wits. Mortified, she took a step away from U. "I didn't mean... I didn't want to-"

To her surprise, U wasn't angry or threatened or revolted. Instead, the unicorn swept Luzi up in his arms. Without uttering a syllable, he dove headfirst back into their kiss. But this time the unicorn's passion was more urgent, as if he was being scorched alive by a fire within. Luzi returned his affection with the same fevered intensity. They clutched in a lovers' embrace, grasping at each other with a desperation that burned stronger with each passing moment. The playful looks disappeared from their faces, replaced by a molten lust that could easily have been mistaken for anger. Starving for each other, they tumbled backwards onto the bed... a mélange of black and tan... a single, striped animal consuming itself.

Soon, Luzi could feel U press against her. She shuddered. They kissed deeply and lingered like that, teasing out the moment, perching on the dewy edge of infinity.

"Are you sure..." he asked, seeking her gaze.

"Yes," she replied, the word like honey water on her lips.

And as the universe exhaled in anticipation, they became one.

If Luzi could have ransomed all the time from then until the end of the world to stay in that moment, she would have.

There was a comfort there she'd never experienced, something pure... something irreplaceable. It was as if she'd tapped into some all-encompassing force of energy which transcended magic or nature. No, she realized, quivering with the sensation. It was as if they *were* energy.

And riding the crest of that beautiful wave, Luzi let herself disappear.

15

"The puppet can only know peace once it learns to love its strings."

– Traditional Nyasian wedding vow

Traversing the Dream Matrix is the province of the weird.

The matrix – what some cultures refer to as the "dream realm" – serves as the skeleton of the universe. A gargantuan tapestry of thought, it connects the consciousness of every sentient being in the world, like mortar between the bricks of a wall.

The laws of reality no longer apply in the depths of the matrix. Spatial relationships and perspectives become unreliable at best, nonexistent at worst. There is no sense of time or place, no border between one dream and the next. One second, you may be standing on a deserted beach. The next, you might find yourself in a crowded bazaar.

Everything is one. One is everything.

Even the most powerful magician can get hopelessly lost in the matrix if they aren't careful. To navigate such a realm requires superhuman resiliency, a steadfast will and a master's understanding of chaos magic.

And *that* was how the Boogeyman carved out his niche as the most feared bounty hunter in the world.

The spectral huntsman navigated his way through the matrix in search of the two marks the Meridian gave him, passing from dream to dream like a ghost. He glided through the infinite maelstrom as few but a Dragnir can, not focusing on *surroundings* so much as *faces*.

As he traveled, the Boogeyman remembered what the Meridian told him about his quarry.

"The primary target is a traitor and former member of my coven," the Meridian had said. "He's a shapeshifter and may not be walking on four legs. Beware... he's a dangerous warrior and will not go quietly. The secondary target is a Nyasian farmgirl with a long, white mane of hair. To the best of my knowledge, she should pose no threat whatsoever."

"And the conditions?" the Boogeyman had asked.

"The task is simple. I want you to bring me back these two marks and any possessions they have on them, right down to the very last clump of lint in their pockets. I do not care if they are dead or alive. But I want them whole. Is that clear?"

"Absolutely, Great Meridian," the Boogeyman had replied. "Although I have to admit the task will not be without its difficulties. As I'm sure you realize, tracking down a unicorn who doesn't want to be found is a dangerous proposition, especially one of such prowess. Regardless, it can be done... providing there is fair recompense, of course."

"Price is no limit," the Meridian had countered. "Gold,

jewels, magic relics... just name a fortune and see it to your pocket."

"I want something else for this task," the Boogeyman had said after a moment. "Something special. Something only you can grant me."

"As you know, in addition to learning how to navigate the realm of dreams, we Dragnir have mastered the ability to possess creatures and inhabit their bodies. I've soared as a gryphon and cantered as a faun. I've swam as a mermaid and fornicated as a Fae. And forgive my boast, but these experiences have brought me to a state of enlightenment that not even a being such as you cannot fathom, mighty Meridian."

The Boogeyman had paused. "Still, there is one creature I have yet to know the exquisite pleasure of possessing. One that's nigh impossible to take against their will."

The Meridian's eyes narrowed. "What is your request, Dragnir?"

"I want to wear the flesh of a unicorn," the Boogeyman had replied, giving the Meridian a sadistic leer. "You will surrender one of your coven mates to me, who will allow me to possess them until I've had my fill. When it is done, we will all go our separate ways – with no retaliation on either side. The price of your bounty will be no more, and no less. Do we have a deal?"

There'd been a long silence before the Meridian answered. When she spoke again, the coyness was gone from her voice, replaced by a tempered steel.

"If you were any other creature in any other circumstance, you would be eviscerated where you stand for even daring to make such a suggestion. But I am not in a position to refuse.

Bring me what I seek, and I will solicit a volunteer for your purpose. You have my word."

"Then consider the contract in motion," he'd declared with an iron certainty, as if the deed were already done.

***

The conversation had taken place a week ago, but in the dream realm, it may as well have been years. In the matrix, time is hollow – like the marrow hole inside a bone.

Patience, the Boogeyman reminded himself as he probed its endless labyrinths, searching for a trace of the traitor or the farmgirl.

Patience.

Finally, the bounty hunter came across a pocket of dreams emanating from a boisterous inn on the border of the elven plains. The source – a portly elven innkeeper – was speaking to two figures. One was a tall, dour human with dark skin. But it was the latter, a white-haired human farmgirl, who attracted the Boogeyman's attention.

It's her! the Boogeyman gleefully realized. *The Nyasian!*

The Dragnir focused intensely, singling the dream out of the swirling chaos like a shark selecting a fish from a school. He aimed himself toward it and pushed forth, grasping the matrix fibers and pulling himself into the elf's consciousness.

Back in the real world, the elf's slumbering body twisted in bed. His body convulsed. His eyes blackened. A gruesome patchwork of bloody lacerations formed on his skin like a rash.

Careful, the Boogeyman reminded himself as the elf's body

struggled with shock symptoms. *Elves are always so tricky to possess. Remember, don't kill the shell while you're still in it or you'll die, too!*

The Dragnir doubled his efforts. Finally, like a roped stallion who decided to surrender, the elf stopped resisting. His bruised body calmed; his struggles ceased.

And just like that, the Boogeyman had control.

In the waking world, the Boogeyman forced the elf's eyes open and slowly got out of bed. He took a few shambling steps in his meat shell, struggling to adapt to his new equilibrium. But it wasn't long before the Boogeyman was able to make the necessary adjustments, and it was with a confident stride that he opened Paz-Ul's bedroom door and made his way down the hallway of the inn.

In front of him, a lobby full of drunken guests carried on, unaware of the terror in their midst, until one by one, the crowd gradually caught sight of the bloody, swollen mess standing before them.

The laughter ceased. A hush spread among the inn's patrons.

Leema stepped forward from the crowd, clutching a bar rag. "Mr. Ul!" she exclaimed, aghast at the sight of her boss. "Are – are you feeling all right?"

The Boogeyman leered at the satyress, a sick jubilation building in his soul. "Time for last call," he croaked, cracking a bloody grin.

And that was when the screams began.

16

"Good pass early. Bad die late. But none alive can flee their fate."

– Abyssinian folk limerick, source unknown

After they finished making love, Luzi and U remained together in bed for a long time, spooning like two matching pieces of a puzzle, until the Nyasian finally fell asleep out of pure exhaustion.

Her repose didn't last long.

Luzi had just begun her slide into the dream realm when a hand clapped across her mouth, jolting her awake. "Mmmph-" she objected, opening her eyes to see U, his armum sword in hand.

After he was certain Luzi wasn't going to yell, U removed his hand from her mouth. But before she could get a word out, the unicorn put a finger over his lips and hissed.

"Listen," he whispered. "Something's wrong."

Luzi focused, unsure what she was supposed to be listening for. But it wasn't long before she heard an awful ruckus coming from the inn's dining hall below them. It was a strange and clangorous mix of sounds: smashed furniture, broken dishes, frenzied yelling. At first, it seemed like the party downstairs had simply gotten out of hand. That illusion was shattered when she began to hear screams of pain and panicked wails among the din. They were animalistic and raw, like livestock being butchered.

And that was when Luzi realized she was listening to people being killed.

Lots of them.

The Nyasian rolled out of bed, her body surging with adrenaline. She hastily dressed and charged herself with Ubamota energy.

"What's going on?" she whispered fiercely, manifesting her armum. "Is it the Overgruk?"

U sniffed at the air. "I don't think so. This is something else. Something I've never smelled before – something bad."

Meanwhile, the screams and struggling continued downstairs, until an eerie silence eventually emerged. Luzi knew that it could only mean one of two things: the threat was neutralized, or everyone downstairs was dead.

That question was soon answered when they heard the slow procession of clunking footsteps coming up the stairs towards their room.

"What now?" Luzi asked in a hushed tone as the thudding drew closer.

U turned to look at Luzi, his eyebrows scrunched with determination. "Whatever killed those poor bastards is here for *us*. No sense in denying it... there's only one way out of this mess."

He brandished his sword.

The footsteps continued down the hallway, getting louder and quicker as they approached, until Luzi felt her heartbeat begin to match their rhythm. Finally, the trudging stopped outside their room. The Nyasian tensed her shield arm, expecting the door to come flying down at any moment.

"Stay behind me," U whispered. "We stick together – whatever comes our way."

Luzi nodded and prepared for hell. But in lieu of a crash, a series of heavy knocks came instead.

U and Luzi exchanged a puzzled glance. The unicorn motioned for her to stay quiet, then moved slowly towards the door. He held up three fingers to Luzi and started a silent countdown. Then – on the count of three – he swung the door open and jumped back with his sword raised.

To their surprise, there wasn't a single monster or mercenary in sight. Instead, an elf stood in front of them, partially obscured in the shadows. But his rotund form and bar apron were unmistakable.

"Paz-Ul!" Luzi exclaimed with a gush of relief. "Are you OK? What's going on downst–"

"Luzi, wait!" U warned sharply. "Look!"

At that moment, the innkeeper took a step forward into the flickering lantern light, giving Luzi her first glimpse of his face. His skin was covered by large fissures; blood oozed from the cracks. His swollen eyes wept pus; a liquid resembling molasses seeped from his ears. And that smell... that awful smell... it was nearly too much to bear.

"Dis help us," Luzi muttered.

As Luzi and U stood gawking, Paz-Ul opened his mouth.

For a second, it looked like the elf was about to speak. But instead, a clutch of thick, black tentacles tipped with razor-sharp barbs exploded out of the elf's mouth. Wriggling madly like hookworms evacuating a carcass, the tentacles hurtled towards them with a startling accuracy, eager to do their master's bidding.

Uchchaihshravas didn't waste a single moment. With uncanny reflexes, he conjured a Deep Magic wall that spanned the room, separating them from the oncoming appendages. The horrid things smashed into the barrier and stopped cold. But Luzi's relief was short-lived when she saw that they had no intention of giving up. The unholy avalanche of meat tendrils smashed into the wall again and again, striking with sledgehammer force and creating a patchwork of rapidly spreading cracks.

U struggled to hold his substantive in place, but it was obvious he wouldn't be able to keep the effort up for long. "He's too strong!" the unicorn grunted. "We're dead if we stay here! We need more space!"

Luzi frantically looked around the windowless room. The only exit was the door, which meant going straight past the creature.

"Where can we go?"

"Down!" U shouted. He gestured with a chopping motion at the floor.

Luzi hesitated. "What about you?"

"Go! I'll be right behind!"

Without further delay, Luzi manifested a Deep Magic axe and started hewing away at the floorboards, sending splinters and sawdust flying into the air. It wasn't long before she heard the wood crack and give way.

"Done!" Luzi yelled as soon as the hole was large enough for them to fit through. She leaped into the gap and tumbled to the main floor below. It was a longer plunge than she'd expected – enough to take her breath away when she landed. Luckily, there was something that broke her fall. Something soft. Something wet.

And that's when Luzi saw she was sprawled out on a heap of dead bodies.

The Nyasian stumbled backwards, taking in the gruesome panorama. An abattoir's worth of flesh was scattered about the inn. There was no way to tell how many bodies there were; not a single corpse was intact. Blood soaked every surface. Jagged bits of bone and skull were driven into the floorboards like carpenters' nails. Offal festooned the walls like confetti.

"No," Luzi whispered, unable to think of anything more poignant to say.

Before she lost herself in the horror of it all, U came crashing down beside her, his sword in hand. "Run!" he cried, pushing her towards the door at the opposite end of the inn.

Luzi and U desperately sprinted for the exit, leaping around bodies and debris as they went. But before they could take a dozen steps, a cluster of tentacles smashed through the ceiling.

"Look out!" U shouted, slicing one of the gruesome appendages in half a split-second before it grabbed them.

"They're everywhere!" Luzi replied, manifesting her shield and chopping at another.

Slashing at the deadly limbs, Luzi and U continued their

mad, serpentine dash across the inn. Just as they reached the door, the innkeeper bashed a hole in the ceiling and dropped through, landing directly in front of them. A fresh swarm of tentacles spewed from Paz-Ul's mouth. With no time to warn Luzi to dodge, U leaped into their path, using his own body as a shield. The deadly coils wrapped around him, pinning his arms at his sides.

That's it – we're dead, Luzi conceded, bracing for the bloodshed to come.

Suddenly, the creature contorted in pain and halted its attack. As Luzi watched in confusion, its deadly tentacles began to turn blue and freeze as a spectral frost crystalized on their surface.

Magic! Luzi realized. *But where's it coming from?*

***

When the Nyasian turned around, her jaw dropped in shock. An assembly of strange and menacing warriors burst through the front door of the inn like a tsunami. There were just seven of them, Luzi would later note, but they may as well have been a full brigade.

At the front of the pack was what could only be described as a werewolf. From afar, he looked like an athletically built young man, dressed in an aristocratic doublet and leather pants. But as he barreled closer, Luzi got a full glimpse of his thick, doglike hair, snarling incisors and steely claws, which tore mercilessly at the tentacles.

Close on his heels was a hulking woodsman, half-covered in piecemeal leather armor. Weather-beaten and ruddy, an unkempt mop of tangled hair and a fire-red beard engulfed his leathery face. The man-bear wielded a fearsome armum axe with a surprising agility, mowing down anything in his way with an ad hoc ballet of deadly strikes.

Next came a strange reptilian creature the likes of which Luzi had never seen in storybooks or dreams. Bone-crushing jaws protruded from its coyote-like face, and a deadly set of retractable claws jutted forth from its fingertips. Moving nimbly on its hind legs, the wiry cryptid flipped and somersaulted among the tentacles with a preternatural ease, almost as if it were able to predict their movements.

Nearby stood a huge, grey, pock-marked troll. She wore no clothing, only a pink ribbon tied into a clump of matted hair. The behemoth's mighty hands – each capable of smashing through stone – flailed like mighty war hammers, battering any tentacle in their path.

No larger than field mice, a pair of tiny pixies zipped above the fray, unleashing Deep Magic energy blasts that seared through the tentacles with a surgical precision. A phosphorescent glow emanated from their delicate bodies, creating a psychedelic trail of light in their wake.

Finally, a grizzled old woman garbed in the velvet robes of a mage stood at the rear of the battle, grimacing as she tried to maintain the spell that had saved U's life.

Distracted by the unexpected onslaught of the warriors seven, the innkeeper loosened his clutches on U, who sucked in a deep, grateful breath. Luzi dashed to her companion's side, ready to cut him free. But the unicorn shook his head as she drew closer, summoning all of his energy to wheeze a frantic warning.

"There!"

Luzi looked to where U pointed. Directly in front of them lay an exposed pathway through the deadly gauntlet of tentacles. It wasn't much – barely wider than the length of a sword – but it was more than enough for a single person to slip through. The window of opportunity was already beginning to close, however, and she knew it would be gone in a few seconds... maybe less.

The Nyasian glanced down at U, who was still struggling to free himself. She looked at the other warriors, who all were fighting battles of their own. A flash of raw, irresistible emotion – perhaps bravery? – exploded in her brain.

This is it, Luzi, she thought, gritting her teeth.

Before her fear could catch up with her courage, she sprinted towards the innkeeper. The next series of movements passed in the space of a single breath. Lithely navigating through the field of churning tentacles, Luzi twirled around with her shield, her long, white mane of hair trailing behind like a banner. Her armum sliced through the top of Paz-Ul's skull. His bisected head thumped to the ground. His body – including the tentacles – instantly followed.

And just like that, the fight was over.

The danger, however, was not. The strangers spun around to face Luzi and U, ready to attack at the slightest provocation. The Nyasian and the unicorn did the same. Their stand-off lasted for a long, uncomfortable minute as the warriors sized each other up.

Finally, the mage lifted a hand in salutation.

"Well, *that* was almost a real all-is-lost moment – wasn't it?" she said with a wink.

***

Luzi's response was less than eloquent: "Who the fucking fuck are you?"

"Omigosh, she's got a dirty fucking mouth!" one of the pixies tittered in amusement.

"Heh – I fucking like her already," the reptile chimed in.

"We're Scions of Dama'run if *that* means anything, young lady" the mage said with authority, giving her companions a stern look. "And believe it or not, we're here to help."

"Wait... you mean, like, *real* Scions of Dama'run?" Luzi repeated, unable to conceal the awe in her voice. Of course, she'd heard of the legendary order of knights. Who hadn't? Culled from the most talented warriors and wizards in the Great Realms, the Scions were famed for their incorruptible oaths to protect the innocent, answering only to the Dama'run Council itself. And their legend reached far – even to Nyasia.

U was less impressed. He squinted suspiciously, like a shopkeeper giving the evil eye to a gang of pickpockets.

"If you're really knights of the mountain city, you won't mind showing us some proof, will you?"

In reply, the wizard removed a small, triangular token made of highly-polished onyx from one of her robe pockets. She held it out for Luzi and U to see. An insignia of an open palm with a glowing, golden eye was magically embossed on its front. On the bottom was a slogan: *Educate the ignorant. Destroy the cruel.*

"Satisfied? Or do you need to check it for an Ubamota aura?"

U grunted.

"Maybe you can put those things away then, huh?" the mage suggested, glancing at their armums. "Keep waving 'em around, someone's liable to get their goddamned eye poked out, don't you think?"

U grudgingly dematerialized his sword; Luzi followed suit with her shield.

The wizard nodded her thanks.

"Now that we're on speaking terms, let me introduce ourselves. I'm Romula Zazzau, captain of the twenty-first squadron of the Scions of Dama'run. And this is my crew."

Romula went down the line, gesturing at each warrior as she called their name.

"To your left is my second-in-command, Anian, formerly of the royal house of Seung."

Luzi watched with curiosity as the battle-scarred werewolf changed back into his human form. As he did, his cuts and bruises magically healed, leaving him without a scratch on his body.

"Next, we have Calypsa and Eureka of the Kalei Faerie."

The pair of pixies zoomed within a foot of Luzi's face and hovered as they examined her, their dragonfly-like wings beating a hundred times per second. Both were clad in gossamer, one-piece gowns made of what appeared to be dyed spider silk, which showed off their pale, downy skin. The more mischievous-looking of the two, Calypsa, had close-cropped, golden hair. Eureka, her innocent-faced companion, had long, pitch-black locks that fluttered behind her like a mane.

Romula moved on to the reptile, who hopped impatiently from foot to foot as he waited for his introduction. "Since his people identify each other by smell and not by name, we've dubbed this upstanding character 'Cobby.' And before you ask, yes... you're looking at a real chupacabra."

The creature winked. Trying to keep her ignorance a secret – she had absolutely no clue what a chupacabra was – Luzi just nodded back awkwardly.

"Over here we have the inimitable Miss Awf'l, the sweetest troll you'll ever have the pleasure of meeting."

Not speaking a word, the hulking grey monster waved shyly from the rear of the party and tried to hide herself behind the others.

"And finally, I give you John Apple, the legendary boozer, brawler and frontiersman," Romula concluded, motioning to the ginger-bearded woodsman.

"Yerp," he succinctly confirmed, twirling his axe absent-mindedly.

U remained nonplussed. "Are we done with this pompous round of introductions yet? If so, how about explaining why you're following us? What do you want, anyway?"

"With you two?" the mage replied coyly, glancing at Luzi. "Nothing. We're looking for the *ring*."

Luzi's heart skipped a beat. "What ring?"

The mage rolled her eyes.

"Come on, kid. Don't treat me like I'm an open book written for stupid people. I assume that I'm talking to Luzinda, daughter of Lara and Lariab, sole inheritor of the Winterstar farm?"

"How'd you know that?" Luzi asked, her head spinning at hearing her parents' names.

"The truth?" Romula admitted. "Dumb fucking luck."

"Many generations ago, one of your ancestors paid the elvish Rundermust a hefty customs fee to travel through the Tuvan Passage. They carried a golden ring wrought in the shape of an Ouroboros... which was logged in great detail. Under Dama'run tax code, the log of that transaction was submitted to the city finance guild as part of the elves' annual tithe. But after the tunnel shut down, it was misplaced and overlooked for centuries, until it was rediscovered by a clerk doing research on inter-realm tax rates. Goddamn *tax rates.* Can you believe it?"

Romula shook her head as if still amazed by the coincidence.

"When the Council of Dama'run learned that they possibly knew the location of one of the Immaculan Rings, they sent me and my crew to collect it and bring it back for safekeeping. We've spent the past few weeks trying to track you down. And luckily for you, we did – right in the nick of time, I'd say."

Romula raised an eyebrow and turned to face U. "I have to admit that we didn't expect a mage, though... let alone *two* of them."

Luzi held her breath, expecting the worst. But Uchchaihshravas was quick with his lie.

"We're not really magicians, we're just farmers who know a few tricks," he told the Scions. "My name is U. I live a few plots down from Luzi. I was helping her with this season's harvest when everything went to hell. Guess I was in the wrong place at the wrong time."

Romula couldn't help but laugh at U's euphemism.

"Wrong place at the wrong time? That's one way of putting it, I guess."

"I don't know how you two managed to kill that unicorn, but you don't know how lucky you were," the mage continued. "The creature that now lays in pieces underneath the rubble of your home was a Monoceros, one of the most powerful creatures in the known realms. And it can only mean one thing – they know you have the ring."

Luzi put her hand to her chest, feeling the ring under her tunic. "So you're here to rob us before they do? Is that it?"

Romula chuckled again. "You've got it all wrong, kid. We're here to *save* you – not rob you."

The mage rubbed her chin thoughtfully. "Let's put it this way," she replied after a moment. "Say that we let you go. What then? What will you do? Where will you take this ring?"

There was a long silence.

"Dama'run," Luzi reluctantly admitted, understanding Romula's point and feeling a little silly about it. "We're taking it to Dama'run."

The mage nodded sagely.

"I thought so. Well, it looks like we all have something in common. So here's what I propose. Let us escort you back to the city. We'll protect you *and* the ring... hell, we'll even let you hold it until as a sign of good faith. All I ask is that you follow my lead and trust my judgement. Sound fair?"

Luzi and U traded a wary glance.

"You expect a lot of faith for strangers," U replied warily. "How do we know we can trust you?"

"Aside from the fact that we just saved your asses from a Dragnir assassin?" Romula replied, as if she were speaking to a pair of children.

"It's pretty simple. I've sworn an oath as a Scion of Dama'run to protect the innocent. And so have the rest of the warriors at my side. This isn't the first time we have laid our lives on the line for this vow, and it won't be the last. We have bled for justice. Some of our friends have *died* for it. Look in our eyes. See what we've lost. If you seek faith, find it there – or nowhere."

Romula put her hands on her hips.

"We don't have long until sunrise. The entire village will find out what happened here in an hour, maybe less. And we'd better be gone long before then. Now, I've got a plan – and it just might give us the edge over the hornheads. But we need to get one thing straight first. Are we foes, or friends?"

Luzi felt her heart speed up. She glanced at U for guidance. But the unicorn just shrugged.

The Nyasian looked to the Scions. She looked to Rom again.

"Life sure has a fucked-up sense of humor, doesn't it?" she said at last. "All right. Let's hear this big secret of yours... friend."

17

"Sometimes you have to change the storyteller to get a different story."

– Pranksy, jester laureate of Dama'run

The weird entourage left the inn an hour before sunrise, the stench of death still fresh on their clothes.

Romula offered more details about her plan as they hastily gathered supplies.

"Here's the problem," she explained. "The unicorns are now able to plot two points on a map: Luzi's home in Nyasia and the inn. It doesn't take a genius to figure out where we're headed – and brains are one thing the Monoceros aren't short on. So we're going to have to chart a new course. And it's got to be one that will throw them completely off our trail... a route that nobody in their right minds would expect."

"Luckily, I think I've got just the thing," the mage added with a grin.

"About a two-day ride from here, there's a desolate stretch of swamp known as Fellwood Fen. Inside lies a powerful magic device known as the Pot of Gold, which can bend the latent Ubamota in rainbows to instantly transport people anywhere in the world... including Dama'run."

"Rainbows?" Luzi inquired, confused.

Romula nodded.

"Among other miracles, rainbows are capable of transporting Ubamota energy – or people – across vast distances in a matter of seconds. The ancient gods would use them to travel the world, leaping from one point to another like sledders zooming down a snowy hill. Sadly, that knowledge was lost when the old gods died. But many years ago, a clan of gnomes known as the Luchrupan found a skull from one of the ancient ones. They dragged it back to their home in Fellwood Fen and forged it into a giant cauldron, which they can use to surf the rainbow just like the old gods did."

"Normally, the Luchrupan wouldn't dream of letting foreigners use their most sacred belonging – you'd have better luck trying to housebreak a yeti," the mage added. "But their king owes me a life debt that he can't refuse. And it seems the time has finally come to collect."

Luzi had more questions, but Romula just hushed her and told her to pack for the ride. U had seemed satisfied with the plan, so not wanting to push her luck more than she already had, the Nyasian bit her lip and remained silent.

For now, anyway, Luzi thought, giving the mage a cautious glance.

* * *

When the group was ready to depart, Romula conjured a

fleet of Deep Magic horses; "spectral steeds," she called them. Each was sized specifically for its rider – even Awf'l had a huge beast to stretch out upon. The only ones without a mount were Calypsa and Eureka, who simply flew alongside the others as they sped across the plains.

The strange assortment of warriors traveled hard, covering nearly as much ground as U and Luzi would have alone. And when Romula finally called for a stop that night in the shadow of a cliff overhang, the exhausted Nyasian didn't offer a word of complaint.

"I'm taking the first watch," Romula declared to her crew, pointing at a rocky crag near their campsite. "Anian will relieve me, and the normal order will follow after that. Please see it done, Mr. Seung."

"Aye," the werewolf replied, giving his mentor a crisp salute.

The mage gave Luzi and U a hard stare, her bloodshot eyes betraying the toll the day's journey had taken.

"As for you two. We're hitting the road the moment the sun breaks over the horizon. I suggest that you get some rest. And don't do anything foolish while I'm gone. Remember, someone will be on watch all night – and the rest of us are light sleepers."

As Romula left to take her post, her crew refilled their canteens in a nearby spring. When the Scions returned, they each removed green, walnut-sized pellets from their travel gear and added a short pour of water. The pellets quickly expanded into spongy loaves, which the Scions tore into pieces and began devouring.

As they dug into their meals, Anian noticed Luzi staring at them curiously – and hungrily.

"They call it bakalaroach," he said, holding out his supper for her to see. "It's a fungus that's farmed as a subsistence crop in Dama'run because it can grow completely without light. The stuff is edible to almost every known species, lasts for months on end, and contains every nutrient that you need for long-term survival. We all eat it while on the road... except Eureka and Calypsa, of course."

"But then again, the rest of us don't have the Fae ability to turn sunlight into energy, do we?" Anian added, glancing at the pixies.

"We stick to light meals," Calypsa joked, earning a giggle from Eureka.

Luzi's stomach growled as she looked at the loaf in Anian's hand.

"What does it taste like?"

"Barnacles scraped off a Kraken's asshole – and that's when it's fresh!" Cobby chortled sarcastically as a hailstorm of food flew out of his mouth.

"Stuff's worse'n Thulian food," John agreed, nonchalantly flicking a crumb of Cobby's bakalaroach from his lap. "An' that's a place where ya eat yer own teeth – then ask fer seconds!"

Anian shrugged, not bothering to refute his comrades' culinary analyses.

"It's an acquired flavor, I'll admit. But don't take our word for it."

The werewolf broke off a hunk of bakalaroach. Reaching into his pack, he retrieved a small glass vial marked

SAFFRON – whatever *that* was, Luzi wondered – and sprinkled a dash on top. Then he handed it to her, offering another piece to U, who politely declined.

Cautiously, Luzi took a deep smell. She risked a cautious bite... then tried her best not to spit it out immediately.

"Oh – it's, ummm... wonderful," the Nyasian managed to squeak as she chewed miserably. "Thank you."

Anian chuckled at her faux politeness.

"Well, I guess it's like the old saying goes: *Taste resides not on the tongue, but in the memory*. But trust me. In the hands of a decent chef, a humble basket of bakalaroach can be turned into a delicacy that few other meals can rival: bakachabaka." [18]

He smiled, lost in a memory.

"Our cook used to make me a big bowl as a special treat whenever I was feeling down in the dumps. I've eaten a lot of fancy meals in my lifetime, but to this day, there's still nothing like a simple bowl of homemade bakachabaka. I guess there were some perks to being royalty, after all."

Luzi raised an eyebrow. "*Royalty?*"

Anian shrugged, remembering that they were sharing their campsite with two strangers.

"Like these other miscreants by my side, Anian Seung was not always the Scion of Dama'run you see before you today. I was once the spoiled son of a noble lineage, raised as a future leader of the oligarchy. A long time ago, anyway."

"That must have been nice," Luzi commented, suddenly aware of her own modest upbringing. "The whole 'noble' thing, I mean."

"Nice? I guess that's one way of putting it," Anian said, shrugging.

"The only comfort my youth lacked was a mother; she died when I was a toddler. My father never remarried – heartbroken, I guess. As his sole heir, I was expected to inherit the entire family estate. It was more money than I could have spent in a lifetime. But it didn't come without strings attached. My father had planned my entire life out to the last hour, the last detail. As for what I wanted? That meant very little. To my father, happiness is something you're *given*, not something you *earn*."

"But a week after my thirteenth birthday, my therianthrope powers emerged," Anian added. "And that's when everything changed."

"Therianthrope?" Luzi asked, confused. "I thought you're a werewolf?"

"I know that's what they call us in Communia," Anian sighed. "But I really wish they wouldn't. We prefer to be called *therianthropes*, mages who can use the Deep Magic to channel the powers of our spirit animals. That includes bears, eagles, sharks and yes – wolves." [19]

The Quiystian pinched the bridge of his nose with a mild frustration, as if he'd discussed the subject many times before.

"I'm sure you've heard all the same old myths about us. But just for the record, most of them simply aren't true. For example, silver doesn't hurt us any more than steel. And we can change to and from our animal forms at any time we want, not just during a full moon... I have no clue how that idiotic rumor got started."

"There is one legend that's true, however," he admitted. "In order to access our powers, a therianthrope must succumb to the animalistic urges that we humans normally repress with all our might. This primal, unfettered energy – *the Raw* – is the source of our magic abilities. But tapping into it comes with a cost.”

“Not all of us are able to master walking this thin line of sanity. Many therianthropes end up going completely feral and completely abandoning their human side. And the rest of us... well... we *all* have our regrets.”

Anian sighed as old sorrows tugged at his heart.

“After my first transformation, I went to my father and told him what happened. He was a stone-faced, mean old bastard – I’d never seen him cry once before that day, not even at our mother’s funeral. But to my surprise, he wept like a baby.

“You have to understand, my father comes from a proud, storied house of diplomats. To call a werewolf his ‘son?’ Admit an entire bloodline was tainted? It would have destroyed a thousand years of status-climbing in a heartbeat. And I saw what my father truly felt in that moment as I looked in his eyes: *shame*. Can you imagine that? A father being ashamed of his own son? Who should feel guiltier?

“For years, he tried to cure my ‘condition’ with every medicine and quackery under the sun, nearly bankrupting our house in the process. Every servant and mercenary who ever took a coin from our family knew what was happening, of course. But my father stubbornly insisted on secrecy and denied it to anyone who asked – not that many had the courage in the first place. When a man can starve out your family at a whim, you tend not to ask a lot of questions.

"I played the dutiful son in this silly theatrical production for a long time, trying my best to keep the Raw inside. But the more I tried to hide what I was becoming, the worse the fits got. I was consumed by it... shaped by it... fed by it. And then – just a few days shy of my eighteenth birthday – everything went to hell."

The Quiystian paused and took a bite of bakalaroach, chewing thoughtfully. His next words were methodical, as if he were analyzing the memory step by step.

"It happened quickly, like so many of these things do. My father and I were arguing. I said something hateful. He slapped me. And before I realized what I was doing, I transformed and lunged for his throat.

"If not for my father's bodyguard, I probably would have killed him. But luckily, she managed to knock me down and put a sword in my shoulder. The pain brought me to my senses. Appalled by what I'd done, I fled like a madman, dashing out the door with nothing more than the tattered clothes on my back. And I haven't set foot in the House of Seung since.

"For a long time, there was nothing to fill my days but anger and shame. I traveled through the countryside for months, a vagabond without a destination or cause. That's when I met Romula. She took mercy on me and taught me how to control my powers, how to channel them for my own purposes instead of being consumed by them. And when the time came, she sponsored me for the Scions. Just like she did for all these other warriors you see here."

Anian looked at his companions with a solemn pride.

"I've been a Scion for almost a decade now alongside Rom

and these other miscreants. Together, we've saved hundreds of lives – maybe thousands. And I couldn't have done it without these powers... I realize that now."

"But the truth is, I still wonder what my father would say if I walked through that front door again?" the werewolf admitted. "I suppose we've all got our weak spots when it comes to family, huh?"

***

Anian's comment earned a friendly chuckle from John Apple.

"Innit a' truth?" he laughed. "I wish Iggy wuz 'round to hear 'at un!"

"Who's Iggy?" Luzi asked naively.

The other Scions sucked in their breath. They turned to look at John anxiously as his hands temporarily clenched into fists. But he soon relaxed, eliciting audible sighs of relief from his companions.

"M'brother," John told Luzi glumly. "He wuz m'brother."

"Our ma n' pa died when we wuz jess youngins," the woodsman explained. "We din't have no other kin, so aft'r they pass'd, me n' Iggy raised each other inna wildr'ness.

"When we git older, we use'ta roam 'round the realms... boozin' it up... tromp'n through the for'st... livin' off'a tha land. It wun't no easy life. But we wuz free, an' we had each other. An' that wuz e'nuff."

A smile bloomed on John's face. He snorted fondly.

"We wuz the same inna lotta ways, me'n Iggy. But he wuz diffrn't, too. Iggs wuz all fuggin' sunshine, no piss – ya know?

Jess happy 'bout ever'thing, alla' time... that boy nev'r met a beast or plant he din't like. But more'n anything, he loved apples. *Them feckin' things c'n save tha world,* he'd say. *They're cheap. They're good eatin.' You kin make 'em inta booze. And the dern things c'n grow jess 'bout anywhere.*

"Fer years before 'e died, Iggy'd plant a dozen apple seeds ever' day, first thing when 'e woke up. After a while, I fell inna tha habit, too. Togeth'r, we musta plant'd thousands a' orchards cross 'o tha Five Realms in jess a few years. It felt good, like'n we wuz really doing somethin' to make tha world a bett'r place, y'know?"

The woodsman's tone darkened. "I shudda fuck'n known bett'r."

"One day, we wuz plantin' a new grove near the west'rn border o' Abyssinia, when we stumbl'd cross a bugbear onna hunt. The big bast'rd attacked withoot warnin.' It wuz either gonna be us 'r him, for sure. But them wuz the days b'fore I knew how ta' use the Deep Magic. An' we wuzn't nearly no match fer a bugbear'n bloodlust."

"We both went at 'im with our axes," John recalled somberly. "It wuz like they wuz toothpicks – he snapped 'em in half wit' a swipe of 'is paw. Then tha bastr'd knock'd me down wit' a kick that damn near broke m'a skull. That wuz when he went fer Iggy. And b'fore I could do anythin' else, my brother wuz torn ta' pieces.

"Whenna' beast came fer me again, I thought I wuz s'good as dead. Then somethin' inside me snapped. I dun't rememb'r too much after that. But when I came to, I wuz standin' there with a magic axe in muh hands, cover'd in bugbear blood."

John spat on the ground in frustration.

"Whatta fuggin' time to learn magic, huh? S' like a cruel joke, ya know? Why'd the gods spare muh life, jess so I could bury my broth'r? I couldn' get the idear out of my head. It wuz too much. So's I did the only thing whut made any sense... start drinkin'."

The woodsman paused his narrative to take a breath. He reached into his vest and pulled out a flask, then took a deep whack. Sighing loudly – his nerves steadied – he capped the flask and put it back.

"The creature took holda me n' it din't let go," John recalled, shame seeping into his voice. "It gimmie a reason to keep livin' – fer a while, 'et least. Then 'bout five years ago, I git thrown in jail after I almost kil't a man in a bar fight. And I might still be rottin' in there today if Rom din't bail me out n' give me a shot ta' make things right again wit' tha Scions."

John looked at the ground sullenly.

"I 'aint so proud'a many things I've done wit' my life. I don't think Iggy woulda been none too proud o' me, either. But I got a lifetime to try to make it up to 'im. An' by the gods, that's jess whut I'm gonna do."

****

As John finished his tale, Luzi heard a tiny snuffle, like a weeping butterfly would make. Puzzled, she looked around for the source, finally realizing it was Eureka.

As the pixie's phosphorescent glow dimmed with sorrow, Calypsa tenderly wiped a tear away from her companion's face and glanced Luzi's way.

"No matter how many times Eureka hears that story,

it always gets to her," Calypsa explained. "She had a little brother once upon a time, too."

"What happened to him?" the Nyasian asked quietly.

Calypsa glanced her partner's way, seeking permission to tell the story. When Eureka nodded her consent, she continued.

"I'm not sure how much you know about Fae society, but we don't have many laws. In fact, there is just one common belief that holds true in every pixie clan: *Love is the root of all evil.* No pixie is ever allowed to fall in love – we're only permitted to procreate. Those who disobey this rule are exiled. No exceptions are made... ever." [20]

"Still, as everyone knows, unjust laws are made to be broken," Calypsa added, squeezing her companion's hand.

"Eureka and I were young when we discovered our connection, only teenagers, really. It began as a friendship, nothing more. But over time, the depth of our feelings for each other began to overwhelm our fear, until one day, we surrendered to the inevitable. So what if we were forced to keep our love secret from the others? For a while – a short while – we were happy."

Calypsa sighed, shaking her head at the memory of those hopeful years.

"I guess it was all doomed to end poorly. But maybe we could have tasted happiness for a while longer... we'll never know. We have the Pied Piper to thank for that."

Both pixies shuddered as Calypsa uttered the name.

"He came to us on his knees, a desperate mercenary-mage on the run from a platoon of Ragnarian bounty hunters. We've had human visitors to Shangri-La before, even hosted the occasional refugee. But when that snake arrived pleading for sanctuary, there wasn't a single one of us – not even the most naïve – who thought it was a good idea."

"Why did he need asylum?" Luzi asked. "What did he do?"

"The Piper? You name it. Fraud, kidnapping, extortion, murder... even alchemy, some say."

"Alchemy?"

"Take our word for it," Calypsa assured Luzi. "They don't fuck around in Ragnaron when it comes to alchemy." [21]

"When the elders refused to grant the Piper amnesty, his laments turned to demands... and then to threats. 'Don't you know who I am?' he raged. 'I'm the Pied Piper! Nobody refuses me! You'll be sorry! By the gods, you'll be sorry!'

"The elders eventually chased him away at the threat of violence. But little did we know that he had every intention of following through on his promise.

"The Piper waited for nightfall, then put his skills to work. Playing his flute in a frequency only the young can hear, he used his power to hypnotize every child and teen in our glen. Then the Piper led them out of the village and straight into a nearby river, where every single one of them drowned... including Eureka's little brother."

Eureka gave a tiny sob at the mention of her sibling. Calypsa stopped, taking a moment to give her companion's hand a squeeze before continuing with her story.

"In the entire glen of Shangri-La, there were just two younglings who survived: Eureka and myself. We'd snuck out into the woods to make love in the moonlight, and were too far away to hear the Piper's song. We had no idea what happened until we returned to the village and heard the wailing of our elders.

"After the mourning was done, the elders asked us why we were alone in the woods that night. When we told them the truth, they exiled us on the spot. As they led us to the borderlands, the old ones asked us if we had any last words. Eureka offered just two: 'no regrets.' And she hasn't spoken again since that day."

"We met Rom, Anian and the others a few years later, and took the Test of Ten to join the Scions shortly afterwards," Calypsa concluded. "But that's another story – and I've already said enough for the evening, I think." [22]

Luzi watched Calypsa and Eureka exchange a long stare, sharing a lifetime of sorrow and triumph in a single moment. They stopped needing words to communicate long ago, the Nyasian realized, unexpectedly envious of their bond as lovers.

"I'm sorry," Luzi told the pixies, not sure what else to say. "That's very sad."

Eureka and Calypsa shook her heads vehemently.

"Sad? We appreciate the sentiment, but there's absolutely no reason for that. Love is a rare prize for the fortunate few who make its acquaintance in their lifetimes. And you should *never* feel bad about falling under its blessing."

As the pixie made her proclamation, Luzi turned to sneak a glance at U. But just then, a thunderous holler sounded out, startling the entire group.

"Huuurrrrggghhhhhrraaaahhhh!"

***

Luzi whipped around, expecting yet another horror in an endless series of calamities. But instead, she saw it was just Awf'l, screaming at the sight of a field rat.

Luzi watched curiously as the troll shrunk away in horror, cowering in fear like a child. It would have been hilarious... if she wasn't so deadly serious.

Almost immediately – as if this was a regular occurrence – Cobby was at Awf'l's side, reassuring the troll in a calm voice. "Sssshhh, it's alright," the chupacabra purred soothingly, shooing the rodent away. "It's gone. Everything will be fine. Why don't you go try to get some sleep? Can you do that for me?"

Awf'l nodded and sniffed, wiping her nose with the back of her hand. She shuffled off and plopped down in a patch of steppe grass, circling the area on all fours like a dog before laying down. Within a minute, the troll was snoring loudly, earning a grin and an eye roll from Cobby.

"Guess that one of us should have warned you about Awf'l's little phobia," he quietly told Luzi and U, trying not to wake her up.

"Romula found Awf'l on a mission near the western forests of Ragnaron about ten years ago when she was just a baby," the chupacabra explained. "Her entire grugg of trolls – dozens in all – had been slaughtered by a pack of manticores." [23]

"Somehow, Awf'l was overlooked during the massacre and hid under a bush. She laid there for almost a week without food or water – watching rats devour her family's corpses the entire time. Now, she can't stand to look at the things. Can't really say that I blame her, either."

As the chupacabra paused for a bite of bakalaroach, Luzi

sat quietly and reflected on his words. There was a different dimension behind the troll now – a surprising vulnerability hidden behind her savage appearance. And Luzi felt ashamed that she ever thought of her as a "monster."

"If you've figured out anything about Rom so far, you know she's not the kind of person who'd leave a helpless child to die... no matter what their race is," Cobby continued. "So needless to say, Awf'l has been on the road with us ever since."

Cobby glanced at the slumbering troll with fondness.

"We've all played babysitter over the past few years – me in particular, I guess. After all, we both lost our families in a massacre. And only someone who's gone through the same thing can know what *that's* like."

Luzi lowered her eyes respectfully.

"I'm sorry. Who did you lose?"

Cobby sighed.

"Everyone," he replied. "I lost everyone."

***

"For many thousands of years, my people lived on an island off the far northern coast of Dama'run," the chupacabra recalled. "It was a paradise, a place where some of the rarest flowers and plants in the world could be found. And *that*, as it turned out, was our curse."

"See, our island was a natural growing environment for Mandrake root, one of the most potent narcotics in the known realms. It's valuable enough that those seeking it will go to great lengths – and do some pretty horrible things – to get their hands on some.

"For a long time, our island's bounty of Mandrake went undiscovered. But about a decade ago, a Ragnarian sailing crew stumbled on our secret when they landed to resupply on our coast. When they returned to their village, their leaders decided to claim our island in the name of destiny. The plan was simple: kill us all and harvest every scrap of Mandrake they could pull out of the ground."

"You've got to understand, my people had no idea what was coming," the reptile explained. "The newcomers didn't have an army. They were outnumbered ten to one. And to my people, those pale prunes clambering out of their boats were more to be pitied than feared."

"Little did they realize that genocide doesn't always come at the point of a sword," he continued morosely.

"The Ragnarians began trading with us, swapping steel tools and medicine for Mandrake. What none of my kin knew – what none of them could have known – was the utter lack of resistance they had to the deadly diseases their new trade partners brought with them from across the ocean. But the Ragnarians knew *exactly* what they were doing; they'd done so many times before. With each contaminated item they handed out, another family's fate was sealed. Hut by hut, village by village, the sickness spread. And by the time my people figured out the source, it was much too late to do anything but die.

"Within a year of their arrival, every chupacabra who lived on our island was dead. Everyone except me. I discovered that I had some sort of freak immunity to the plague – a one in a billion chance. But instead of salvation, it was a punishment."

Cobby shook his head sadly.

"I stayed on the island until the last of them was gone, doing what I could to ease their suffering. It wasn't much. I'm a better clown than a nurse, as it turns out. I finally had to flee when the Ragnarians moved in to take the island en masse. I roamed the Dama'run coastline for months, searching for survivors. But to this day, I've never met another of my kind. And as far as I know, I'm the last chupacabra in the world."

"That's awful," Luzi consoled, not sure what else to say. "I'm so sorry."

"You keep telling us that," the chupacabra replied in a mock-offended voice, winking at his comrades. "Keep it up and you're liable to run out of sorry."

"How did you join the Scions?" Luci asked, eager to change the subject.

"Ah – well... it's a little embarrassing," the reptile said, snickering at the memory. "Romula caught me sucking blood from goats."

Lucy felt her eyes widen.

"Ummm... what?"

Cobby dug into a small travel satchel at his side, removing a tiny vial filled with a red liquid. He tapped the glass gingerly, as if examining a magic potion.

"We chupacabras have evolved a natural clairvoyance over the years. Normally, it's not much – just a few fractions of a blink. But there's something in goat blood that seems to supercharge this ability. When I drink it, I can stretch those tiny fragments of time into several seconds – more than enough to dodge an arrow.

"I found this out by mistake when I fled to the mainland. The first goat I ate was out of pure desperation. We didn't have the goddamn things on our island, you understand? After that, it turned into a real feast. But I got greedy. I got careless. And the local farmers started to catch on.

"Eventually, a group of villagers appealed to the Scions of Dama'run for aid. They were paid up on their taxes, so Rom was dispatched to hunt down 'the goat-sucking monster.' It didn't take her long. But instead of *killing* their monster, she *recruited* me."

Cobby removed the cap from his vial and took a snort of goat's blood, smacking his lips with pleasure.

"Goes to show you what a poor judge of character our fearless leader is, I suppose... hahaha!"

***

Just then, a cloud shifted above and a burst of moonlight illuminated the nearby hill where Romula was sitting. The mage's silhouette loomed mysteriously over the plains, like a wendigo howling to the heavens.

Luzi looked up at Romula, alone on the craggy bluff.

"Does she always take watch by herself like that?"

"Who, Rom?" Cobby replied. "Yeah, she's a real lone wolf sometimes."

"She *likes* it 'et way," John concurred.

"Can you blame her?" Anian quizzed his fellow Scions. "She's been doing her shifts like this ever since that day in Avalon. Ever since we lost Red Riding Hood."

"Fucking Avalon," Cobby said, shaking his head mournfully.

"Fucking Avalon," the others replied, sharing his moment of pain.

"What happened in Avalon?" Luzi butted in, unable to overcome her curiosity. But her question hit a brick wall.

"Oh no, you don't," Anian said, holding up his hands. "I'm not touching this one with a twenty-foot halberd. If you want to know about Avalon, go ask Romula."

"Yeah, I'm sure she'll be thrilled to tell you all about it," Cobby joked.

"The only challenge will be getting her to shut up," Calypsa agreed.

"Har har har!" John concurred.

Luzi glanced towards the bluff as the Scions continued laughing. Suddenly, an impulse flashed in her brain, and she felt her feet follow. "Fine... I'll go ask," she said, getting up from her seat.

Horrified expressions broke out on the Scions' faces.

"Hey, wait, we were just kidding," Anian implored as she started walking over to the bluff.

"Luzi!" U chimed in, trying to catch her attention. "Maybe it's better if you-"

But the Nyasian couldn't hear what he said next, because she was already on her way up the hill.

When Luzi reached the top, she found Romula sitting cross-legged on the ground. The mage stared out at the horizon, unblinking and unflinching, as if she didn't even know Luzi was there. It wasn't until Luzi opened her mouth to speak that Rom acknowledged her presence at all.

"What are *you* doing here?" the mage growled, not bothering to turn her head.

"Sorry if I startled you," Luzi apologized.

Rom clicked her tongue.

"Startled? I heard you coming from a league away. The only surprising thing is that you'd have the guts to distract me from watch duty in the first place."

"Fair enough," a flustered Luzi admitted. "Um... I was wondering... um..."

"Gods be damned – spit it out, kid! What the hell do you need?"

"Do you want some company?"

Romula finally turned around to face Luzi. She wrinkled her brow, clearly not expecting such a request. For a moment, Luzi thought she was going to get another mouthful of swears and a swat upside the head. But after a long pause, Romula gestured for the Nyasian to come sit beside her.

"Not a peep," the mage ordered gruffly, turning back to the horizon.

"Not a problem," Luzi replied, sitting down.

For several minutes, neither of them said another word. It was an awkward and heavy silence, the sort that had always made the Nyasian squirm. *How are you ever going to break the ice with this woman?* she wondered, stealing a glance at Romula. *What do we possibly have in common?*

That question was answered when – as Luzi shifted positions – a hastily chewed chunk of bakalaroach gurgled somewhere inside her guts.

BRAAPPPPP!

The sound of Luzi's flatulence echoed in the silent night, embarrassingly loud and impossible to ignore. Finally roused from her watch duties, Romula gave Luzi an icy stare. At first, the Nyasian's cheeks turned red with humiliation. But after a moment, the blood disappeared from her face as she thought about the absurdity of her shame.

You're being chased by killer unicorns... the fate of the world is on the line... everything you've ever known has been turned upside down... and you're worried about a FART?

Almost involuntarily, Luzi felt her lips perk up in a smile. Soon, a tiny snicker squeaked out, evolving into a chuckle despite her best efforts. "Sorry," Luzi sheepishly apologized to Romula, trying unsuccessfully to wipe the grin off her face.

The Nyasian fully expected to be chased off with a stern admonishing. But to her surprise, something else burst forth from the battle-hardened mage: laughter.

"Aw, hell, don't worry about it," Romula told Luzi when her snickering had died down. "The road diet has never done wonders for my stomach, either."

"Still embarrassing," Luzi said, shrugging.

"You should *never* be ashamed about laughing at a fart, kid. I don't know much – but I'm pretty sure about that."

The mage chuckled a few more times, indulging an inner craving that she'd ignored for way too long. "Tell me something. How old are you, anyway?"

"I've seen twenty-two winters, Luzi replied defensively. "And a spring on top of them, too."

"Twenty-two," Romula sighed wistfully, thinking of better times. "My daughter would have been just three years older than you if she were still with us. And gods be damned if she didn't crack up whenever she heard someone break wind... right up until the end."

"How did she pass away?" Luzi asked, the smile fading from her face.

Romula bit her lip, the wound still as sore as the day it was inflicted. Her voice darkened, returning to its typical, grim timbre.

"Pass away, hell. She was *murdered*."

"I come from a long line of mages that span generations," the mage continued. "My family specialized in healing magic – what some call the 'blue arts.' And for the first half of my life, I didn't kill anything that didn't cluck, low or oink.

"I lived with my husband and our little girl in a seaside village near the western border of Ragnaron. We made our home in the village lighthouse. My husband served as care-taker, while I did my healing magic for the locals in exchange for a bit of pocket money. We weren't rich, but we were happy. I thought nothing would ever change."

"And then that goddamned unicorn showed up on our doorstep," the mage recalled bitterly.

"A unicorn?" Luzi asked, feeling a sudden twinge of anx-iety. She resisted the urge to glance back at U.

Romula nodded.

"Ironically, it was my success as a healer that drew her my way in the first place. Somehow, she learned about my prowess in the blue arts, and came to demand that I use my abilities to help her get pregnant. When I explained to her that was impossible – that the Monoceros birth drought was infinitely beyond my ability to heal – the unicorn would hear none of it. Once again, she demanded that I cure her infer-tility or she would kill my family. And once again, pleading with her for understanding and mercy, I told her that I could do no such thing.

"The unicorn fell silent then, as if the reality of the situation had finally sunk in after all those long years. Finally, she turned to me and said three, short words: *I believe you.*

"In a flash – before any of us could even scream – the unicorn tore open my husband's throat, growling and shaking her head as the blood soaked the ground. When the thing had ripped him to shreds, she turned her attention to me. I dashed for the bedroom in a mad attempt to reach my daughter. But the unicorn lashed out with a kick that sent me flying straight through the lighthouse window. I fell fifty feet onto the sand below, hitting the ground hard. I remember very little about what happened next, except one thing... the sound of my child screaming."

The mage paused, wincing as the memories washed over her like god-fire.

"I woke up several days later in my neighbors' home. They'd found me and patched me up the best they could, but I'd been broken into a hundred pieces and was beyond even my own healing powers. Still, as bad as the pain was, the mental anguish was a thousand times worse.

"But eventually, as I lay there with no choice but to mend, the anger in my soul began to outweigh my sorrow. *That unicorn is still out there – and nobody will ever make her pay for what she did*, I told myself, obsessing over the sick truth of it all. And that was when I realized what needed to be done."

Romula's eyes narrowed.

"They told me it would take a hundred years to track that wretched unicorn down. They were wrong... it only took seven. The journey was long, but I used to learn every scrap of battle magic I came across. And by the time I was done with that goddamned hornhead, there wasn't even a pile of ashes left to piss on."

Luzi looked at the grizzled old wizard, seeing the same hate she once had for U reflected in the mage's weary, brown eyes. It was like the Nyasian was getting a glimpse into a version of her own future that might have come to pass – and still could, if she let it.

"So... um... did it help?" Luzi asked tentatively. "Getting revenge, I mean."

The sorcerer raised an eyebrow. "You ask some weird questions, you know that, kid?"

"So I've been told."

Rom chuckled sardonically. "Fine. You want to know about revenge, Luzi Winterstar? If I had to sum it up in one word, it would be... hollow."

"During those seven years, the only thought that churned through my mind was the deaths of my husband and child. And over time, that awful memory slowly eclipsed the reasons I loved them in the first place. When I think of them now, it conjures anger, fear, grief – but less and less 'love' as the years drag on. It's the final, cruelest part of their murders. And I'm the only one who can be blamed."

"But at least you acted nobly in their names," Luzi pointed out.

Romula just shook her head.

"Noble? No... any truly noble act requires sacrifice. There was no sacrifice in what I did. Just anger. And as a result, my life has become little more than revenge disguised as charity.

The Scions you see down there? They're noble people. Me? I'm just *pretending* to be one."

A prairie owl hooted softly in the distance. The mage immediately snapped to attention, turning her gaze to the plains below in search of possible threats, but finding none.

"Can I ask you one last question?" the Nyasian cautiously inquired when Rom had settled back down.

"Yes?"

"What happened in Avalon?"

Romula gave Luzi a curious look. "That crew of mine has some loose lips, don't they?" But after a moment, she sighed in resignation and looked up at the stars.

"A few years ago, we had a swordfighter named Red Riding Hood on our crew. We were on assignment in Avalon near the outlands of Quiyst when something went wrong — very wrong. And we... I... was forced to leave her behind."

The mage paused.

"Sometimes fate comes easy. Other times, it comes really goddamn hard. Red didn't deserve to go out like that. Neither did my daughter or my husband. But I can tell you one thing — I'll die before I let it ever happen again. And you can tell them all down below that's *exactly* what I said."

With this final proclamation, the old mage returned to her watch duties, motioning for Luzi to rejoin the group below.

"Go on, kid," she urged. "Get some shuteye if you can. We ride at first light, and we've got a long trip ahead of us before we reach the fen."

Luzi nodded, then got up and walked down to the campsite below. The other Scions glanced her way as she passed, each curiously pondering what the conversation was about... but too smart to ask.

U, however, had no such compunction.

"And what did you two chat about?"

Luzi looked back up at Romula, keeping watch over the camp from her lonely perch on the hill.

"Just some friendly advice from one lost soul to another," she replied quietly. "Come on... I'll tell you all about it over a handful of bakalaroach."

18

"Fortune favors the bold. But then again, so does disaster."

— General Su Ai, famed hero of the 2nd Cyclops War

As Romula promised, they departed at the crack of dawn, their spectral steeds glowing brightly as they streaked across the plains.

The group rode for hours, watching the environment gradually change with every mile they logged. The air grew fetid and briny. The ground transformed to mud. The surrounding flora got damper, lusher. Creeping, crawling things began to lurk in the shadows. And eventually, Luzi realized that they'd left the Elven Plains altogether.

We're entering a different world, she noted, gazing uneasily at their surroundings as they slogged through the wetlands.

Finally, late in the afternoon, they arrived at a massive stretch of forest that blocked their way forward. The twisted, warty woods towered so high, they seemed more sky than earth. Everything inside was completely hidden by the dense overgrowth, a mystery nobody in their right mind would want to solve. And Luzi knew what she was looking at before Romula uttered a single word.

Fellwood Fen.

"What's it like in there?" the Nyasian asked, peering into the darkness and trying to sound brave.

"I'm not going to lie," Romula warned, refusing to pull her punches. "You're going to hate every minute of it."

"Nearly anything you bump into in that forest has the ability to kill you: venomous insects, festering diseases, deadly quicksand. That's not even to mention the wild beasts that would love nothing better than to devour us and turn us into dung: the hide-behind, the basilisk, and if rumors are true, even the dreaded bunyip."

"But those who have entered Fellwood Fen and lived to tell the tale – and there aren't many of us – have all said the same thing," Romula cautioned. "The most insidious danger in that awful place isn't the beasts *or* the bogs... it's exhaustion."

"Don't worry about me," Luzi promised, her pride flaring up. "I can take anything this goddamn swamp can dish out."

Romula nodded approvingly, as if she knew her comment would put fire into the Nyasian's belly.

"Hold onto that courage, kid," she said. "You're going to need it."

And with that final exchange, they proceeded into the forest's murky depths. [24]

***

Despite her bravado, traversing the fen proved to be a test of endurance that Luzi nearly failed.

The swamp was every bit as miserable as Romula had promised it would be. A thick cover of trees blotted out the sun like a solar eclipse, except for a few scattered beams of sunlight that poked timidly through holes in the canopy. Inky-black marshes stretched as far as the eye could see, turning the ground beneath their feet into soup. As they trudged through the bog, hordes of stinging insects hovered around their faces, harassing them out of pure spite. A network of thorny overgrowth ripped at their ankles with every step. Each slimy lungful of air was accompanied by a scummy mix of swamp gas and feculence and decomposing flesh that assaulted their noses. And an unknown army of sinister things skulked about in the darkness, croaking and slurping in a grotesque anti-lullaby.

We're as welcome here as a shit fairy at a debutante ball, Luzi observed uneasily, cringing at every sight and sound. [25]

For hours, they trudged through the muck like soldiers in a muddy trench. Luckily, the mage's sense of direction was infallible. She led them over hidden land bridges... through twisting passages in the brambles... past deadly quicksand pits... around giant, hundred-year-old hornets' nests. And more than once, a burst of Deep Magic from her fingertips sent some dark shape scurrying into the shadows after it ventured too close.

But even with Romula's uncanny skills as a guide, the group's journey through the undergrowth was excruciatingly slow. The humid, vampiric heat of the fen stretched time like taffy. Each step took more energy than the last. And after only a few miles, Luzi already felt like she couldn't go on.

The Nyasian was on the verge of having to beg for a break

when she heard John's booming voice call out to the other Scions: "Ey! 'Ere's sumthin' y'all need tuh see!"

As Luzi and the others gathered around John, the woodsman pointed to a thick, large tree, where a menacing claw mark was dug into the trunk. The scratches were several inches deep and nearly as wide, and could easily have been mistaken for sword scores if not for their ragged edges.

"At's 'n ironwood tree. At' damn bark is 'bout tough as steel, give 'r take. Bout the only way tuh cut 'em down is wit' fire."

"So what the hell could have done *that*, Johnny Appleseed?" Cobby whispered in awe.

"I tol' ya not ta call me 'at, ya fuggin' lizr'd," the woodsman whispered back.

"John!" Romula chastised, urging him back to the task at hand.

"I dunno," he replied, scratching his beard and squinting at the mutilated tree trunk. "I jess dunno – but I dun' like it."

"Rom?" Anian inquired, sharing his fellow Scion's concern. "What now?"

The mage opened her mouth to speak. But before she could say a word, a terrible howl belted forth from the depths of the forest. It sounded like a baby and a wildcat trying to outscream each other – Luzi had never heard anything like it. Another hellish ululation quickly followed... and another... and another. Soon there were dozens of the things, all shrieking like demons and getting closer by the second.

Suddenly, they heard a snap of a twig behind them. The group conjured their armums and readied for battle. But to their surprise, nothing was there.

"What the f-" Luzi started to ask, but U grabbed her arm and put his finger up to his lips. He pointed towards a nearby tree; Luzi nodded that she understood.

The unicorn gestured to the others, then began to slowly creep forward with his sword upright. As he reached the tree, he paused for a moment, glancing back at the Scions purposefully. Then acting quickly – faster than a cobra striking a rat – he stabbed into its trunk, driving his blade clean through to the other side.

A terrifying howl issued from behind the tree, followed by a huge, arterial spray of blood. Uchchaihshravas swiftly withdrew his armum, cocking back for another swing if it was necessary.

It wasn't.

A strange, skinny creature slumped to the ground, dead as a doornail. A disturbingly proportioned cross between a sloth and a monkey, the creature was as tall as U, with foul-smelling black fur covering its body. Luzi's gaze gravitated towards its menacing, three-pronged claws and long, sinewy arms.

"What *is* it?" Calypsa gasped, as she and Eureka held their noses.

"It's called a hide-behind," Romula said, moving over to the creature and giving it a kick to make sure it was dead. She scanned the treeline, looking for others.

"I've never seen one myself, but I've heard about them. According to legend, they have a preternatural ability to hide in a forest and ambush their victims. It makes them some of the deadliest predators in the fen. Apparently, they have a fondness for raw intestines – hence the smell."

As if replying to Rom's last statement, a loud round of hooting resounded in the trees.

"We must be in their hunting territory," the mage continued. "They've marked us as prey. Soon, there'll be dozens of them here. And they'll all be just as hungry as our friend down there on the ground."

"How should we play this?" Anian asked Romula, running through battle scenarios in his mind. "Panther's Paw formation? Or maybe Lamia's Revenge?"

But the wizard just shook her head.

"You've learned a lot over the past years, but you still forget one thing, Anian. The best way to win a fight is not to have it in the first place."

She turned to John. "How much liquor do you have on you?"

"Not much, jess two flasks o' tha good stuff."

"That'll do. Hand it over, please."

John reluctantly surrendered his prized hooch, only to gasp when Romula opened one of the containers and emptied it on her head.

"Hide-behinds can't stand the smell of alcohol," the mage explained, passing the flasks down the line. "It's like breathing in sulfur to them... they can't be within a mile of it. Hurry now – douse yourselves good. We won't have much time before the rest of the pack catches up with us."

True to her prediction, it wasn't long before more hide-behinds began to dart behind the trees all around them. With their prey alerted to their presence, the creatures became more brazen about revealing themselves, allowing the group to catch fleeting glimpses of them as they ducked for cover.

They're trying to scare us into making a run for it, Luzi realized, knowing the creatures would pick off anyone who left the safety of the group.

Soon, the footsteps drew within arrow range... then javelin range. Together, the Scions stared out into the treeline defiantly, ready to fight to the death if need be. But to their surprise, no attack followed. Instead, the hide-behinds shuffled away into the forest, gagging in disgust as they went. Gradually, the sounds of the fen started up around them again. And after just a few minutes, it was as if they were never there in the first place.

"Gods be damned," Anian told Romula, shaking his head incredulously. "Don't you ever get tired of being right?"

"I still say it's a waste of good whiskey," John muttered, morosely peering into an empty flask.

Romula patted him on the shoulder sympathetically. "When we get back to Dama'run, I owe you a round of thousand-year-old brandy at the Stewed Pooka... with a dragon breath chaser, if you want."

"Let's keep moving," the mage told her crew, glancing overhead at the faint daylight breaking the canopy. "We've got a while to travel, and not much light left."

Luzi and the Scions turned to leave. But as they did, Romula inconspicuously gripped U by the elbow.

"That was some damn fine sword work for a farmhand – my compliments," she commented quietly.

"Credit my father," U replied. "He served with the local magistrate before I was born, passed on what he learned to me. It's not much... but it gets the job done."

Romula nodded in agreement.

"You and Luzi managed to kill an alpha-level unicorn back in Nyasia. I'd say that qualifies as *getting the job done*."

U smiled politely, trying to end the conversation.

"Luck... all luck. But thankfully, you and the Scions are here now. And I feel much better knowing that some *real* warriors are at our side."

Without another word, U turned and joined the others, leaving Romula behind. As he left, the smile faded from the mage's face. She paused to watch him for a split second more, biting her lip in contemplation.

And with a final glance at U, she rejoined her crew.

*****

Just as the last of the meager daylight began to give way to the night, the exhausted troupe arrived at a large grove of strange trees.

Gnarled and ominous, the trees had wrinkled trunks that bore an uncanny resemblance to human torsos. Their branches stretched directly upwards, like spindly hands grasping for the heavens. Luzi had never seen anything like them. There was a sinister familiarity about the things she couldn't quite place... something ancient... something evil.

Romula, however, was strangely relieved to see the creepy stretch of woods. "They're known as body trees," she explained. "And there's only one place in the known realms where they grow – the Luchrupan homeland." [26]

Luzi looked at the grove with new eyes. She turned to Romula, almost afraid to say the words.

"You mean... we're *here*?"

The mage allowed herself a curt smile. "We're here. But let's not start kissing our own asses just yet. We still need to make it through the grove, after all."

"The grove?" Luzi queried, raising an eyebrow.

"Unlike Nyasians, the Luchrupan don't bury their dead. Instead, to honor the fallen, they ritually consume their flesh and make sculptures out of their bones. The grove we're about to enter is the place where they display the finished works of art. And they are fiercely protective of it."

"Wait a minute," Luzi remarked warily. "You mean we're walking into a goddamn *cannibal graveyard?*"

"It's really not as bad as it sounds," the mage offered with a shrug.

"Yeah right – said the bird to the worm," Luzi countered.

Rom grinned.

"You've got a future as a poet in case this warrior thing doesn't work out, kid. Let's move out."

***

They'd barely walked a hundred feet before they came across the first death sculpture.

Standing waist-high with Luzi, the skeleton was arranged in a heroic posture, as if it was posing victorious on a battle-field. The bones – thicker and stouter than a human's – were expertly flensed and polished to the point of gleaming. It was the work of an artisan, not a butcher, which only made it more frightening.

Even "The Royal Child" doesn't hold a candle to this awfulness, Luzi thought, shivering. [27]

It wasn't long before they encountered another of the bizarre sculptures. This time, the subject was a juvenile Luchrupan – possibly a child. The youngling's skeleton was posed in mid-skip, as if the artist had deliberately tried to capture them at their most vivid. A few steps away, there was another skeleton, this one belonging to an elderly member of the tribe. The Luchrupan's arms were outstretched, as if preparing to embrace a loved one. Soon, Luzi could see thousands of the things scattered around the grove... a veritable army of the dead. And as she looked around with a growing unease, Luzi felt like she was trapped in some demented storybook that couldn't possibly have a happy ending.

Suddenly, Luzi heard a voice call out in Communia from the treetops somewhere in front of them. It was vaguely human-sounding, but with a higher pitch and a menacing vibrato.

"Who goes there?" he demanded. "Speak now, intruders!"

Hissing accusations echoed throughout the woods.

"Who, indeed?"

"Who, indeed?"

"Who, indeed?"

Luzi felt her heart thump. *Gods help us, we're surrounded!*

"Show yourself!" Romula called out with authority. "What is the meaning of this?"

"You're in *our* grove, strangers," the voice repeated, this time with a decidedly threatening edge. "You'll answer *our* questions. And right now, we have only one. WHO ARE YOU?"

"My name is Romula Zazzau, and the warriors at my side are Scions of Dama'run," the mage replied. "We come in peace, seeking an audience with your Psychopomp. I'm an old acquaintance of his, and I promise you that when I'm finally granted an audience, he will frown on the disrespect we have already endured. Now I tell you one last time, show yourself!"

There was a pause before the voice answered. "You're outnumbered and uninvited," it warned. "Remember that before you make any sudden moves."

In a moment, a gnome dropped out of a nearby tree with an effortless nimbleness. The size of a human child, he was clad in a tattered loincloth and nothing else. His leathery green skin was crossed with layers of wrinkles, almost like an armadillo. Pike-sharp eyebrows arched above a pair of clever, calculating eyes.

The gnome rubbed his hands together, grinning like a loan shark on collection day.

"Allow me to introduce myself. I am Silas de El'ya, right hand to the Psychopomp of Fellwood Fen. And in his absence, I have authority here. Now tell me... what business do you have with our king?"

"With all respect, Lord Silas, that's an answer I reserve for him, and him alone."

The Luchrupan crooked a hairy eyebrow with suspicion.

"You say you're friends of the Psychopomp. But you skulk unannounced through our sacred grove like bandits and refuse to tell us why you're here. It's a vexing paradox, indeed. How do we know this is true? What proof do you have of your claim?"

Romula paused for a second, then uttered one, simple word: "Eimear."

The mage's response ignited a wave of whispers and muttering among the anonymous masses in the trees.

"Eimear!"

"Eimear!"

"Eimear!"

Silas gave Romula a sour, confused look, like a street fighter who'd been challenged to a chess match.

"You are either very brave or very foolish to bring up that name," he said, hedging his bet with a tinge of respect. "But something tells me the Psychopomp will want to figure that out for himself."

"Send a runner ahead of us and let our king know some old 'friends' are on the way," Silas called out into the trees. "And make sure to mention they cited our late queen as proof of their camaraderie."

Luzi saw branches rustle as one of the hidden Luchrupan rushed off.

Silas made a fist. A golden, magical flame ignited around his hand. At his cue, dozens of diminutive warriors dropped out of the trees and surrounded the intruders, each as battle-ready as their captain.

"Our village is just a few minutes away," Silas said. "Follow me and keep up – we move fast. But understand this. My clan is everywhere in these woods. This is our *home*. And the moment any of us suspect you're a threat, you'll be cut down where you stand... friends of our king or not."

∗∗∗

Flanked by dozens of gnomes, Luzi, U and the Scions followed Silas into the grove.

Luzi felt the hair stand up on the back of her neck as they approached the village. *Who knows what's waiting for us in there?* Luzi shuddered, the gruesome graveyard of skeletons still fresh in her mind. She steeled herself for buildings made of bone and parapets made of flesh, a necropolis of fear and terror.

But instead, she found something completely different: treehouses.

As they drew closer, Luzi saw there were hundreds of circular thatched huts built directly into the forest understory. Each was connected to the others via a series of narrow walkways. Here and there, tiny hearth fires glowed, creating a tapestry of orange in the otherwise gloomy treetops. It was a quaint sight, something from out of a child's fairy tale.

Down below, dozens of Luchrupan moved about their daily routines, blissfully unaware that catastrophe now walked among them. There were a scattering of soldiers among the crowd, but the bulk of the gnomes were noncombatants, too young or unskilled in war to pose any real threat. There were workers with spades and rakes... elders carrying water jugs... children whooping and playing.

No skeletons. No corpses. Just a village.

As they passed by each cluster of homes, Silas called out a short phrase in the Luchrupans' native tongue: "Nir anädaela!"

"What is he yelling?" Luzi whispered to Rom.

"Strangers passing through," the mage quietly translated.

The villagers stopped in their tracks and stared with open mouths when they caught sight of the strange caravan.

One by one, the gnomes dropped whatever they were doing and trailed along after the group, forming an impromptu mob that continued to grow larger as they go. But to Luzi's surprise, the Luchrupan didn't have expressions of fear, only curiosity. It was like they were watching a circus coming to town instead of a platoon of potential assassins.

This is our home, Silas had said when they entered the grove. And as Luzi looked around the village, she finally understood what he meant.

They weren't an army – they were a family.

The weird entourage continued marching until they came to a large, open space at the center of the grove. The forest canopy had been cleared in one spot, just enough for a large swath of moonlight to make its way through. Underneath sat a huge, ivory cauldron with a large ankh carved into the front. The vessel was covered in mystic runes and crammed to the lid with thousands of shiny, yellow coins.

The Pot of Gold! Luzi marveled, glancing at it as they passed.

Waiting for them at the opposite end of the clearing was a corpulent Luchrupan with a golden crown balanced on his head of gray, greasy hair. He sat on a throne carved into a living body tree, smoking a long, curved pipe – just like Luzi's father used to enjoy.

"Well well well, indeed... what do we have here?" he inquired curiously as the group came closer.

Silas led them slowly to the foot of the throne where a pair of large bodyguards stood, framing their king like burly bookends. "Psychopomp," he announced with a swift, respectful bow. "These are the humans we caught trespassing in the Sacred Grove."

The elderly Luchrupan scrutinized Romula, taking a long puff on his pipe and slowly exhaling a big, grey cloud. "Romula Zazzau," he commented at last, his voice vacillating between worry and relief. "I never thought I'd see *you* again."

The mage offered a brief curtsy. "Likewise, good king. But as fate would have it, here I stand."

The Psychopomp glanced at the crew beside her.

"And who are your companions? You must have moved up in the world, to command such a crew as this, eh?"

"The warriors you see here are my fellow Scions," Romula said, introducing each of them in turn.

"And these other two?"

"They are our... guests."

The Psychopomp chuckled. "Guests? Fine, Romula – I'll play along. So tell me, what calamity brings you to us this time?"

Romula dipped her head in deference. "I apologize for our unannounced visit. But there's no way to tiptoe around my request, so I'm just going to say it."

The mage pointed at the cauldron in the middle of the clearing.

"We need to use the Pot of Gold. And we need to use it *now*."

Romula's declaration set off a round of murmurs among the Luchrupan. The congeniality evaporated from the Psychopomp's face like a spilled beer on a hot summer day.

"You know what my people have decreed. No outsiders may use the cauldron. So tell me... why would I allow you to access that which we've denied monarchs and royalty, oh humble Scion of Dama'run?"

"Because I'm calling in a favor," Romula continued. "One that was promised to me decades ago in the name of your wife, Eimear."

The Psychopomp squinted his eyes in pain. It was as if the mage had pierced his chest with a dagger.

"I haven't heard the name of my queen spoken aloud in many years – many years, indeed," he said, his sorrow palpable. "I'd almost forgotten what it sounded like."

Romula didn't allow the Luchrupan the chance to reflect on the memory.

"It's not my intention to reopen ancient wounds, but we stand in urgent need. We're being pursued by a coven of unicorns. And the Pot of Gold is our only chance at escape."

The Psychopomp's eyes opened wide.

"Unicorns? And you come *here*? Do you value our lives that little?"

Romula held up her hand, as if swearing an oath.

"I know we've delivered a dire liability to your doorstep. And I am truly sorry for that. But believe me when I say that many other lives are at stake, not just our own. We wouldn't have come here otherwise. So as soon as you've sent us on our way, we can-"

"You presume action before commitment," the Psychopomp interrupted. "Tell me something, Romula. There are many reasons why the Monoceros would want you dead. But which is it this time?"

The question stymied Romula. She said nothing.

The Psychopomp narrowed his bushy eyebrows.

"Your silence puts your cause in serious jeopardy. I suggest that you either find your tongue fast or get the fuck out of our forest. Now, I'm going to ask you one more time. *Why are they chasing you?"*

Romula pursed her lips. "We have one of the Immaculan Rings," she said after a long pause.

The mage's words touched off another round of fierce murmurs among the Luchrupan.

The Psychopomp stared at Romula with disbelief. "An Immaculan Ring? You're lying."

In reply, Romula nodded at Luzi. *I hope you know what you're doing,* the Nyasian thought, reaching under her tunic.

As Luzi held the thing out for all to see, the Psychopomp gazed at it silently, as if he couldn't believe what he was beholding.

"Gods be damned," the gnome whispered.

"It gets worse," Rom admitted. "We think that a coven of unicorns has the other ring. And if they catch up with us, one of the mightiest weapons in the known realms will be under the control of history's most notorious killers. Now you see why we've been forced to seek your aid. The world is in danger every second we remain here. And I promise that unless you help us, *nobody* will be safe from the slaughter to come. Not the humans... not the elves... not even the Luchrupan."

The Psychopomp chewed on Romula's words, his pipe ember flaring several times as he mulled her proposal. After a minute, the Psychopomp motioned for Silas to approach the throne. He leaned close to his lieutenant's ear and whispered a question. Silas peeked at the Scions with a sour look, then whispered a reply to his king. Nodding sagely, the Psychopomp turned back to Romula with a stern expression cemented on his face.

"As much as I hate to admit it, you're right," he told the mage. "There's no question that it's in all our best interests to get you out of here as quickly and quietly as possible, indeed. And although I regret making such a hasty promise, I cannot renege on the pledge I made to you all those years ago."

Romula's left eyebrow arched. "You mean—"

"We will grant your request," the Psychopomp answered, cutting her off. "The Pot of Gold is yours to use."

The Psychopomp gives the mage a wary look.

"If it were anyone else in this world that wandered in here like this, things would have turned out very differently indeed. I grant this favor in the name of my late queen. Consider my debt to you repaid."

The declaration set off another round of murmurs from the Luchrupan.

"Repaid, indeed!"

"Repaid, indeed!"

"Repaid, indeed!"

The Luchrupan king rapped his knuckles on the arm of this throne for silence.

"I'd send you on your way this very minute if it were in my power," the Psychopomp said. "But the Pot of Gold can only be used during daylight. You need the sun to create a rainbow, after all."

He looked up at the night sky through the clearing in the trees.

"We have about eight hours left until sunrise. You can wait here until then as my guests. And as long as you can find the patience to sit still and avoid causing any more trouble, there's a good chance we'll all make it out of this alive – a good chance, indeed."

As the Psychopomp said these last words, Luzi noticed him put out his pipe abruptly, even though it still had a good ember to it. The gesture caught her eye; it was the same idiosyncrasy her father used to have... whenever he was trying to keep a secret from her.

Luzi looked over at the others to see if they noticed anything wrong. But none of them showed any sign of suspicion, so she bit her tongue. *You're just being paranoid*, she told herself.

"Find a place for our new friends to rest while they wait," the Psychopomp ordered Silas. He turned back to Romula. "I'll send someone to let you know when it's time for the ceremony. If you require anything in the meanwhile, just speak the words."

Romula bowed in respect.

"The world is in your debt, Psychopomp. We shall see you anon."

Silas gestured for them to follow and began leading them away from the throne. Romula and the others trailed behind, the tittering of the Luchrupan mob echoing in their wake.

Before they went, Luzi couldn't help but glance back at the Psychopomp, unable to shake her earlier paranoia. Eerily, he was looking right at her, matching her stare with his own. Their eyes only met for a moment before the gnome hastily averted his gaze. But it was long enough for Luzi to see something the king couldn't hide.

Fear.

***

Silas guided the group across the clearing, where a makeshift campsite carved out of tree stumps was arranged around a firepit. A generous bed of coals awaited them, emanating a warm, inviting light. As a half-dozen Luchrupan warriors formed a perimeter around their guests, a few younglings rushed to set up some wash bowls and pitchers of water. Meanwhile, Silas beckoned Romula and the others to sit down and make themselves at home.

"I apologize for the crudeness of the accommodations," he said in a not-so-sorry voice. "As the Psychopomp mentioned, if you need anything, just call. Guards will be within earshot... *at all times.*"

Romula forced a big, insincere smile at the veiled threat.

"We'll be fine. Our gratitude for your hospitality."

"Let's hope it's not a consideration worn thin," Silas responded, his voice sharp as a dagger. "Look for my coming at the break of dawn."

Giving the group a final, *I'm-watching-you* glare, the Luchrupan slowly walked away, leaving them under the vigilant gaze of his kin.

Romula shrugged and walked over to a bowl of water. She dunked her head in, swirling it around for a moment before surfacing with an immense "Aaaaaahhhhhhhh!" Then, as casually as if she was sitting down in her own living room, the mage plopped down on a tree stump and pulled a hunk of bakalaroach out of her pocket.

"Go on," she encouraged the others, munching away as she spoke. "We've got a while until sunrise. There isn't any sense in making the trip hungry."

One by one, they followed Romula's lead, breaking out their travel packs of bakalaroach and indulging in a quiet, weary meal. There was just one who didn't eat: Luzi.

Her anxiety didn't escape Romula's gaze.

"Alright, spit it out," the mage said with a sigh. "What's bothering you, kid?"

For a brief moment, Luzi considered telling her everything. But suddenly, the flimsiness of her evidence hit her square in the face. *After all, what proof do I really have other than a sideways squint and a stubbed-out pipe?* she admitted to herself.

"I guess that I'm just curious why the Luchrupan would let us use the Pot of Gold," Luzi finally asked Romula, cautiously probing for more information. "How did you meet the Psychopomp, anyway?"

"Like I said earlier, he owes me a life debt."

"Yes, but for *what*?"

"To be honest, I'm curious about that myself," Anian chimed in, nodding respectfully to his mentor.

Romula glanced at her crew – each of whom bore the same expression – then turned back to Luzi.

"Fair enough. The answer is simple... I killed his wife."

The mage held up her hands, fending off a half-dozen shocked stares. She lowered her voice, glancing at the Luchrupan guards around them.

"Let me explain. The Pot of Gold is one of the most powerful magical relics in the Great Realms, but it has one major drawback: it requires a massive amount of gold – the single-best conductor of Deep Magic in the world. And I don't know if you've noticed, but there isn't a single hunk of it within a hundred miles of this entire godforsaken swamp. So the Luchrupan have been forced to entreat with some pretty shady sources to get what they need.

"About three decades ago, the Psychopomp brokered a deal with a baron in the Quiystian province of Muu, one of the gold-richest territories in the world. He agreed to provide the Luchrupan with 10,000 bars of pure bullion – enough to power the Pot of Gold for a century. In exchange, the baron's soldiers were allowed to use the pot to launch a surprise attack on a horde of bandits that had been plaguing the Quiystian roadways.

"Naturally, the attack went off without a hitch... not a single hijacker survived. But when the gnomes went to collect their fee, the baron refused to surrender a single doubloon. Perhaps he got arrogant, or perhaps he never intended to pay in the first place, nobody knows for sure. The only thing that matters is what happened next.

"The Luchrupan queen, a powerful mage named Eimear, recruited a war party and journeyed to the baron's homeland to demand payment of the debt. But troops were waiting for them in ambush. Eimear and the Luchrupan never stood a chance.

"Only two of the gnomish war party survived. One was Eimear, who had her mind wiped clean during a psychic fight with a stronger magician. The other was her personal body-guard, who was able to escape and bring his queen's still-breathing body back to Fellwood Fen."

"So what does this all have to do with *you*?" Luzi asked.

The mage sighed, muddy memories stirring up in the muck of her psyche.

"Three years later, the Dama'run Council sent me to

Fellwood Fen to try and broker a similar deal with the Luchrupan. When I finally battled my way to the Luchrupan grove, I was ready for a cold reception, perhaps a fight or two. Imagine my surprise when I was immediately taken to the royal yurt to meet their comatose queen."

"Wait a minute!" Cobby remarked. "She was still *alive*?"

Romula nodded.

"The attack left her mind ruined, but her body remained whole. So the Luchrupan continued to feed, water and groom their queen with an unceasing devotion, many of them fully convinced that she might wake up at any time."

"I don't get it," Anian asked, scrunching an eyebrow. "Why didn't they kill her?"

"Not all cultures are as nonchalant as Quiystians when it comes to euthanasia," Romula explained. "The Luchrupan code forbids the killing of a clanmate under any circumstance... even in the name of mercy. However, as outsiders, we were able to do what they could not. So at her husband's request, I agreed to send their queen to the next life with dignity."

"It was painless," the mage added calmly. "She never felt a thing."

Romula's cool recollection at taking a life gave Luzi a chill. *How many times has she done something like this?* the Nyasian wondered.

"In the end, the Luchrupan denied the council's request to use the Pot of Gold, ruling that no foreigner would ever be granted the privilege again," Romula continued. "But before I left the fen, the Psychopomp swore to me that if I ever personally needed a favor – anything – I had but to ask. So today, I asked."

"I know the Psychopomp seems like a real sonovabitch," the mage admitted. "I get that. I really do. But he truly loved his queen. I saw it in his eyes. And if he's willing to help us in her name, that's all the proof I need."

The Scions exchanged glances, unsure of how to respond until Luzi blurted out what was on all their minds.

"I just hope you know what you're doing. For all our sakes."

"Me too, kid – me too," Romula replied, flashing a rare grin at her honesty. "Now get some rest if you can. We've got a long trip ahead of us tomorrow – and a big celebration to prepare for when we get there."

19

"Oaths are but words, and words are but wind."

– Azizig-Balewa, elvish shaman

The Psychopomp stood alone in his yurt, perched on the edge of eternity.

The gnome king had ordered his guards to wait outside, giving them explicit instructions not to disturb him. But the truth was, even if someone *were* to walk in at that moment, he wouldn't have noticed.

With the calculated dread of a lion trainer entering a cage, the Psychopomp trudged over to a wooden chest tucked away in the corner of the room. He opened the trunk and flipped a concealed trigger, which sprung a secret compartment in the bottom. There was only one item inside: a purple gemstone pendant carved in the shape of a teardrop.

The Meridian's sigil.

The Psychopomp thought back to seven summers ago, when she came to the fen in secret – even from the other Overgruk – seeking to form an alliance between the Monoceros and the Luchrupan. When the gnomes rejected her offer, the Meridian insisted they keep one of her sigils... just in case.

"You are not the only holdovers from the Age Fantastic we have made this offer to," the alpha unicorn hinted mysteriously. "There will soon come a time when your clan will have to choose sides – the humans or us. And when it does, I promise that I will be benevolent and forget the poor decision you have made here today."

It had been more than three years since that day, but the Psychopomp still thought of it often – in private. He knew the others would not condone the sigil's use; all but a select few were unaware it even remained in the village. There were rules, after all. *Still, there are times when rules need to be broken,* he told himself. *For the honor of the family.*

The Luchrupan king paused and looked down at the pendant with a terror building in his heart. *Once you do this, there's no going back,* the Psychopomp warned himself. But it was a facetious gesture; his mind was made up as soon as he saw the ring.

There is no other way.

Do it.

Do it.

Taking a deep breath, the Psychopomp squeezed the pendant in his hand. He closed his eyes and focused his mind.

"Great Meridian," the Luchrupan whispered fiercely, as the jewel glowed with an eerie, spectral light. "I beg you, hear my call!"

An irresistible presence instantly flooded into his head, plumbing every crevasse of his brain. "Psychopomp," an unmistakable voice boomed. "It's been a long time. Does this mean you've reconsidered my offer?"

The gnome couldn't help but cringe.

"Mighty Meridian, please forgive my reply, but no. My people have decreed that the Pot of Gold shall not aid any foreigner. I cannot move against their desires. I must refuse... with every possible due respect, indeed."

He could feel the unicorn's impatience simmering.

"So tell me, little king. Why are we speaking?"

"I offer you something else of value: information," the Psychopomp added hastily. "A cohort of Scions of Dama'run have ventured into our grove with a pair of Nyasian farmers in tow. And they have something you might be interested in... an Immaculan Ring."

At the mention of the ring, the Psychopomp felt a sharp twinge in his head. He realized the Meridian was creating a psychic wall in his mind, preventing him from severing their mental tether. The urge to flee crackled like lightning. But of course, it was much too late for that.

"Why are you telling me this?" the unicorn queried suspiciously. "What's in it for you?"

The Luchrupan King clenched his hands. Despite his fear, a fire broiled in the gnome's eyes, born of hate and suffering and loneliness.

"As you know, many years ago, my queen – *my wife* – was murdered by a Quiystian baron by the name of Odna Han. And every night since her death, I've begged the gods to deliver me a way to punish that filth-monger for what he's done. But my prayers have gone unanswered. Han is too strong, too wealthy, too well-allied. My people wouldn't stand a chance in open combat against his troops, even with the Pot of Gold at our disposal."

The Psychopomp paused, gathering his courage.

"You ask what I stand to gain by calling on you?" the Luchrupan asked, every word dripping with venom. "The answer is simple... revenge. Once you have the ring in your possession, I want your coven to kill every last member of the Han family. Wipe them out to the last child. Remove every trace of their accursed bloodline from this world. Promise me that – and guarantee that you won't use the rings to harm any of my family – and I am at your command, oh mighty Meridian."

When the Meridian replied, there was a grudging respect in her voice.

"Your request is honorable, Luchrupan. The Hans are as good as dead. And not a single Luchrupan will be slain when I have the rings – you have my word."

"Then what do you require of me, Great Meridian?"

"As we speak, my most trusted lieutenant and a murder of my swiftest kin are on their way to Fellwood Fen. I need you to guide them to the exact location of your village. Send an emissary into the treetops with a signal so they can see it from above. But whatever you do, be conspicuous. The humans must suspect nothing until we're in striking range."

"Do you want my warriors to help take them into custody?"

"No," the Meridian retorted sharply. "Your 'warriors' will just get in the way. Tell your people to stay hidden until it's all over. My kin need no assistance. They *love* what they do. And they're *good* at it."

A shiver ran down the Psychopomp's spine.

"I can keep them here until sunrise before they figure out I'm trying to stall them," the Psychopomp said. "But delaying them any further may be difficult without rousing suspicion. Can your warriors make it here by the morning?"

"They will be there," the Meridian replied with a chilling certainty. "I hope for *your* sake that my quarry is present as well. Contact me again when my brothers and sisters arrive. And whatever you do, don't speak of this to anyone... Luchrupan, human or anything in between."

With this final warning, the Meridian withdrew from the Psychopomp's mind. The pendant abruptly stopped glowing. And in the blink of an eye, the Psychopomp was alone again.

The gnome basked for a moment in the cold comfort of the Meridian's promise. "Revenge is finally ours, my queen," he murmured, the words empty and hollow as his heart.

And the Luchrupan King slunk away from his hut before he could find the courage to weep.

2 0

*"If you can't afford to stop for death, the reaper will stop for
you."*

–Balewa Bin Saud, chirurgeon general of Dama'run

Luzi spent the rest of the evening in silence alongside
U and the Scions, swaddled in a blanket of anxieties as she
waited for the dawn.

Naturally, she didn't sleep a wink.

But eventually – with an excruciating laziness – a few,
faint rays of sunlight crept their way through the treetops and
onto the forest floor. And gradually, a new day in Fellwood
Fen slouched into existence.

As the Scions yawned and stretched, U looked Luzi's way,
expecting her to partake in a hasty breakfast like the rest of
them. But the arrival of the dawn had set a strange cocktail of
emotions churning in Luzi's stomach that food couldn't settle.

Rising from her stump, she walked over to a solitary sunbeam and closed her eyes. Luzi placed her hand on the ring
that hung around her chest and traced the cold metal of the

"

chain with her fingers. She stood like that for several minutes – perched on the edge of a dream – until U nudged her back to reality.

"Is everything all right?" he asked tentatively.

Slowly, Luzi opened her eyes.

"Just remembering," she said, waiting a long moment before speaking again.

"I was thirteen-years-old when my mother gave me this ring," she said, hushed with nostalgia. "I remember it like it was yesterday, though. Normally in the outback, ninety-nine out of a hundred days are flawlessly clear and sunny. But it was gloomy and grey that morning... almost exactly like today."

Luzi chuckled, remembering the dumb fire of her adolescence.

"I was such a little pissant back then. Always questioning, always complaining, always full of aimless angst. I remember griping about the lousy weather on our way to the fields: *If the sun doesn't have the guts to show up to work, why should we?* And that was when my mother told me something I'll remember for the rest of my life."

"Courage isn't always a blazing sunrise – sometimes it's just a candle in the gloom," Luzi recalled, hearing her mother's voice as she spoke the words.

The Nyasian gazed up into the sunbeam for a long moment, savoring it like a fine brandy. "I wish the old lady was here to see this," she mused with a melancholy smile. "Papa too. They would have appreciated it."

Luzi felt U's hand tenderly touch her shoulder.

"They'd be proud of you," the unicorn assured her. "You know that, right?"

"Sure... but that doesn't make me miss them any less."

"No, I don't suppose it would," U conceded, lowering his chin sadly.

Suddenly, Romula's deep alto voice abruptly cut the air, silencing them both.

"Everyone look sharp! We've got a problem!"

***

The startled Scions seemed as confused about the alert as Luzi and U.

"What's wrong?" Anian whispered, the hair on the back of his neck dancing as he scanned their surroundings.

"Unicorns?" Calypsa inquired, nervously glowing brighter as she said the word.

"Can't be," a puzzled Cobby commented, flaring his nostrils. "I don't see anything at all... or smell anything, either."

"Yes – and *that's* the problem," Romula admonished, clicking her tongue like they were schoolchildren and she was an exasperated professor.

"Take a look around," the mage chastised. "Quickly... what's missing?"

Simultaneously, eight pairs of necks rotated on their shoulders.

"Umm... where did our guards go?" Luzi commented as the others came to the same realization.

Romula pursed her lips.

"Exactly. They were all here a few minutes ago – at least half a dozen. When I turned around, they were gone. And that's not all."

She gestured around at the empty village square, where just a few minutes ago, hundreds of leprechauns had stood. There were no clanking breakfast pots... no laughing children... none of the bustle from the previous day. Even the sounds of the surrounding forest were mysteriously dimmed, as if the entire grove was holding its breath. But eerily, several signs of the gnomes' recent presence lingered: still-crackling fires, fresh footprints, half-full water buckets. It was as if the entire village had been quarantined. *Or evacuated*, Luzi thought uneasily.

And that's when she noticed the fog.

It was easy to overlook in the dim light of the fen at first, grey and misty as the rest of the murk in that accursed swamp. But this particular patch of brume was moving faster than the wind – and in the opposite direction. Even worse, it was headed straight for them.

Luzi turned to warn the others, but the ever-alert Romula beat her to the punch.

"Scions – we're under attack!" she hollered, conjuring a pair of deadly looking Ubamota short swords.

The others followed Romula's lead, manifesting their own armums and preparing for battle... all except U. Instead, he calmly stepped forward and pointed a finger at the cloud of mist.

"Enough theatrics!" he shouted. "Show yourselves – if you have the courage!"

At that exact moment, as if she had been waiting for the right time to make her presence known, a screeching voice called out in Communia.

"Well, *that's* a funny choice of words coming from a traitor."

Before Luzi's unbelieving eyes, a platoon of equine figures emerged from the fog, stepping forth from the mist as if birthed from the aether. The shapes began to consolidate... hooves, heads, horns. And in a matter of moments – barely enough time for Luzi to gasp – a full murder of unicorns stood in front of her with their murderous eyes ablaze.

As the shocked group of adventurers watched with a dawning panic, a leering, one-eyed unicorn stepped forward from the pack and slowly spread her wings. She paused for a long moment and sniffed at the air, as if savoring a meal to come. Then – jutting her chest forward like a prized show horse – she let loose a tremendous whinny that shook the entire forest.

And despite her best efforts, Luzi couldn't help but gasp with fear.

***

The sun had only been up for a few minutes when the Psychopomp heard a piercing bellow resound from outside his yurt.

It's begun, he realized, his heart sinking.

The gnome waited alone. A squad of his most trusted guards patrolled outside the hut. They had not been pleased with their orders; several were still unable to look him in the eye. And the Psychopomp saw he'd lost their confidence.

No matter, he rationalized. *I'll gain it back. I'll make them understand why I did it. And in the end, they'll thank me. ALL of them.*

The Meridian's sigil sat on a table before him. The

Luchrupan scrutinized it for a moment, as if the thing has a life of its own. A wisp of regret seeped into his heart, but he forced it out, lest it sap his courage for what needed to be done next.

Without further delay, the Psychopomp picked up the pendant. As soon as it touched his bare hand, a jolt of electricity hit his brain. And in less time than it took to cringe, SHE was inside his mind.

"What news?" the Meridian demanded telepathically, not bothering to disguise her eagerness.

"Your warriors are at the task as we speak," the Psychopomp replied. "It should be over soon."

"You have done well," the Meridian said, the satisfaction unmistakable in her voice. "And soon enough, you shall reap your reward. I just have one more question. Did you tell anyone else about our bargain? *Anyone*?"

"As you commanded, Great Meridian, my tongue has been stayed."

There was a silence as the Meridian weighed whether he was telling the truth. "Good," the unicorn said, content with her conclusion. "Then the secret of what happened here today will die with you."

Suddenly, the Psychopomp heard the sound of yelling and struggling outside the yurt. After a few moments, the door burst open with a crash, as if something immeasurably strong kicked it down. "Who dares–" the Luchrupan king shouted. But when he saw what lay outside, he froze in horror.

Each of his guards was brutally slaughtered. Their bodies lay torn to bits on the ground, eviscerated beyond recognition.

What's happening? the Psychopomp wondered, aghast at the crude pile of flesh that used to be his most loyal warriors.

On cue, an invisible unicorn materialized on the threshold of the hut, emerging from out of thin air as he negated his cloaking powers. Slender as a whip and with a white stripe running down his face, the unicorn flashed a bloody grin and slowly walked toward the Psychopomp. His hooves clomped loudly on the floor of the hut, like hammers driving nails into a coffin.

"Meridian!" the Psychopomp yelled telepathically, clutching her sigil in his trembling hand. "Why are you doing this?"

"It's very simple," the alpha unicorn replied dispassionately. "Nobody can know that we have both rings. Not yet, anyway. And unfortunately, the guaranteed silence of your people is exponentially more valuable than any service the Pot of Gold could have ever provided us. The arithmetic is simple: you've all got to die."

The Overgruk assassin creeped closer to the gnome, gnashing his teeth in anticipation.

The Psychopomp broke out in a cold sweat, his eyes transfixed on the approaching unicorn. "But I thought we had an understanding – an alliance! You promised none of us would be killed once you have the rings... you promised!"

The Meridian snickered.

"And none of you will, little king. Because you're all going to die *today*."

"If it's any consolation, I do intend to keep my other half of the bargain," she continued. "The bloodline of Odna Han will feel my wrath. I will exterminate every single one of those rotten Quiystians, just as I pledged. After all, a Monoceros is nothing if not for their word."

"You evil goddamn–"

"Goodbye, Psychopomp," the Meridian interrupted disinterestedly. "I'll let the Hans know you send your regards."

The Psychopomp felt the alpha unicorn withdraw from his mind. He opened his mouth to scream, the agony of betrayal stinging his lips like a million bees. But before a sound could pass his lips, the Meridian's minion lunged towards him, sinking his razor-sharp teeth into the gnome's pudgy throat.

The Luchrupan king had time for a final prayer, flung out to any god who happened to be listening: *Please let it be quick.*

But to his horror, it wasn't.

21

"Fortune is like a star made of glass; just when it gleams bright-est, it shatters."

– Skuuld, son of Simael (Ragnarian representative on the Grand Council of Dama'run)

When a tsunami hits, most people will instinctually try to run away. But a tiny percentage of them – just a fraction of a fraction – will freeze and stare into the wave, enraptured by its sheer power.

There was no mistaking what camp Luzi was in.

Despite her fear, she couldn't help but be amazed by the majesty and diversity of the Monoceros. The beast with one eye stood at the forefront of the battle line, grinning with an-ticipation. An auburn unicorn at her side impatiently shifted from hoof to hoof, his horn ablaze like a torch. A lanky uni-corn behind them bristled with deadly spikes, licking her lips at the prospect of combat. And a full assembly of their kin – all just as menacing – paced and snorted beside them.

Glorious, was all Luzi could think as she gazed at the Overgruk… until she remembered they were there to kill her.

"Uchchaihshravas, my compliments on the flesh costume," the one-eyed unicorn quipped coyly.

"Karkadiann," he replied in turn, spitting out the name like a mouthful of poison. "I should have known the Meridian would send *you*."

"I wasn't sure we'd be able to get this close without you detecting our presence, even cloaked by PhoPa's fog powers," Karkadiann needled. "But I guess that spending a week in the company of a stinking, mewling ape has hobbled your senses more than either of us thought possible."

Romula and the other Scions stared at U, the savage truth hitting home.

"What does she mean? Who *are* you?"

Karkadiann laughed cruelly as U's bravado was sapped away in an instant. "Go on… show them!" she brayed, amused at the pitiful look in her former coven mate's eyes. "You might have lived like a human these final days, Uchchaihshravas. But at least you can die like a Monoceros."

U turned to the Scions. He stood defiant, a prisoner in a hostile courtroom with no chance of acquittal.

"It's not Luzi's fault," U implored sadly. And with that final plea, he transformed.

The Scions' response was not one of clemency.

"Bastard!" Romula snarled. "I'll kill you myself!" She took a step towards U, intent on ending him with a single blow. But as the mage lifted her twin swords, a deafening scream blasted across the battlefield.

"Back, wizard – he's mine!"

Moving in perfect concert, the unicorns activated their powers. The auburn unicorn burst into living fire, becoming a sentient torch. Another Monoceros manifested a shimmering, diamond skin that covered its body like a suit of armor. Yet another unicorn crackled with a golden, lightning-like energy.

As her coven mates transformed into living weapons, Karkadiann triggered her own power. There was a loud popping sound, like a cork being yanked out of a gargantuan wine bottle. A moment later – completely flaunting the laws of reality – an identical copy of Karkadiann was standing beside the original. Every detail of the unicorn was exactly the same, right down to her scooped-out eyeball. Then, in less time than it took to blink, each of those versions split in half again... and again... and again. Soon there were dozens of doppelgangers, each as ferocious as their maker. The copies joined the Monoceros ranks, swelling them to insane proportions.

"Don't worry, this will all be over soon," Karkadiann jeered, each doppelganger speaking in unison – a chorus from hell. "But first, my mistress requests an audience with the traitor."

A purple pendant hanging around her neck started to glow.

"No!" U hollered, lunging forward desperately. But before he could reach it, an irresistible wave of Deep Magic coursed out from the stone. And in the space of a breath, the Meridian seized control of their minds.

Luzi felt her limbs stiffen as the alpha unicorn's psychic powers flooded her brain. *I can't move!* she panicked. Out of the corner of her eyes, she saw U and the Scions, each stricken with the same magical paralysis. Somehow, the Nyasian could feel them connected to her own mind. That's when she realized the awful truth: they were all sharing a single consciousness... and the Meridian was in the driver's seat.

And suddenly, they were no longer in the fen at all.

***

Romula knew where she was as soon as she saw the glow.

To be fair, the lighthouse had *always* been there in the back of her mind. In many ways, she'd never left it that day. But there it was – right in front of her – its humongous gas lamps fully ablaze and beckoning homeward.

There was nowhere to go but forward.

As the gentle lapping of the ocean sounded nearby, Romula climbed the hundred and twelve steps that led to the lighthouse keep, counting each one as she passed. When she reached the top, she slowly pushed open the door and peered inside.

"Oh," she muttered involuntarily, taking a step back in horror.

A young girl and a bearded man were inside, sitting at the kitchen table and quietly singing a nursery rhyme. They looked up at Romula as she stood in the doorway, unsurprised, as if they'd been expecting her. The man was too thin – gaunt from worry or malnutrition. The girl seemed listless, uncharacteristically languid and dull. But it was them, no doubt.

It was them.

"Are you going to sit down, or are you going to abandon us... again?" the man asked, gesturing towards an empty chair. The girl looked up and gave a lackluster smile.

Romula sat down, a defiant frown masking her thumping heartbeat. The mage dug her fingernails into her palms, trying to wake herself up.

"You're not real. I'm obviously trapped in some sort of psychic hallucination. Let me guess... you're supposed to be my worst fear come to life? My husband and child resurrected to haunt me? Pretty cliché stuff. *This* is the best torture you unicorns are able to conjure? Pathetic."

The man laughed dryly.

"Same old Romula. Everyone loves a warrior until they stop fighting, huh? Relax, my love. We're not here to torture you. We're here to welcome you home."

"No..."

"Yes. Look into your daughter's eyes. See the darkness, see the cold. You can't remember her as a person anymore. She's just an ideal to you, something from a past life that gives you a reason to justify your hate. And so am I. You've forgotten all about us."

"No!" Romula insisted, her veneer of cool melting away despite her best attempts. "Don't you get it? Everything I've done – *everything* – has been to honor your memory. It's how I keep you alive. It's the only thing that makes me a hero. The only thing!"

The mage's plea elicited a weak snicker.

"Heroism isn't born from tragedy, Rom. Only villains. And you've got enough blood on your hands to fill an entire rogue's gallery."

Her husband tilted his head, teasing Romula with a half-grin.

"You have failed, unicorn-slayer. The game is over. It's time to concede defeat and join us honorably in the afterlife. You owe us *that*, at least."

"No!" the mage insisted, narrowing her eyes in determination. "This is a lie! None of this is real! None of this is real!"

"Then why do I miss you so much, mama?" her daughter asked morosely, speaking for the first time.

And even though she knew it was all fake, Romula felt her heart shatter just the same.

***

Anian awoke in the Great Hall of the House of Seung... his least favorite room in the palace.

No expense had been spared in its creation: marble floors... chamber ceilings... ornate rugs... antique furniture. The Great Hall was swept and dusted at least twice a day, and it was so large that a shout echoed for precisely four seconds when hollered from the entrance.

That was where his father stood now, dressed in that ridiculous purple surcoat of his and leaning on a diamond-handled cane. He also wore his trademark smirk, the one that reminded Anian he would never quite measure up to expectations.

"Welcome home, son," the elder Seung jabbed. "It's been a long time."

"I don't suppose that you've been keeping up with your Huo?" the old man chided, sizing up his son like a tailor measuring a suit. "From the looks of it, you've replaced your morning ablutions with a roll in the pigpen." [28]

"Father, I don't understand-"

"Oh, for the love of Kyii – it's a *metaphor*, Anian. You abandoned us. You abandoned your responsibilities, your heritage. And now you're a foreigner in your own home."

"I left for your own good!" Anian pleaded, feeling like a child begging not to be punished. "I didn't want to hurt you! Don't you see that?"

The old man laughed.

"Is that what you tell yourself? Your shameful exodus was for *our* benefit? You left home because you were scared, Anian. Because you didn't have the guts to do what was needed to keep our house in order. Because you're too weak to control your emotions."

"No... it wasn't my fault... I couldn't help it..."

"You never would have succeeded as my heir, even without your affliction," Anian's father continued mockingly. "You were always too feckless. I see that now. You're a sheep... a slug... a wiffle-waffle of the highest degree. Worst of all, you're a coward. And calling you my son is a shame I'll take to my grave."

Then his father began to laugh. It was a cruel, mocking chortle that reverberated in Anian's heart.

"Stop it," the Scion begged, putting his palms against his temples. "Please! Father!"

Old feelings began to well in Anian's heart... bad feelings. His blood pressure skyrocketed. The hairs on his arm jumped with electricity. His incisors swelled, becoming mini-daggers in his mouth.

The Raw.

Not again! he pleaded. *Not again!*

But it was too late. As his father's laughter continued,

Anian transformed into his monstrous alter ego, ending the violent metamorphosis with a blood-curdling howl. Reason fled from his mind. Salivating at the mouth, he leaped forward at his father with outstretched claws. He felt them sink into flesh. He felt the meat give way.

Lost in a bestial rage, Anian slashed again... and again... and again. He tried to scream, but couldn't form words. Instead, all he could do was howl.

So that's what he did.

***

To call Shangri-La "beautiful" would be a criminal understatement. The homeland of the Kalei Faerie is an unchained melody that vibrates to its own mystic frequency. Everything sparkles in the forest of the Kalei. Everything hums.

But for Calypsa and Eureka, there was nothing that reminded them more of home than the river.

The pixies sat together on a tree branch, listening to the breath of the water on the riverbed as if it were a symphony conducted just for them. It was so calming that neither gave much thought to why – or how – they were there in the first place. It was as if they were napping together and had just woken up.

Then they heard it.

The soft, lulling melody of a shawm carried towards them on the wind, coming from some indeterminate origin downstream. It played no discernable song – only a haunting, thirteen-note pattern – but there was something primal to the music that felt gut-churningly familiar.

"By the Deep," Calypsa whispered to Eureka. "It's the Piper."

The two were on their feet at once. Eureka reached out to her partner, trying to get her attention. But to the pixie's shock, her hand passed clear through Calypsa as if she was a ghost. Equally as surprised, Calypsa reached out to touch Eureka... with the same result.

"What's happening?" the tow-headed Fae questioned with a shaky voice. "What is this?"

The pixies' confusion took a back seat to terror when they caught a glimpse of a youngling emerging from the forest. The little one sleepily fluttered out from the trees like a drunken moth, her wings beating with a lackluster malaise that couldn't quite keep her airborne. As she neared the river, the pixie child began to drift lower, until she touched down into the water and sank below the surface with a soft "Glurp."

"No!" Calypsa cried out, following Eureka as she rushed to the river's edge. They desperately tried to fish her out, but their ghostly hands simply passed through the youngling's body. Helpless, they watched the little one drift downstream – completely submerged – powerless to do anything to save her.

Unable to avert her gaze, Calypsa stared downstream in a near-catatonia until Eureka managed to get her attention with frantic waves of her arms. The pixie turned to where she was pointing, then gasped. A massive exodus of Fae children followed in the first youngling's wake, floating out of the forest towards the river. There were hundreds of them – thousands, even – all seemingly without a sentient thought in their heads as they drifted to their deaths.

And all the while, the Piper's song called them closer.

Calypsa screamed. Eureka glowed frantically. They tried desperately to stop the younglings... to grab them... to hold them. But it was all for naught. One by one, the Fae children dropped down into the river. One by one, they were swallowed up.

Bloop.

Glomp.

Blurp.

Then, to the pixies' horror, another figure emerged from the woods: Eureka's brother. He followed the rest, lost in a mindless fugue state and completely unaware of his sister's presence as he sank into the water.

The heartrending cry that issued from Eureka nearly destroyed Calypsa.

Crushed, the two kneeled weeping on the riverbank, unable to even hold each other for comfort. Both felt something wrong about all of it, of course... something very wrong. But in that moment, it didn't matter. There was only one sensation, one possibility, one reality.

Agony.

***

The sonovabitch knew how to wield an axe... that much, John Apple could admit.

It was a good thing the tavern was vacant; the collateral damage would have been gruesome. Mugs crashed against walls. Tables splintered like plywood. Lanterns smashed to the ground.

John's foe stood his equal, both in skill and stature. Clad in a black hood that hid his face, he matched the woodsman's every expert attack... and then some. John feinted left; the masked man dodged right. John swung high; the masked man dodged low. Even his secret "trap n' slice" move – the one he and his brother had invented all those years ago – failed to draw a single drop of blood.

For some reason, John couldn't remember how long he'd been dueling with the hooded menace, or even why they were fighting in the first place. But there wasn't time to reflect on such things. Not when a razor-sharp hunk of steel was being swung at his face, anyway.

"Who th' hell are ya?" John huffed at last, backing into a defensive stance to catch his breath.

The stranger let his guard drop. Lifting his hands, he removed his hood and exposed his face.

John gasped, turning white with terror. "Et's *you!*"

His assailant laughed. When he spoke, it was without the slightest hint of an accent – in flawless, textbook Communia.

"Hello, brother. It's a pleasure to see you."

"Iggy... why're ya talkin' like 'at?" a puzzled John asked, unable to process what he was hearing. "Whuts happenin'? Am I losin' muh feckin' mind?"

"*Am I losin' muh feckin' mind?*" Iggy mocked sarcastically, imitating his sibling. "Leave it to my big brother to remain pathetically stereotypical, even in his hallucinations. I mean, what's next? Soon you'll be saying, '*This can't be real!*' or '*By the hairy balls of Dis!*' or some other ridiculous goddamn thing."

"Stup it, Iggs! Pleez, lil' bruh... why're ya doin this?"

"It should have been you," his sibling hissed. "If it had been you in my place, I would have made a difference with my life. But look at what *you've* done. Look at all the hate and misery and death you can lay claim to as part of your legacy. The wrong brother died that day. You're a loser, John. And you know what losers do?"

"Whut?"

"They *lose*."

Iggy raised his axe again, grinning fiendishly.

"You know the funny thing? I used to look up to you. You were my hero. And now look at us... a couple of brothers fighting to the death. So I guess no matter who wins, you've failed!"

"Iggs! Dun' do it!"

But John's plea went unheeded. His brother lunged forward with a mighty chop of his axe, barely missing the woodsman's face. Iggy pressed his advantage, dropping his arm back for another hack. Acting on instinct, John swung his own weapon at his brother's overexposed shoulder. His aim was true; the entire arm was lopped off with a sickening ssshhhluuuunnnk.

As Iggy's arm crashed to the ground – still clutching his axe – the expression on his face didn't change. He leaned down and picked the weapon up with his other hand, laughing all the while.

And back he came with his one good arm, swinging for John's head.

＊＊＊

If there was one thing that Cobby hated, it was nothing.

The chupacabra woke on a deserted shore, somewhere un-recognizable and desolate and cold. Listless waves lapped on the beach. Clouds obscured the sky, casting a dreary shroud over the sun. And an endless stretch of horizon stretched out before him, leading somewhere – or perhaps nowhere, from the looks of it.

Not a soul was in sight, friend or foe. Not a single living creature crawled, flew or flopped as far as the eye could see.

Nothing. Empty. Boring.

"So I guess I'm fucking *dead* or something?" Cobby quipped, the sound of his voice echoing along the shoreline.

"Fucking dead... what a bummer," the chupacabra muttered quietly.

Not sure where he was going, Cobby picked a random direction and began walking slowly down the coast. The tide swallowed up his four-toed tracks as he went, erasing any evidence of his presence, almost as if the land didn't want him there at all.

As he plodded along, he told himself some jokes, trying to break the awful silence:

"What creature is constantly getting lost? A where-wolf!"

"How do you turn bread into butter? Feed it to a cow!"

"What did the elephant say to the human? How do you breathe through that tiny thing?"

But no matter how awful the joke was, nobody laughed. Nobody smiled. Nobody told him to shut up. And suddenly, Cobby realized that this was it – *the afterlife* – and it was just as dull as he'd been afraid it would be.

He was alone. He was bored.

Forever.

"Ha ha fucking-ha," the chupacabra whispered. "This isn't funny at all."

And with a pathetic sigh, he continued trudging along the shore.

****

For Awf'l, the nightmare was simple.

Rats.

Thousands and thousands of hungry, dirty rats.

They crawled all over her – violating every privacy – chattering and gnawing with the tiny daggers in their mouths. Their tails wriggled like sentient bullwhips; their eyes glowed red as blood moons. The troll didn't dare scream for fear they'd crawl in her mouth. So all she could manage was a sustained, terrified whimper: "Muhmuhmuhmuhmuhmuh-muhmuhmuh..."

As the creatures continued to swarm, Awf'l forced herself to concentrate on a coping technique that Cobby once taught her... the Happy Green, he called it. "There's just one thing you need to remember," he said. "If things ever get scary and none of us are around to help, I want you to think of *ten green things* – anything, just as long as they're green. Think hard about each one. Say the words to yourself. And I promise you'll feel better when you're done."

With Cobby's pledge in mind, the troll closed her eyes tight and feverishly began putting her limited knowledge of Communia to work.

Green apple, she thought, as a rodent skittered across her stomach.

Green tree, she told herself, trying to ignore the chewing on her neck.

Green froggy, she imagined, cringing as a rat's tail whisked around in her nostril.

It helped – for a little while, at least. But the rats kept up their inexhaustible assault, steadily nipping away at the troll's sanity with each bite of their incisors.

Tears ran down Awf'l's face. A tiny whimper escaped her lips, the sound almost inaudible among the scurrying of tiny, clawed feet.

And someplace far away, a cruel voice laughed.

***

Meanwhile, Luzi and U stood gazing down into hell: Mount Meruum.

Standing nearly twenty miles high, the massive volcano is the largest of its kind in the known realms. Inside its core, billions of tons of lava roil and churn, an ocean of fire ready to destroy anything it touches... even unicorns.

Luzi blinked her eyes like a sleepwalker, trying to adjust to her new surroundings. "Wha- what's happening?" she asked, gradually regaining her senses.

"We're in astral form," U replied with dismay. "The Meridian has trapped us inside our own memories with her psychic abilities. The others are battling their own nightmares, no doubt. And knowing my mistress, they're just as terrible as this one."

"I don't understand," Luzi said, glancing around at the mountain. "Where are we?"

U sighed.

"Many years ago, when I was still a young stallion, my cursed vision almost drove me to madness. I came here to Mount Meruum to end it all, like many other unicorns have. But just as I was about to leap into the magma, the Meridian managed to track me down. She stood beside me – right where you are now – and told me something that saved my life. 'If you never know the joy of seeing a living flower, you will never suffer the sorrow of seeing it die,' she said. 'Fate has *spared* you, not *spurned* you.' And for a long time, I believed her. It gave me a way to face another day, a way to make sense of my curse. There was no other alternative. There was no sense in hoping for one."

He looked Luzi's way. "Until I knew that *you* existed, Luzi."

At that very moment, as if she'd been waiting for her cue to enter, the Meridian's voice boomed out:

"WELL IF *THAT* ISN'T TRUE LOVE, I DON'T KNOW WHAT IS."

In an instant, the alpha unicorn materialized in astral form on the opposite rim of the volcano. Strangely, she didn't seem angry. Instead, there was an expression of mild amusement on her face, as if she was the only attendee at a surprise party thrown in Luzi and U's honor.

Even from that distance, Luzi couldn't help but be captivated. Unlike U, the Meridian made no attempt to hide her grandeur, spreading out her immense wings to intimidate them as she approached.

Those who have seen her in repose have described her as beatific. Those who have seen her in combat have called her terrifying. None – friend or foe – have ever called her ordinary.

"So *this* is the Nyasian girl you're willing to throw away the future of your entire race for?" the Meridian heckled. "I'm not impressed. To be honest, I thought she'd be taller."

"As for you, my erstwhile champion, I have to admit to a certain level of disappointment. Surely you understood what had to happen here today... and what will have to happen tomorrow? The humans must die. There's no other choice. And it was very silly for you to ally yourself with them."

"Be ready for anything," U warned Luzi as the Meridian strolled closer, ignoring her taunts. "She has near-unlimited power here, and won't be afraid to use it."

"Oh, don't be so dramatic," the alpha unicorn chastised. "I didn't bring you here to fight, Uchchaihshravas. What would be the point to that?"

"So why *are* we here, my mistress?"

"Because I have a proposition for you," the Meridian replied coyly.

"I was wrong about the Nyasian," she continued. "I see that now. I should have given you the chance to probe your unique... connection. I almost robbed you of that. So as penance, I am prepared to grant you an incredible boon. Mercy.

"If you abandon this doomed resistance and surrender the ring, I swear on my honor as a Monoceros that your lives and safety are guaranteed. There will be tolls that must be rendered, of course, amends that must be made. But you shall both live to the end of your natural days as long as you follow Overgruk law."

"By the Deep... you're serious, aren't you?" U said, dumbfounded.

The Meridian nodded.

"The end is coming soon. *Io-X'likon'sh* is at hand; I've seen it, I've felt it. And we will need soldiers like yourself to see it done. The Third Age of the world ends today. When I have both rings in my possession, a Fourth Age will begin – that of the unicorn. Their deaths... so *we* may live."

"But you don't understand!" U protested. "There's a chance of co-existing with the humans. We've been wrong, all this time. This doesn't have to end in war – for any of us!"

The Meridian tsssked in disappointment.

"Oh, Uchchaihshravas. You still don't get it, even after all these years. This isn't about war or diplomacy. It never has been. It's about *evolution*."

"But mistress!"

The Meridian rose to her full height, towering above them in the sunlight.

"Enough! I've made my offer. The only thing remaining is your reply. What do you say? Shall we go home? Or do we see this through to the end? Weal or woe, Uchchaihshravas? Speak now!"

For a moment, U just stared back at her, matching the alpha unicorn's gaze. Suddenly, the corners of his mouth ticked up in a smile.

The Meridian's eyes narrowed.

"What's so amusing?"

"You were right to choose this memory, you know," U told her, a clever assertiveness creeping into his voice. "It was the worst moment of my life. I still remember every second of it. I'll *never* forget. You stood right there – right in that goddamned spot – and told me that my death vision was a blessing. You said fate had spared me, not spurned me. And I ate it up."

"I remember, Uchchaihshravas. It was all true. Every word of it."

U's smile twisted upside down with a sudden menace.

"Well, maybe it's time to judge that for yourself, my mistress."

Before the Meridian could stop him, U opened a space in the back of his mind that he'd been hiding in reserve. Instantaneously, a tsunami of memories flooded over the Meridian, completely overwhelming her. In all her long years, she'd never felt such an agony.

BARREN FORESTS DESICCATED RIVERS BLEACHING BONES DESERT DUNES CRACKING EARTH EMPTY FIELDS FRIENDLESS DEATH HOLLOW BATTLE MASSACRE PITS BODIES EMPTY BELLIES FOOTPRINTS FADING WORM-EATEN DUSTY PAGES CRUMBLING TUNNELS BRIDGES COLLAPSING FALLOW OCEANS GREY GAUNT SHADOW SEARCHING SALLOW WILTED WITHERED ABSENCE VOID MISSING PIECES LOST ALONE DARKNESS DESPAIR...

"What... is... this?" she gasped, struggling in vain to regain her senses as the images continued to explode in her head.

"The Dying Eyes," U replied grimly. "You're experiencing seven millennia of despair and isolation distilled into a single moment. You've been inside my mind so many times, I've lost count. But you never bothered to actually see the world through my eyes even once, did you? *Did you?*"

As the Meridian thrashed in agony, the astral plane trembled with her reply.

"STOP!"

U tried his best to shield Luzi and the Scions from the psychic feedback. But the inevitable spillover hit them as well. They were seized by the onslaught, held captive by its sheer gravity. In the process, the unicorn's memories became completely exposed to Luzi and the Scions. Every single moment of his life – including his relationship with Luzi – was laid bare before them in an instant. One by one, they bore witness to his childhood. His battles. His murders. His fears. His loves.

Everything.

But there was no time to dwell on any of it. Unable to contain the immense energy coursing through it, the pendant hanging around Karkadiann's neck exploded into a million shards. There was a brilliant, brief flash of light, like an ember crackling in a campfire.

Nine pairs of eyes opened. Nine sets of lungs took a collective breath.

We're free! Luzi gleefully realized.

She wasn't alone. The others turned to face each other in a daze. But before anyone could speak a word, Romula grabbed Anian's arm.

"I was wrong about the unicorn," the grizzled old mage whispered to her lieutenant. "Get them out of here, Anian. *All* of them. And forgive me for what I'm about to do."

With that final declaration, Romula squared around to face the Overgruk. In the space of a breath, she soaked up all the available Deep Magic around her, igniting with a golden glow that blazed like the beacon of a lighthouse.

Somewhere, a man and a girl nodded with approval.

"Scions!" Romula hollered. "Give these bastards hell!"

"No!" Anian yelled, finally understanding his mentor's plan.

"They've broken free!" Karkadiann screamed to her peers as she saw what was happening. "Kill the wizard! Kill her now!"

By then, it was too late – for either side. Loosing a bellow equal to the mightiest Ragnarian berserker, Romula released every iota of the Ubamota energy she'd gathered, aiming it in a circle around the Scions. Like a magnifying lens burning up ants, the massive blast expanded outward, vaporizing half of the unicorns in its wake. It was an awe-inspiring sight... the stuff of legends... the stuff of heroes.

But just as she knew it would, the effort proved too much for Romula to bear. The massive force of the Deep Magic explosion coursed through her body, ripping it apart and turning it into a flesh-colored mist that drifted away into the air. In the space of a second – maybe less – it was as if the mage never existed.

And that was the last the world ever saw of Romula Zazzau.

22

"Rom!" the Scions cried out in unison, their grief making Luzi's heart skip a beat.

Seizing the element of surprise – Romula's final gift to them – the remaining six Scions rushed into battle. The warriors reacted as a single unit, like they'd done so many times before. But this time, it was with a fury they'd never known they were capable of.

Anian was the first into the fray, shredding the throat of a charging unicorn with a single pass of his claws. The stabbing horn of another punctured his shoulder from behind, but he quickly recovered, took its jaw off with a roundhouse swipe, and leaped back in the thick of battle.

John also took the offensive directly to the unicorns, barreling into their midst like a mad bull. The woodsman rushed at them with his glowing axe, mowing down a unicorn with a series of vicious chops. On the final hit, he hurled his axe at another charging unicorn, which lodged in its withers and dropped the beast to the ground.

Nearby, Cobby bounded and catapulted across the battlefield with an uncanny agility, slicing with his claws in every direction and making his presence known in a thousand ways. Awf'l followed closely in his wake with her granite fists flailing in circles, moving with a nimbleness that belied her size.

Meanwhile, Calypsa and Eureka hovered over the battlefield, creating substantive force shields to cover their comrades' backs. A unicorn spotted them and leaped into the air with its mouth wide open, intent on gnawing them to bits. But the pixies suddenly cut course and zipped through the beast's eyeballs – one in each socket – exploding out its ears like self-guided crossbow bolts.

It was a valiant effort. It was fearsome... brutal... inspired. But it wasn't enough.

It wasn't nearly enough.

Bolstered by an endless supply of Karkadiann's dopplegangers, the Overgruk encircled the Scions, tightening their ranks like a noose around a condemned prisoner's neck. Flames burst in the air. Shrapnel whooshed by their heads. And everywhere were snapping jaws and crushing hooves, all craving one thing: death.

Just then, there was a tremendous commotion from the surrounding forest. For a moment, Luzi expected to see some kind of awful, new unicorn emerge from the woods. But when she spotted the source of the ruckus, the Nyasian's heart jumped in her chest.

Dis be praised! she marveled, her jaw dropping at the sight.

Dozens of Luchrupan warriors charged forward, each wielding armum weapons and screaming like banshees. At the front of the pack was Silas, leading the attack with an unflappable confidence. Both fists glowing with golden fire – the same he'd threatened the Scions with just hours earlier – Silas unleashed an expertly aimed blast of Ubamota energy that seared a hole through a unicorn's head, dropping it to the ground like a sack of potubers.

"Defend the grove!" he hollered to his peers, diving into the midst of the fight.

The abrupt assault divided the unicorn ranks. Some hesitated, unsure if they should continue the battle against the Scions or confront the new threat. Others had no such confusion, immediately counter-attacking the Luchrupan. Their retribution was swift and cruel. One Monoceros bit a large chunk out of a gnome's torso, leaving the ghastly leftovers twitching on the ground. A pair of Karkadiann's doppelgangers tore an unlucky Luchrupan in half between their snapping jaws. Some of the gnomes were seared to the bone by Deep Magic energy blasts. Others were stomped to jelly beneath steel hooves.

While the Luchrupan's attack provided a temporary distraction, it also added complications. Suddenly, there was no safe harbor amid the pandemonium; an errant step in any direction could mean certain death.

"Where can we go?" Luzi yelled. "They're everywhere!"

U was about to retort when a third voice called out, startling them both.

"I wouldn't worry about *them*," it said, hissing with malice. "You've got your own misery to deal with."

***

As the battle raged around them, Luzi and U spun around to face their assailant: Karkadiann.

The unicorn grinned cockily, like a cat that cornered a pair of mice.

"Just for the record, we had the drop on you almost an hour ago," she sneered. "We could have slaughtered you all as you snoozed by the fire, and you couldn't have done a thing about it. But I refused to give the command."

U was unimpressed. "How magnanimous of you. So why are we still alive?"

Karkadiann tossed her head back and laughed, amused at his defiance.

"Oh, Uchchaihshravas. Did you really think I'd let you pass from this world without allowing me to reclaim the honor you stole all those years ago?"

"I beat you in a fair fight, Karkadiann," U countered. "I could have killed you. I took your eye instead. And you'd remember that mercy now if there's a shred of empathy left in that callow heart of yours."

The empty socket in Karkadiann's head twitched.

"You call what you did mercy?" the unicorn snarled. "You *ate my eyeball*, Uchchaihshravas! To leave me scarred forever with my failure was a fate worse than death, and you know it. If the Meridian hadn't forbidden our rematch, you would have been worm food long ago."

"There was a time I would have given anything to relieve the torment you so graciously gifted me," Karkadiann continued. "But do you know what? Over the many years I've been waiting for my revenge – as the drudgery of two thousand years in the caves has taken its toll – I've finally come to realize something about the pain."

The corners of her mouth curled into a sick smile. "I *like* it."

"Karkadiann... please. I beg you."

The Meridian's lieutenant chortled at U's plea.

"*Please?* Pathetic. You're even beginning to talk like them, traitor. The warrior I once knew is truly gone, isn't he? Well, I'll just have to try and salvage whatever honor I can from this." [29]

Karkadiann began to multiply, creating fresh doppelgangers with her powers. Soon, dozens stood before them, a platoon of killers united under one mind. They slowly surrounded Luzi and U, each hoof step deliberate as a nail in a coffin.

"Do you have any last words before we send you on your journey to oblivion?" Karkadiann asked.

"That's funny," U replied, digging his hooves into the ground for traction. "I was about to ask you the same thing."

Karkadiann grinned. And with dozens of simultaneous whinnies, the doppelgangers rushed forward for the kill.

***

If Luzi hadn't been combat-trained by U's own hand, she never would have stood a chance against the onslaught. Staring down a charging unicorn is like standing in front of an oncoming avalanche... a raging firestorm. And many has been the warrior who failed that merciless test of fortitude.

As she watched the army of doppelgangers rush towards her, dread gripped Luzi's heart like a vice. But the events of the past week had altered something deep within her, and fear no longer had the paralyzing effect it once did.

When one of the beasts tried to impale Luzi on its horn, she planted her feet, like a tree holding fast against a hurricane. *This is it!* she told herself, remembering her training. The unicorn lowered its head and thrust at Luzi. At the last moment, she nimbly hopped to the side and swung her shield, decapitating the creature with a single hack. It was a textbook strike – just like she'd been taught to make. But to her shock, instead of spouting a torrent of blood, the severed head and torso instantly disintegrated in a sinister puff of smoke. And in a moment, it was as if the unicorn was never there at all.

A fake! Luzi realized.

But there was no time to try and sort out her next target; *it* chose *her*. She whipped around in time to ward off another onslaught, barely dodging out of the way of a jabbing horn. In the same motion, Luzi spun around and sliced at the doppelganger with a single, clean stroke. Again, the body went up in smoke.

Damn you! the Nyasian huffed, her frustration mounting.

Nearby, U pounced on the nearest doppelganger with a preternatural speed, driving his horn straight through the beast's brain. The renegade Monoceros didn't take a single moment to gloat. In the blink of an eye, he spun around and faced off against another doppelganger, lashing out with a savage kick to its throat.

Meanwhile, yet another duplicate creeped up behind U, ready to plunge its horn through the back of his head. And if not for Luzi, it would have succeeded. "Look out!" she hollered, catching sight of the attack from the corner of her eye.

Without a moment's hesitation, the Nyasian hurled her shield forward like a giant discus. The armum soared through the air, spinning violently until it connected with the doppelganger's neck.

POOF!

Luzi immediately tried to manifest another shield. But halfway through, another clone lunged forward, snipping at her still-extended hand. With a savage chomp, it bit off the tip of Luzi's index finger, slicing clean through the bone.

The Nyasian grimaced as blood spurted from the wound. As her concentration shattered, Luzi's half-formed armum disappeared, leaving her defenseless.

The doppelganger saw its chance. It sprung for her throat, intent on ending the battle with a single bite. There was only time for one, desperate move. Swelling with adrenaline – acting purely on instinct – Luzi rematerialized her shield in her unwounded hand. In the same motion, she sliced forward with an uppercut. The blow connected through sheer luck, bifurcating the doppelganger's head.

Take THAT, you motherfucker! Luzi gasped as it vanished.

The Nyasian peeked backwards in a desperate attempt to see if U was still alive. But there was no time to get her bearings; another clone was upon her in the space of a heartbeat.

The remaining doppelgangers circled Luzi and U, assailing them relentlessly with a syncopated, hive mentality. Fighting the creatures off was a losing proposition from the very start. For each of Karkadiann's copies they destroyed, two more stepped up to take their place. All they could do was keep swinging away or die. And Luzi knew it was only a matter of time before they both made a fatal mistake.

As she continued to hack at the clones, Luzi frantically searched the battlefield for any sign of the real Karkadiann. But each copy was perfectly identical. There wasn't one physical difference between any of them. It was hopeless... goddamn hopeless.

And that's when Luzi noticed something that made her suck in her breath.

As each doppelganger attacked, it gnashed its teeth and narrowed its eyes in a display of mercilessness, a crucial component of the unicorn fear factor. But all the way across the battlefield – to the right and rear of the group – one of the unicorns had a different expression on its face.

A smile.

As Luzi's jaw dropped, the smiler met her eyes. Abruptly, Karkadiann's grin disappeared as she realized she'd been spotted. Digging her hooves in the ground, the unicorn prepared to dash into the safety of the crowd once again.

There was no time for the Nyasian to second guess herself.

With the bravado of a doomed gladiator, Luzi barreled straight ahead at full steam. It was madness, she knew. Or perhaps stubbornness – they were impossible to tell apart any more. She slipped past a few desperate jaw snaps from the duplicates, no longer astounded at her own abilities. When Luzi reached Karkadiann, she swung her shield with all her might at the creature's horn. The unicorn recoiled in a last-ditch effort to dodge the blow, and for a horrifying moment, Luzi thought she'd miscalculated the distance. But then there was a bright explosion of sparks, like a knife hitting a grind-stone, and a terrifying shriek that chilled her to the bone.

In slow motion – almost like she was dreaming – Luzi watched Karkadiann's body crumple to the ground. As the unicorn landed with a thump in the dirt, the remaining clones instantly dissipated. Odious smoke clouds wafted across the battlefield and vanished into the air.

Karkadiann lay still, silver streams of blood spurting out of the stump on her head like liquid mercury. The fire had left the unicorn; she was a popped bubble, emptied of all vitality.

Taking a deep breath, Luzi moved to finish her off. But before the Nyasian could make the killing strike, a hand touched her shoulder.

Luzi looked back to see U, who had returned to his human form.

"Wait... I should be the one who sees this through," he said solemnly. "I owe her that much, at least."

Luzi nodded and stepped back.

U moved up to take her place. He raised his sword and looked down at Karkadiann. The dying unicorn gazed up at U, gurgling on a throatful of blood.

"Your time will come soon," she wheezed. "Remember that, traitor."

"I will, my sister," U replied. "Travel well."

And with a single, swift stroke, he lopped off her head.

***

After U dealt the death blow, he and Luzi turned back to the battle, expecting to see a field of corpses and a dozen waiting unicorns. But to their surprise, the fight raged on – and so did the Scions.

"Gods be damned, they're still alive!" U muttered with astonishment.

If it had been any other six warriors who stood against a murder of unicorns, the fight would have been over before it began, Luzi realized. That they'd survived this long was a testament to their skill – and guts. But despite their valiant resistance, it was clear the Scions wouldn't last much longer without help.

Unless someone does something about it.

Luzi turned to U, expecting an argument. But to her surprise, the unicorn just raised his armum in a warrior's salute and smiled in that inscrutable way of his, as if everything was going exactly the way he'd planned it all along.

"No regrets," he said, nodding.

"No regrets," she concurred, her eyes blazing with resolve.

And with the confidence that only certain death provides, they rushed into the fray.

The battle raged for several more minutes. The screams of agony echoed endlessly in the bloody morning, blending together in a surreal fugue. Through it all, Luzi kept swinging, determined to kill just one more unicorn before she met her end. *I'm not afraid,* she told herself, expecting every breath to be her last. *I'm not afraid.*

Then, just as her exhausted muscles began to seize up, she cocked back her arm for another strike – only to find there was nothing left to attack.

"By the gnarled nards of Dis," she whispered to herself in astonishment. "Did we just fucking win?"

Luzi looked out on the battlefield, taking in the full scope of the carnage for the first time. Mutilated bodies – both unicorn and Luchrupan – were strewn about the field in various states of dismemberment. The musty, salty smell of blood hung in the air, inescapable and unignorable. *I was wrong,* she realized with dismay. *There are no winners here at all.*

Suddenly, a relieved voice called out from across the gore and doom.

"Luzi!"

The Nyasian turned around and saw U sprinting towards her. Her nerves numb, her tongue tied, Luzi could only watch as he swept her into his arms, hugging her so tightly she feared she might pop.

"Thank you thank you thank you," the unicorn muttered gratefully.

Luzi must have groaned or whimpered, because U came to his senses and pulled away from their embrace. A sudden worry in his eyes, he looked her up and down, his gaze finally settling on the bloody stump where her fingertip used to be.

"Oh! Your hand!"

Fussing nervously, U ripped a piece of cloth from Luzi's tunic and wrapped a makeshift tourniquet around her severed finger. "Does it hurt?" he asked, holding her hand tenderly as he worked. "I should have been paying more attention. It's all my fault. If I'd just have-"

"Ssshhh," Luzi told him, gently pressing one of her unbloodied fingers to his lips. "It doesn't hurt. Not anymore."

The pair looked at each other, acknowledging the true depth of their connection for the first time. It isn't longevity that makes such feelings exist. Some couples can cohabit each other's lives for years and never truly know each other. Others need but hours. What Luzi and U shared in that moment was beyond thought or time, transcended magic or science. It was the end and beginning of all things, the alpha *and* omega. And "love" is too cheap a word to describe it.

Unable to stop themselves, lost in their own gravity, they leaned in for a kiss. But their moment of epiphany was short-lived. Mere seconds after their lips touched, a familiar voice cut the air.

"Well, I have to admit, *this* isn't what I expected to find."

Startled, U and Luzi turned around to see the Scions. Each had a grimace on their face to match their myriad cuts and bruises. Beside them stood Silas, flanked by a crew of his bloody and beaten kin.

"I'm sorry to interrupt such a tender moment," Anian said. "But we really need to talk."

23

You can't balance the scales of fate by weighing the wind."

– Ahmed Ata, 78th imam supreme of Abyssinia

Separating from their embrace, Luzi and U shifted into fighting stances and prepared for the worst. For a long time, nobody said anything. Swamp crickets chirped. Leaves rustled in the trees.

Finally, U broke the tense silence with a simple declaration.

"If you're planning on killing us, you're going to need a lot more firepower, don't you think?"

Gritting her teeth at U's lack of diplomacy, Luzi braced for a violent reprisal. But Anian just shook his head in exhaustion.

"It's been an unbelievably terrible day," he pleaded. "Do you think we can skip the 'If we wanted you dead, you'd be dead already' speech?"

Not letting his guard down, U turned to Silas.

"And what about you? Shall we trade words or blood?"

Silas gestured about the battlefield.

"There's been too much sorrow today – too much, indeed," he replied, holding up his hands in surrender. "Like the were-wolf said, all we want to do is talk."

Luzi and U exchanged a long, wary look.

"For the sake of argument, let's pretend that we believe you," U begrudgingly granted. "What happens now?"

"That's a no-brainer," Anain replied. "We're headed back to Dama'run with that ring... just like we planned to do all along."

"You, Nyasian, are welcome to accompany us back," he continued, glancing at Luzi. "Hell, the city council will probably give you a medal for what you've done."

Anian turned his attention back to U.

"*You*, however, are hardly a humdrum conundrum, unicorn. We've seen inside your mind. We know what you've done. Your past is stained with so much blood that I don't think you can ever be washed clean of it."

The werewolf folded his arms across his chest.

"But we also know what you've done to protect this ring – what it's cost you. And if anyone can appreciate the need for a second chance, it's us."

"So what do you think, Lord Seung?" U asked boldly, as if he didn't care what the answer was. "Do I deserve redemption, or not?"

Anian tapped his foot as he pondered his reply.

"Do you know what Romula told me before she died?" he said at last. "*Get them to safety... all of them.* And if she believed in you, I suppose that I can try, too. I say let the Dama'run Council decide your fate. They'll most likely execute you, of course. But if you're willing to accept the risk, I'm willing to testify on your behalf – whatever that's worth."

The werewolf turned to his companions.

"Still, my opinion is just one of six. What about the rest of you?"

There was a brief silence, then John stepped forward. As he spoke, the woodsman struggled to control his deep, backwoods accent. It was a valiant effort; Luzi could almost understand nearly two of every three words.

"Y'all know me. I dun abide by many ethik'l codes. But if't weren't fer this feckin' unicorn, this ring'd be settin' on a unicorn's horn right 'bout now. We all owe'm a blud det, and it's one ah'm meanin' tah repay."

John held out his hand to U. "Blud det. Ah' mean it."

U shook the woodsman's meaty paw solemnly.

Anian gestured to Calypsa and Eureka. "And what about you two?"

The pixies wordlessly conferred with each other, communicating by shifting the colors of their glowing wings.

"This unicorn has maimed and murdered on a scale that we've only had a slight glimpse into," Calypsa replied at last. "We ignore that fact at our own peril."

"But we've also seen what kind of compassion he's capable of," Calypsa continued. "It reminds Eureka and me of all the reasons why we left Shangri-La in the first place. People are transformed not by being loved, but by learning to love others. It's more powerful than the deepest hate or fear or tradition. Nothing can stand in its way – not even the gods. And certainly not us. We vote yes."

Eureka glowed brightly in agreement and proudly took her partner's hand.

Anian rubbed his chin thoughtfully. "What about you, Cobby?"

The chupacabra nodded approvingly at U. "That bastard over there knows what it feels like to be a castaway, just like the rest of us. That's gotta be worth something."

"Besides," Cobby added with a sad, mischievous smile. "It'll really piss off the council if we bring him along. It's *exactly* what Rom would have wanted."

Anian turned to Awf'l, seeking a final vote.

"How about you, Aw-"

But before he could finish his sentence, the troll lunged forward and engulfed U in a huge hug.

"Hrrrawrggh!" she gushed enthusiastically.

"It looks like you have the official Awf'l seal of approval," Anian said, chuckling as U tried to nonchalantly wipe gobs of drool off his cloak.

The unicorn lowered his eyes humbly.

"Thank you," he said softly. "I won't let you down, I swear it. And when we reach safety, I'll personally-"

The werewolf held up his hands.

"Not to be rude, but let's save the gratitude for later if you don't mind. Right now, we've got another problem to solve. Namely, getting the hell out of here before any more of your coven mates arrive."

The Scions glanced uneasily at each other.

"Anian's right," Calypsa agreed. "We need to get on the road as soon as possible. Every minute we linger here brings us closer to death."

"But we're still a week's journey from Dama'run," Cobby protested. "Even if we ride without stopping, we'll never make it there before the Overgruk get another chance to hit us."

U nodded.

"The chupacabra is right. And next time, we won't be so lucky... I guarantee it."

"We've got to do *something*," Anian insisted.

"Yes... but what?"

Silas cleared his throat.

"Allow me to make a suggestion. Perhaps it's best that you leave our grove the way you originally planned to... through the Pot of Gold."

A round of laughter resounded from the Scions.

"You must be fucking mad!" Anian replied, speaking on their behalf. "Why in the name of the Seven Unholy Gates would we trust you after what just happened?"

Silas shrugged.

"I know you must doubt our intentions at this point. You'd be fools if you didn't, indeed. But although you can never truly trust someone acting out of magnanimity, you can *always* believe someone acting out of self-interest."

"Oh, really?" Anian asked skeptically. "And what's in this for you?"

"Our lives!" Silas spat out, finally losing his cool. "By the gods! Are you really this daft, or are you just yanking my globes?"

Silas shot Luzi an icy look.

"We all know the Meridian will never stop coming for that thing hanging around the Nyasian's neck. And as long as it remains within an eagle's flight of our grove, my people will never be safe. But if we can get the ring to Dama'run as quickly as possible, maybe – just maybe – her wrath will follow. It's the only hope. *For all of us.*"

Anian jabbed his finger at the gnome.

"How do we even know this is a genuine offer? Where is your coward of a king, anyway? Let's hear the words from his own mouth – take us to him!"

"I'm afraid we can't do that," Silas answered.

"Why not?"

"Because he's *dead.*"

The Luchrupan's statement took the entire group by surprise.

"We found the Psychopomp and his personal guards with their throats torn out shortly after the unicorns arrived," Silas explained. "Apparently, the Overgruk were planning to double-cross us as soon as they got their hands on the ring. It seems they started with our king."

"Was *that* part of your plan?" Cobby quipped, not bothering to disguise his sarcasm.

"My kin and I had nothing to do with this!" Silas vehemently retorted. "Only the Psychopomp and his guards knew about the ambush. The rest of us didn't find out until the Monoceros were already in the village. If we'd have known, we'd never would have allowed it. He betrayed us ... just the same as he betrayed you."

"Do you really expect us to believe that?"

The Luchrupan nodded. "I do, indeed. Because it's the *truth.*"

The Scions glanced at each other cautiously. In the past, Romula had always been the one to make these decisions. And now – in this moment – they felt her absence profoundly. But a choice needed to be made. There was no time to argue.

Together, they looked Anian's way.

"Dammit, I never asked to be in charge!" he insisted, backpedaling. "All I've ever wanted to do was get us all back home alive!"

"And that's exactly what makes you a good leader," Calypsa pointed out, as Eureka nodded in agreement. "You're first in command now, Anian. This is *your* call. We'll stand by you, either way. Just like we did for Rom."

"Fuggin' right," John confirmed.

"We got your back, furbag," Cobby added, punching him on the shoulder. "Just make sure to bring us some souvenirs when you get back from your power trip, huh?"

Buoyed by his comrades' faith, Anian paused in thought. When the Quiystian spoke, he could almost hear his mentor's voice, as if the old, cantankerous mage were speaking through him from beyond the grave.

"Fine, Lord Silas – we'll do it your way... the Pot of Gold it is. I guess that if you have to eat shit, it's best to take big bites, huh?"

Cobby hung his head dejectedly. "Anian just told a joke? *Now* I'm worried."

"But I want you to keep one thing in mind," the werewolf warned Silas. "Make one move to cross us – or give me a glimmer of suspicion that you're even contemplating it – and I personally guarantee you'll be the first to die."

The gnome gave him a grim nod.

"That seems to be the price of trust these days. Now follow

me. You're about to see a miracle only a small handful of outsiders have had the privilege of witnessing."

"What's that?" Luzi asked with wide eyes.

The Luchrupan smiled.

"We're going to summon a rainbow," he said.

***

As the group proceeded to the Pot of Gold, some of the gnomes fanned out toward the village perimeter, calling to their peers as they went: "Anrud o'din! Anrud o'din!"

"What are they saying?" Anian suspiciously asked Silas, watching them scurry off into the distance.

"There's no direct translation from our tongue," the Luchrupan replied. "But if you had to put it into Communia, I suppose you could call it the Sacrament of Colors." [30]

When the group arrived at the Pot of Gold, Silas clustered them around it. Meanwhile, the Luchrupan arranged themselves in widening, concentric circles. In just a few minutes, hundreds of gnomes from all corners of the village had assembled around the Pot of Gold, with more stragglers arriving every second. The process was meticulous and solemn. As each gnome took their place in the formation, they remained reverently silent... a far cry from their curious and playful dispositions from earlier.

"How long will this take?" Cobby asked Silas, unable to keep his impatience on ice any longer.

"Summoning a rainbow requires a critical mass of believers," the Luchrupan responded, holding up his hand for patience. "We must wait for the others."

"The others?" Cobby queried. "How many?"

Silas glanced at him sideways. "*All* of them."

Eventually, when the last of the Luchrupan were assembled around the Pot of Gold, Silas lifted his hands up high, like the conductor of a band striking up a tune. "My family!" he called out, turning in a circle as he spoke. "Our guests carry an item of great evil with them. Creatures of even greater malevolence seek to claim it as their own. And there is only one way to make sure they fail in their endeavor. We must summon the Anrud o'din!"

"Anrud o'din!" his kinfolk echoed. "Anrud o'din!"

Silas gestured for silence.

"I know your hearts are still reeling from what happened this day, but time is of the essence. I ask you to follow me now. Let your voices reach the heavens and bring the rainbow back with them!"

The gnome turned in the direction of the cauldron.

"To the old gods... to the new gods... to the gods who never were... we beseech you... we command you... hear our call!"

Without further pomp, he began to chant. The noise that issued forth from the Luchrupan was like nothing Luzi expected to hear. It was resonant and deep, like the low of a bull camel, yet with the gentle, sustained vibrato of a monk's *ohm*. With a practiced unity, the other gnomes joined Silas's one-note song. Within a few moments, the entire assembly – fathers, mothers, children – were locked into the supernatural hymn.

And that's when the magic happened.

Before Luzi's unbelieving eyes, the gold coins inside the pot melted into magma. As the Luchrupan continued their chant, slowly increasing in volume and speed, the liquid gold started swirling to match the rhythm. It was mesmerizing... dazzling... divine.

Suddenly, a shimmering burst of rainbow erupted from the cauldron. The unstoppable medley of light rocketed upwards, piercing through the gloomy canopy of the fen with an explosion of glitz. The rainbow hovered in the air, so bright it illuminated the entire forest floor.

As the other gnomes continued chanting, Silas stepped to the edge of the Pot of Gold. He beckoned the group to come closer. They each took a step towards the cauldron, the light from the rainbow reflecting off their faces.

"What now?" Anian asked quietly, equally as smitten by the display as the others.

"Climb into the cauldron and submerge yourself like it's a bath," Silas replied. "Once you're in the gold, the trip will be almost instantaneous, so don't be shocked by how quickly it happens. We don't have exact control over where you'll emerge in the city, but it'll be within a body of water, so be prepared to get wet. Other than that, all you have to do is relax. We'll take care of everything else."

Silas gestured at the Pot of Gold. "There's only one question left. Who goes first?"

Anian turned to Luzi.

"It seems fitting that the one who started this quest also ends it," the werewolf told her. "The honor is yours... if you want it."

Luzi stared into the shimmering rainbow. A million shades of emotion flashed through the Nyasian's brain. There was so much to be said... so much to confess... so much to celebrate.

But there wasn't time to explain any of it, and even if there was, she didn't have the words.

Mustering all of her courage, Luzi walked over to the Pot of Gold and placed her hands on the edge, preparing to climb inside. But as she got ready to enter the cauldron, an urgent impulse flashed in her mind.

"Wait!" she blurted, turning back to U. "Before we get into that thing – while we still have a chance – I need to tell you something."

"Since this journey began, I've questioned everything I thought I knew," Luzi explained. "Every belief I held, every truth I embraced, all of it now dwells in the past. And it seems only ambiguity stands vigil over the future."

"There's one thing that I am sure of, though. I finally get it, U. My parents weren't keeping me from finding my real home, they *were* my real home. That's all a home is... the people you care about. And when you think of it like that, none of us are ever as alone as we're afraid we are."

An enormous, goofy grin blossomed on U's face, as if he was surprised he still had the capacity to experience new emotions after all these years.

"When you put it like that, I guess we aren't," he replied, his eyes glittering in the light of the rainbow.

Luzi looked at the unicorn, recalling that not-so-long-ago moment when they first met. An angry farmgirl with delusions of grandeur. A stranger cloaked in shadow and malaise. Both of them lost... and both of them found.

She smiled and extended her hand. He stepped forward and took it.

And together, they climbed into the Pot of Gold.

24

"Who reads the eulogy when the preacher is dead?"

– Bozza Black, president of the Undertakers Guild of Dama'run

The Meridian reclined on her subterranean throne, each beat of her mighty heart echoing like a war drum in the empty stillness of her chambers.

Before her lay a tiny obsidian box engraved with dozens of intricate, fractal hexes – each a deadly magical booby trap. The treasure inside filled the alpha unicorn with a taunting hope, like a life preserver tossed just beyond the reach of someone who was drowning. Such power, right in front of her. And yet, so frustratingly useless.

Once again, fate has fucked the Monoceros! she rued.

Before long, the clapping of hooves echoed in the distance. The sound didn't faze the Meridian, who continued to lounge undisturbed, staring at the box with unblinking eyes. Eventually, a slender unicorn with a stripe of white running down its face emerged from the darkness. The junior Monoceros paused at the foot of the Meridian's throne and bowed respectfully. He said nothing, waiting for his mistress to acknowledge him.

"Sharkaash," she said after a long, deliberate hesitation. "You return at last. And *without* your sisters and brothers."

Sharkaash lowered his eyes.

"Mistress. After I killed the Psychopomp, the Luchrupan turned against us, rising to the aid of the traitor and the Scions. We fought with all we had, and they suffered great losses – but it was not enough. I alone escaped to bring you news of the assault."

The Meridian was unimpressed.

"Word of your defeat proceeds your arrival by hours. I have already received confirmation about the ring's arrival in Dama'rum from our spy in the city. The council has it in their possession as we speak. Uchchaihshravas and the Nyasian are beyond my grasp. You have failed."

There was a silence, then Sharkaash spoke, dreading the answer but having to ask.

"What shall my penance be, mistress?"

But the Meridian's answer surprised him. "There will be no punishment," she said. "Worry not. You will soon have ample opportunity to redeem your disgrace."

"Mistress?"

"I have spoken to the leaders of the other covens. Almost all have pledged allegiance to our cause, and the last holdouts will be with us soon enough. War is coming – THE war – and they know it. The *Io-X'likon'sh* has begun."

"But... the humans... they will fight... won't they?"

The alpha unicorn chuckled.

"Let me tell you something that I've learned about the apes.

Very powerful humans have something in common with very stupid ones: they both alter the facts to fit their worldview instead of the other way around. The Council of Dama'run has grown docile, overconfident. They have no clue what is headed their way. How *could* they?"

The Meridian gazed at her subordinate, her onyx eyes alight with a dark fire.

"This was a long time coming, rings or not. For thousands of years – ever since we were forced underground to this stinking cave – the world has been shaped by rulers seeking to govern through the odious apparatus of reason. As a result, it has descended into chaos and self-interest. The world doesn't need reason. It needs *fear*. And soon, we shall remind it of this savage truth it's had the audacity to forget."

The Meridian breathed deep, like she was inhaling the scent of a battlefield after a war.

"Can't you feel it? The universe cries out for renewal. The time has come for the Monoceros to take our rightful place again as rulers of the world, or die trying. If these are truly our last days, we will meet them with a scream, not a whimper. And it will be glorious, either way."

She turned away from Sharkaash.

"Now leave me alone before I change my mind about you. And tell the others I will address them shortly."

"Yes, mistress," the junior unicorn said reverently. In a moment – like fox fleeing a farmer – he was gone.

When Sharkaash had departed her chambers, the Meridian fixed her attention on the box in front of her again. A long moment passed. Then, focusing her mind, she used her telekinetic powers to deactivate the traps and flip the lid of the device open. Inside lay a ring, carved in the shape of a serpent. Wrought in immaculate detail, the unworldly, golden metal shined independent of the light in the Meridian's chambers, a star in the midst of an empty night sky.

Like a reformed alcoholic remembering her last drink, the Meridian allowed herself a brief indulgence in a taboo she hadn't tasted in years: hope.

Soon, she gloated, imagining the sensation of sunlight on her skin.

Soon.

25

FOOTNOTES

[Footnote 1] It's worth noting that the Monoceros titles of "brother" and "sister" refer to clan membership, not blood.

Indeed, it's the rare Monoceros who gets a chance to know their parents or siblings at all. Immediately after birth – before the youngling can get the chance to bond – the infant is surrendered to the custody of the coven. They're raised communally from that day until adulthood, with the group teaching them how to survive... whom to love... whom to hate. And at no point are they ever introduced to the biological parent who sired them.

The penalty for any Monoceros who reveals the secret is a swift and brutal death – with an emphasis on the latter.

[Footnote 2] There are five great realms that encompass the whole of the known world, each recognized with its own seat on the Dama'run Council.

The Elven Plains, ruled by a loose tribal affiliation called the Rundermust, is the oldest civilization of them all. Next came Abyssinia, the forest monarchy of the south, where humans have learned to live in peace with nature instead of conquering it. In turn came the island federation of Ragnaron, where war and weapons are the currency of the land. Finally came the mountainous domain of Quiyst, where scholars outnumber soldiers. The fifth realm, "The Otherworlds," encompasses the many races who lived among the forests and in the mountains and in the oceans long before they were settled by human or elf, as well as the lesser populated nations such as Nyasia. And to all but a dwindling few, that is the entirety of the known world.

Of course, there is a sixth realm which appears on no maps, a dark land where no light has shone for a hundred thousand years, and no whisper has ever been spoken. But that's a story best left for another time.

[Footnote 3] The famed Riders of Zinn hail from a village-city in Abyssinia, which holds an annual horse race to determine the fastest rider in town. The winner is then put in charge of warning the entire village in case of an attack – a great honor and solemn responsibility.

Their fame has given rise to fables about "half-human, half-horses" called centaurs who live in the village, existing side by side with their fully human neighbors. The myths have never been proven true, of course.

But then again, they've never been disproven, either.

[Footnote 4] "Uchchaihshravas" is only a general approximation of U's true name, of course. The unabridged versions of Monoceros names are a hyper-complex mix of phonetics, numerals and cadences beyond the human tongue, ear or quill. The closest one can come to transcribing U's true name would look something like: Uchuchchaihsssshravasss Ueei-ohm'yinn-i Mo'youn'r'r'-o-loä-i-muörr Z'I'o-lk... dei unguntz!... dem>uu'lOvyer!gruuggök-8,894.

Unsurprisingly, unicorns rarely use their formal names.

[Footnote 5] The Monoceros are well known throughout the realms for their love, respect and fear of poetry.

Although they have no written language – all of their history is passed down orally or telepathically – the Monoceros consider poetry to be one of the five essential arts, alongside sculpture, performance, architecture and war. Unicorns who are unable to appreciate its subtleties are seldom able to rise in clan stature, unless they're particularly powerful or cruel.

The best Monoceros poets are able to wield words like weapons, as a long legacy of tragedy demonstrates. A sonnet from MkumboRar once inspired an entire monastery of monks to jump off a mountain to their deaths. An anti-ballad from Gor-El-Sid poisoned the "incorruptible" marriage of the emir and emira of Jinn. And a single cycle of iambic pentameter from the Monoceros bard known only as "I" sparked a bloody coup that leveled the storied House of Damascus.

As the infamous alpha unicorn Ly the Poet once said: "Poetry is the humility that makes fools of monarchs... the heart that beats in darkness... the liar who speaks the truth... and even we Monoceros are its victims."

[Footnote 6] A product of the primordial first age of the world, dragons were virtually extinct when unicorns rose to dominance in the Great Realms. As such, the two never occupied the same eon, and never had to compete for a seat at the head of the food chain.

Many a scholarly debate and bar argument has been waged over what species would have emerged victorious, with no argument ever gaining a definitive foothold over the others. But everyone agrees on one thing.

It would have been a hell of a fight.

[Footnote 7] At its zenith, the Tuvan Passageway was the third-most-travelled crossing in the history of the Great Realms.

The second-most-traveled was the legendary underground tunnel of Sirinan, which connected Quiyst with one of Ragnaron's largest outlying islands, Gwarrk (until the Great Quake swept every trace of it away eight hundred years ago).

The most-traveled crossing that ever existed – and the only one of the three still in use – is the Vavsoliar Gate. A massive bridge that has no rival, it is the sole way in or out of Dama'run. More fortunes have passed over it than can be counted in a million lifetimes. As the late city councilor Adirok Hix once said: "The Vavsoliar Gate is more than a bridge, it is the very soul of our city – and it will stand as long as a single coin remains in the depositories of our hearts."

[Footnote 8] The Ten Wonders of the Great Realms, in no particular order, include:

    1) The Mountain City of Dama'run

    2) The Tuvan Passage

3) The Xibalban Catacombs, which contains thousands of unclaimed bodies from the Quiystian Red Purge

4) The Themiscyrian Highway, the longest trade road in the known realms

5) Shambhala, the temple that houses the famed Göbekli monks

6) The Tower That Izz, a sentient ziggurat in Western Abyssinia

7) The Invisible Pyramids of Leva, which cannot be seen until one is inside them

8) The Gardens of Soab, with their legendary moaning orchids

9) Pandaemonium Hall, the infamous concert venue for music sorcery

10) The Gundian Courthouses, the triple towers made of bone

[Footnote 9] Blantises, one of the most despised scourges of the Nyasian outback, pose little physical threat to a human. The problem lies in the lizard's rapacious appetite. The eggs of the blantis are fast-hatching and plentiful, and their young are ravenous from birth, devouring twice their weight in food every day. Blantises can eat almost anything, including sand (if they must). But most of all they love potubers – the main crop of almost all Nyasian farmers.

When the outback was first settled, the united commission of provinces spent decades trying to find a solution to the blantis dilemma, even offering a bounty of a gold piece for anyone who turned in a hundred lizard tails. But the commission gave it up after the effort nearly bankrupted them, declaring that the blantis was simply another challenge of life in the desert.

You just can't kill your way out of some problems, it seems.

[Footnote 10] Unbeknownst to U and Luzi, the myth that hummingdragons can grant wishes is true, but incredibly rare. In fact, there have been only three beings in the history of the Great Realms who were pure enough of heart to have a boon granted by a hummingdragon.

The first – a hungry, orphaned elvish girl – wished for a loaf of bread.

The second – an elderly farmer from the Abyssinian borderlands – wished that he would not outlive his beloved wife.

The identity of the third – who wished to "remain humble" – isn't known, or ever will be.

[Footnote 11] It's a proven fact that Monoceros prefer to attack during rainstorms. Some say it's because they're "evil," which isn't remotely true. Much like a tiger hunting its prey in thick steppe grasses, unicorns love to use their impeccable darksight to their advantage. In addition, the booming thunder of a storm creates the perfect stalking environment, often ending a hunt before it ever begins.

And *this* is why so many stories involving unicorns take place on a "dark and stormy night."

[Footnote 12] It's worth noting that unicorns seldom bemoan their position in the coven hierarchy.

There are many ways to advance or sully one's station in Monoceros society: wisdom, bravery, cowardice, martial prowess, contests of might, displays of the five essential arts, and a million tiny gestures that mean nothing to a human... but everything to a unicorn.

It's not uncommon for a beta unicorn to rise to alpha status – and vice versa – every few decades. So unlike humans or elves, most unicorns know what it's like to live as a servant *and* a lord. And the Monoceros aren't the only races in the Great Realms who say this system is fairer than anything humanity has invented.

[Footnote 13] The Phangorian Inn is well-known for its eponymously named wine, which is brewed from the Phangor flower. The resulting beverage has a considerable kick, which is masked by its unobtrusively robust flavor. And many a traveler has woken up on the floor, wondering what the hell happened the previous night.

But the real reason that Phangor wine is the inn's best-seller has nothing to do with its taste or its potency. When fermented into a liquid, the Phangor flower acts as a powerful prophylactic. In particular, it counteracts a dreaded, sexually transmitted fungal parasite common to the plains known as "Puppetmaster Crud," which spreads to its victim's brain and rots their mind from the inside out.

The inn also brews ale. Nobody's raving about *that*, though.

[Footnote 14] There has been a growing demand for a world monetary standard among merchants and finance guilds throughout the Great Realms.

After many centuries, gold has become the coin of choice in Ragnaron, Quiyst and Abyssinia, largely due to its rarity and applications in magic. But adoption of the gold standard has been thwarted by the disproportionate influence of the Dama'run kachma on the world market, as well as the Elvish Rundermust, which has refused to budge from their long-established use of the "britt," a rare type of ore found mainly within their borders.

Ehnansi Tembe, the Abyssinian representative on the Grand Council of Dama'run, is among the most vigorous voices on the topic, arguing not only for a gold standard, but a consensus on other units of measurement such as weight, length and volume... a "revolution of centimeters," as he calls it.

[Footnote 15] As the civil war between the Rundermust and the Yali enters a new decade, both camps have been pressing for funds to fuel their side of the battle. And a rising number of innkeepers along the southern border of the Elven Plains have found themselves financing a war they never wanted to be part of in the first place.

To avoid war taxes, vast segments of the local economy have gone underground. But inns and taverns – many of which double as the only bank in a hundred-league radius – have not been able to escape the tax collector's eye.

It isn't only money changing services that attract attention to the taverns, however. It's common for an inn to also serve as a post office... an apothecary... a grocery depot... a library... a theater... a town hall.

As Paz-Ul, the proprietor of the Phangoriann Inn, is fond of saying: "For the true spirit of a nation, look not to its courtrooms or palaces, but to its bars."

[Footnote 16] She's not wrong.

[Footnote 17] True to U's claim, there are almost no known cases of Monoceros engaging in inter-species relations. But that doesn't mean it hasn't happened.

According to one myth, long before the unicorn birth drought began, there was a unicorn coven that decided to renounce lives of violence. The coven – who called themselves the Pegg – exiled themselves to a far corner of the world, settling in the outlands beyond the Great Realms in a place without a name. There, they began mating with local packs of wild horses. The hornless offspring had the strength, speed and wings of unicorns, but the feral intelligence of horses. They became known as the Pegasus: the children of the Pegg.

Over time, the Pegasus continued to breed with wild horses, until eventually – after thousands of years – their blood became so co-mingled that even a Monoceros wouldn't be able to tell the difference. Or so the story goes, anyway.

Ask a hundred Monoceros about this legend and ninety-nine will deny it. Such tales are kept strictly in the realm of whispers by shame or pride – or perhaps a little of both. But the truth is, there are many among the horned ones who believe in the existence of the Pegasus.

Maybe more than they'd dare to admit.

[Footnote 18] The standard recipe for a bowl of bakach-abaka prepared in traditional Quiystian style follows below (feeds one):

Dice a half-pound slab of raw bakalaroach, making sure to

remove any unripe gills. Place the pieces in a baking pan and drizzle with a tablespoon of cramboo oil. Roast over a high fire for ten minutes, flipping them halfway through (until the fungus is tender).

Meanwhile, mix a cup of milk, a quarter cup of sugar, a fresh comb of honeyskeeter nectar and a dash of myrtle extract in a saucepan. Stir over medium heat until the mixture fully dissolves. The resulting sauce should be the same color as a plucked poison-feather bird.

When the bakalaroach is roasted, add it to the saucepan and stir well. Eat directly from the pot – preferably with a big-ass kitchen spoon.

[Footnote 19] Some say that an old Ragnarian fairy tale known as "The Wolf and the Wife" is actually based on the true story of a therianthrope who fell in love with a woman above his station.

It goes like this:

Once upon a time, a ferocious wolf fell in love with the beautiful daughter of a village steward. Struggling against every fiber of his being, the wolf went to the steward, proclaiming his love and asking permission for his daughter's hand in marriage.

The steward told the wolf that he would be pleased to give his blessing – under one condition.

"My daughter is innocent in the ways of love. I cherish her more than I care for my own life. And I'm afraid that in the vehemence of your affection, you might do her harm. But if you would let the village surgeon remove your claws and extract your teeth, I'm sure you would be able to embrace her properly. If you agree to this, I would gladly assent to her marriage."

The wolf, lost in his love for the steward's daughter, happily agreed to the proposition. Without further delay, the village surgeon was summoned and worked her craft upon the willing suitor. When the beast was defanged, declawed and helpless as the day he was born, he appealed again to his would-be father-in-law.

"As you see, I stand enfeebled before you," the wolf said. "I pose no threat to a small rodent, let alone your beautiful daughter. It is as you asked, is it not?"

"It is," replied the steward. And he promptly called for his warriors, who came running out and trapped the wolf in a net.

When the wolf was subdued, the steward took out his hunting knife and held it to the creature's belly. "It seems that love can tame even the wildest beast," he whispered cruelly.

And he cut deep and wide.

[Footnote 20] The Fae suspicion about "love" stems from their belief that it affects logic and judgement to a dangerous degree. Many consider it a mental malady... an affliction more contagious than the worst plague.

[Footnote 21] Alchemy has been banned in every city-state across Ragnaron, with a mandatory punishment of death for anyone dumb, desperate or greedy enough to ignore the decree. Other governments across the Great Realms have also prohibited the science, albeit at lesser penalties.

The bans have been inspired by the alchemist's ultimate dream: turning lead into gold.

The fear isn't without cause, of course. If someone were to actually accomplish the task, any nation with a gold-based economy would be instantly plunged into financial chaos – something that the Ragnarians are keenly aware of.

Despite the steep penalties for dabbling in the "dark science" of alchemy, many people in the Northern Lands continue to seek the elusive formula. And they continue to pay the price for their efforts. The most recent annual execution count for alchemy charges in Ragnaron stood at sixty-seven... up twelve from the year before.

[Footnote 22] The Test of Ten is one of the whispered-of legends that make the Scions of Dama'run one of the most prestigious fighting forces in the known realms.

Every candidate for their order is put to a final exam that few can pass. Acting without rest or aid, each must battle ten veteran Scions in a row... without a rest. Any warrior who fails to remain standing is dismissed with prejudice and can never apply again.

While the Test of Ten is supposed to be non-lethal, there have been no shortage of deaths from heart attacks, errant blows and other mishaps over the years. In these cases, the deceased is given the posthumous rank of "Scion mortem" and is buried with full honors.

For many centuries, the Test of Ten ensured that only the very best warriors and mages were accepted into the order of the Scions. But in recent years – as a chronic recruitment shortage continues to decimate the corps' numbers – there has been grumbling among many veterans who claim they've been told to "pull their punches" during the test. This is not something discussed with outsiders, of course. And only those who have taken part in the test know if it's true... or just another cynical rumor in an increasingly suspicious world.

[Footnote 23] There are several theories about why manticores hate trolls so much. But the leading hypothesis holds that the lion-scorpion hybrids, who prefer to ambush their prey in tall grasses near rivers and lakes, are simply trying to preserve their favorite hunting habitats. Trolls – who are strict vegetarians – can eat a third of their weight in grass every day, and often leave wide stretches of riverbank stripped bare in their wake.

[Footnote 24] Throughout the ages, hundreds of attempts have been made to seek the Pot of Gold. All but a few have ended in disaster.

Seasoned cartographer Yomira de Estafania got trapped in a patch of quicksand and drowned after an epic, two-day struggle. Ruthless conquistador Corpizarro was slain along with the rest of his company when they launched a foolish attack on a nest of hide-behinds. And the tale of famed adventurer Will Sawyer – who was bit by a parasitic julu fly and slowly consumed groin-first by carnivorous larvae – is one even the drunkest and crudest of fauns hesitates to tell.

So the stories go... and go... and go.

[Footnote 25] Almost all the sub-races of Fae – and there are many – are welcomed with open arms throughout the known realms... except shit fairies, of course.

While most branches of the Fae family tree eventually evolved into sentient, elegant beings, the creatures commonly known as shit fairies never rose above an insect intelligence. Unlike their kin, who photosynthesize their energy, the aptly named Fae subsist on dung, which contains a crucial nutrient they need to process Deep Magic.

Shit fairies tend to follow herds of grazing animals, or settle near large cities, where they present a constant nuisance for local gongfarmers and dung gatherers. They are also a chronic issue at the River Styx, the infamous sewer-river of Dama'run, where they've been linked to several outbreaks of the plague over the past few centuries.

[Footnote 26] There are but a dwindling handful of humans and elves left in the world who can understand the complex and obtuse language of trees. And according to those who can, there isn't much to tell in the first place.

Trees only say two things over and over, they say; one is a question and the other an answer.

Are you OK?

I'm OK... are you OK?

All except for the body tree grove in Fellwood Fen, of course. Those accursed trees – or perhaps they're not trees at all, but damned spirits – only say one thing:

Beware.

[Footnote 27] As a whole, the people of Ragnaron aren't known for their art. But even Nyasian potuber farmers know about the legend of "The Royal Child," which many call the most awful painting ever created – and the most important.

A massive effort that stretches over more than five hundred-feet of canvas, the painting was created from the blood of a thousand dead warriors, collected after an ancient battle near the Ragnarian city-state of Vargg. It depicts a mother nursing her newborn child: a strange contradiction to foreigners, considering its origin. But such dualities are natural to Ragnarians. Life is beauty and horror... birth and death... good and evil.

And those who believe there are "shades of grey" are to be pitied as fools.

[Footnote 28] The House of Seung is one of a dwindling few in Quiyst which still practice the art of Huo.

Intended to be a way for warriors to focus themselves before a battle and be at peace in the event of their demise, Huo is a way of living – of thinking – a deliberate calm and dignity to one's actions that elevates the nobility above the commonfolk... or so the theory goes.

Once a fact-of-life in the Quiystian aristocracy, the ways of Huo have been slowly dying out among the younger generations. That includes one of its most important rituals, the "morning ablutions," which require a five-point cleaning of one's body and spirit that can often last for several flips of the hourglass.

[Footnote 29] There is no word in the Monoceros vocabulary for "please." The unicorns consider the term to be a sign of weakness, and scorn any culture who uses it.

[Footnote 30] There aren't many sounds – whether they be hymn or song – which can compare to the Luchrupan

Sacrament of Colors. But if anything come close, it's the chant of the Göbekli monks.

Cloistered in a temple deep within the highlands of Quiyst, the monks have been reciting the same sutra for 2,000 years without stopping. Exactly thirty-three are on duty at any given time, rotating out of the circle when they're forced to eat, piss or sleep. If one loses their voice, another will take their place. When one dies, another is born in their stead.

The monks believe that if their chant ever stops, the world will end in a fiery cataclysm and all of existence will cease.

Luckily, their faith has never been put to the test.

– END –

Want more Eric Kiefer stuff? Check out books, music, comics and more at **www.TheKiefer.com**

Also available for sale at retailers such as Amazon, Apple, Barnes and Noble, Smashwords, Bandcamp and more:

The Soft Exile

The New Zeitgeist: Songs From The Zombie Apocalypse
The New Zeitgeist: A Tale From The Zombie Apocalypse

Spoken Word For The Doomed

Your Seed For The Moon

The Spectre And The Dozer

Life Is Soup. I'm A Fork.

www.ingramcontent.com/pod-product-compliance
Lightning Source LLC
Chambersburg PA
CBHW071238300726

48975CB00002B/472